MY DEAR VET

JM DRAGON

Define Destiny Series
Haunting Shadows
In Pursuit of Dreams
Actions and Consequences
All Our Tomorrows
Two Steps Forward One Back
A World of Change

When Hell Meets Heaven Series
When Hell Meets Heaven
Fatal Hesitation

JM DRAGON & ERIN O'REILLY COLLABORATIONS

Say You Won't Go
Racing for Love
Against All Odds
Take Me as I am
Echoes of the Past
The End Game
Requiem
Earthbound
New Beginnings
Atonement

MY DEAR VET

JM DRAGON

Affinity
Rainbow Publications

2020

My Dear Vet
© 2020 by JM Dragon

Affinity E-Book Press NZ LTD
Canterbury, New Zealand

1st Edition

ISBN: 978-1-98-858885-8

Editor: Raven's Eye, CK King
Proof Editor: Alexis Smith
Cover Design: Irish Dragon Design
Production Design: Affinity Publication Services

ACKNOWLEDGMENTS

Thank you to all the readers who come back and read my novels. I can't say that I would give up writing if no one ever read my work, because I've always written stories from a very early age. I do feel an immense rush of pride when someone takes the time to read my stories. It makes me very humble. I began writing *My Dear Vet* several years ago. Personal issues made it impossible for me to finish in a reasonable time. Even with a publishing deadline this year, I still managed to be three months late. I have a very forgiving team behind me, and I acknowledge their support.

The inspiration for this story came from my own experiences with vet care as a patient's parent over many years. Of course, this is fiction, though some events resonate or are even true. I love my animals, chickens, cats, alpacas, dogs…I guess any animal. They deserve an incredibly special mention. Where would we be without our companions?

Nancy, thank you for the attention to detail I missed. Particularly picking up on my rather Brit terms when I'm writing from a US point of view. I just can't help myself!

My editor deserves her pay; I always make it difficult but not intentionally.

The meticulous Alexis Smith, thank you.

DEDICATION

I want to dedicate this book to my Affinity management colleagues. We have had a tough couple of years, challenging us on business and personal issues. Ten years together, I know we will do what we can to keep the wheels rolling, because we love what we do and the authors we support.

TABLE OF CONTENTS

CHAPTER ONE

Ava Grace Lawrence climbed out of her Jeep and looked down the main street of Sterling, a town nestled in a rich, rural community. A signboard at the town's entrance boasted around ten thousand residents; it was a nice small town.

Ava sighed, taking several leaden steps to the door marked *Best vet surgery for miles-Welcome.* "Sure, it is. It's the only one for fifty miles." Opening the door, the smell of dog pee mixed with cat excrement made her gag. Not exactly welcoming, no matter what the sign said. Nostrils pinched, she stepped toward the reception counter. An explosion of voices halted her progress.

"Shit Jerry, she's gonna kill us both. I thought I said you needed to keep the dogs and cats apart. Ain't my fault if you lose your job over this. She doesn't take kindly to mistakes, remember Gloria?"

A timid male voice replied. "Naw, she ain't that bad, Pam. Doc Lawrence wouldn't allow it. Besides, Gloria wasn't a nice lady."

"Old man Rush's bullmastiff almost ate Mayor Blaine's beloved cat. I know that cat's expensive, cuz, Sheena Blaine mentions it at every bridge meeting. That cat cost more than I make in two years. Some African name, saint or something...."

"A Savannah." Ava spoke out and watched several expressions cross Pam's face, guilt the most telling. She set her bag on the floor and stared at the receptionist.

"Oh, didn't think you would be back yet. How did it go?"

"It went as well as you would expect from a constipated goat."

"Aw well, you don't have many patients...maybe three or four. The first one isn't due for fifteen minutes."

Ava narrowed her eyes and crinkled her nose. "What's gone on here? I left two hours ago, and the place was pristine. Now." She waved her hands around, pointing at dishevelled shelves and merchandise all over the floor. "Someone had a skunk party, and I wasn't invited?"

"We don't allow skunks. They are vermin. Jerry accidentally introduced Misty Blaine, the mayor's cat, to Tom Rush's bullmastiff, Rock Rush." She waved her hands in the air. "This is the result." Pam scowled.

Ava swivelled around, coming face to face with a young man who looked to her like a cross between a rat and bull. He was strangely handsome in an odd way.

"Jerry, your version?"

The silence stretched for a good five minutes. Ava watched the man, who had the IQ of a ten-year-old. *What was my uncle thinking, employing him? Damn useless the lot of them.*

2

"I didn't do nothing wrong Doctor Missy Lawrence. Just forgot Rock was off his lead."

Ava could feel the tightening on her forehead. Damn, I'm frowning again. I hate this place. It's putting at least ten years on me.

Picking up her bag, she shook her head. "Staff meeting after the consults, and don't either of you disappear." She strode off toward the door marked Doctor Lawrence, entered, and slammed the door behind her.

†

Minnie Barrington took a bowl of corn from the utility room. As soon as she opened the door, the chickens came running. She smiled. What had been six chickens when she first started her hobby had become over forty, after introducing the first rooster. She never had the heart to cull the baby roosters.

Fifteen minutes later, after filling the feeders and making sure water was available, she looked around. Her veggie patch was doing okay, not great; the chickens kept flying over the three-foot-high fence. "I really should have cut the wing feathers like the book said." Minnie grimaced. Hurting or damaging any life was abhorrent to her.

A raucous sound caught her attention, and she ran toward the disturbance. Minnie's hand flew to her mouth. Gertrude, her very first hen, a Sussex bantam, lay on her side, heavily panting.

"Gertie, what's happened darling?" She bent and inspected the bird as best she could. Something protruded from the rear end. "Oh no." *What do I do?* Minnie carefully lifted the bird, who gave a pathetic cry. "It will be ok, Gertie,

3

I promise." Heading back to the house, she carefully laid Gertie in the wicker laundry basket close at hand, thankful she didn't protest or try to get out. "I'll be back. Rest little Gertie."

Minnie left the laundry area and sped to the phone hanging on the wall. She spotted the local phone book under a scattered pile of advertisements and scrambled through the pages to find the location of the nearest vet. Her mother had taken care of vets in the past. Frankly, Minnie didn't have a clue who to call.

Just then, the phone rang. Minnie frowned. *Let it ring or take it...damn.* "Yeah?"

"God, did you get up on the wrong side of the bed this morning?"

Minnie closed her eyes. "Mom, it's eleven here. What do you want? It's early for you to call?"

"Now that's a loving daughter's welcome, I must say. It's not that early...well maybe."

Minnie looked at the clock on the wall. Her mother never called before five. "I need to make a call, Mom, what do you need?"

Minnie heard a heavy sigh and closed her eyes.

"I don't need anything, but... Yes, I know you always say there's a but, this time there really is."

"Mom, get on with it. I need to call a vet. Gertie is injured."

"You're taking a chicken to the vets? What brains do you have left, darling? Are they scrambled from living with all those chickens? You don't take a chicken to the vets; you wring it's neck."

Minnie bit her top lip. This was her mom, after all, anyone else she'd have verbally taken their head off. "That's my decision. What do you want?" A feeble croak floated in the air. *Oh no, I might be too late.*

"I'm sorry, Minnie, you've always had a soft heart. Lawrence Veterinary on Taylor Street. He's the best and the only one for miles."

"Thanks Mom. So, why did you call?"

"Take your chicken to the vet, and I'll call you tomorrow. Hope she gets better."

The call ended. Minnie held the phone next to her ear, still expecting to hear more than the distressed sounds in the background. Rallied her to her main purpose, she grabbed the car keys from the wall rack, collected Gertie, and headed out.

†

Jackie Cochran sang out of tune to Taylor Swift's newest release, smiling as she checked on a beautiful ginger tom cat. He'd decided to trap his tail in a door, and now he was sans tail and ornery. He meowed loudly, as she blew him a kiss and moved on to the next patient, a kitten rescued from a wheat silo. Almost suffocated, she now had eight lives left, that they knew of. All the kitty needed was a home if you could get over her antsy behaviour. She needed a loving and forgiving owner.

The door to the hospital recovery opened, and Jerry ambled in. He looked upset.

"Hey, Jerry, why so sad?"

"Not."

Jackie stroked her nose and walked toward the gentle giant. He was six five, at least, and built like a line backer, but he had such a gentle personality. *Pity he isn't that bright; he'd have had the world at his feet.* "Bad day. I heard about

5

the problems with Rock Rush. He can be boisterous." She smiled and wished she hadn't when tears appeared in Jerry's eyes. "Hey Jerry, why don't you tell me what's upset you. I'll help if I can."

Jerry gave her a misty gaze. "Doctor Missy Lawrence wants a meeting. I think…" He shrugged.

"Yeah, what do you think?"

"Well, Pam said I might not have a job."

Jackie moved closer and placed a hand on his shoulder. "Pam knows nothing. Is it a staff meeting?"

Jerry frowned. "I don't know. She said no one was to leave."

"Good. Means I'll be there. Don't worry, we're buddies, right?" She lifted a hand in a high- five gesture. Seconds later, Jerry weakly tapped her hand. "Great, now dry those tears. We don't want Doctor Missy Lawrence or Pam to see them, right?"

Jerry smiled, and for a moment, Jackie lost herself in that smile. *Gorgeous, and I'm not even attracted to men.* "Hey, go see Mr. Ginge. He needs company and only responds to you."

Jerry nodded and wandered to the cage. Soon, the ornery cat was purring like he'd been given the world. *Yeah, that's Jerry. Just a wonderful human being. Animals always know.*

CHAPTER TWO

Ava stared at the motley crew of what was supposedly the best vet's office for miles. In location terms, that was true. She stopped herself, by a whisker, from shaking her head. She forced a smile.

"I haven't received threatening calls from the mayor or Tom Rush, which is a good thing." She watched them all smile and allowed their brief respite, for a few seconds. "Who the hell was responsible for the mess? Not only the stink of the place, the untidy appearance, and of course the supervision of the animals."

Pam immediately opened her mouth, and for a moment, Ava thought the woman was going to admit she wasn't innocent of all doing. *Ah no.* Pam closed her mouth just as quickly and folded her arms across an ample bosom, her expression defiant.

7

Jerry shuffled around looking like a dog about to be put down.

"Want to say something Jerry?" He looks like he could crap himself.

"I think it was a total misunderstanding, Doc. Lawrence. Jerry would never put an animal in harm's way, you know that, right?"

Ava balled her hands and turned to the senior vet nurse. "And you know this how, Ms. Cochran? The facts are that Jerry is responsible for allowing the situation to happen."

The glare Jackie Cochran gave Pam threw daggers. "He has a gentle heart he would never intentionally put any animal in harm's way." Jackie shrugged.

"I see. You don't actually know what happened other than third party gossip, right?" Ava noted Jackie's bland expression.

"Pam, you were there. What happened?" Jackie glared at the receptionist.

An exaggerated sigh came from Pam. "Jerry released Rock Rush from his leash in the reception area. Lizzy, the mayor's daughter, was sitting quietly in the cat area with Misty. Rocky smelt the eternal foe and went berserk and pushed her carrier over, the latch opened, and Misty ran around the reception area. We eventually managed to put Rocky on his lead, and Lizzy said everything was fine, once Misty was back in her carrier, she did look traumatised." Pam shrugged.

Ava rolled her eyes. "Well said Pam. Have you thought that perhaps you need to be a writer with prose like that?" She focused her attention squarely on Jerry. "Is that how it happened Jerry?"

Jerry didn't answer; his head was down. *Guilty as charged, I guess.* "I wouldn't do anything to hurt my friends."

"Your friends, as in?"

"He means the animals. All the animals, even humans, though god knows why he thinks that, with the people he mixes with around here," Jackie muttered, her eyes on Pam.

Ava glared at the nurse. "If I wanted your opinion, Ms. Cochran, I'd have asked for it. Jerry, it appears you are responsible. That, of course, means—" The sound of the bell ringing insistently drew Ava's attention away from the matter. "We are closed for the day; it's the half day. Can't people read around here?"

"I'll go see what the problem is." Jackie quietly slid out of the room.

Ava frowned and looked at her inherited staff. *God only knows what else could happen around here. Uncle Gerry is in big trouble when he comes back from his world tour.* She took a few minutes to digest what she knew or didn't. "Where was I... ah right, Jerry."

The door opened, and Jackie popped her head inside. "We have an emergency. Minnie Barrington has brought in Gertie. She looks really sick to me."

Scratching the back of her neck, Ava pursed her lips. "Place her in the treatment room." She turned to Jerry. "This isn't the end. We will resolve this tomorrow."

†

"Sorry, sorry, but Gertie is really in bad shape." Minnie scratched her forehead, as she looked at the distressed chicken in the cat carrier she used for this kind of occasion.

9

"Doc. Lawrence will fix it Minnie, for sure." Jackie placed a hand on Minnie's arm.

"Oh, my mother said he was the best around, and that's what's on the door."

A painful squawk from the bird startled both women. "Let me go check what's keeping the doc."

Jackie left the consulting room.

Minnie gave what she thought were soothing sounds to Gertie, her attention so taken with her bird she didn't hear the whisper quiet entrance of another person into the room.

"Is this the patient?"

Minnie looked up in surprise, at the woman at least a foot taller than herself, with an intimidating expression. "Yes."

"What's the problem?"

Minnie shifted her focus to the reason she was there. "I found her distressed. It's her rear. I think her guts are falling out. Can you help me?"

"Let's get her out of the cage, then I can examine her."

Minnie carefully pulled Gertie out of the cat cage. In a slight effort to protest, Gertie's beak moved with no sound. "She's in pain, please help her."

Minnie watched, as deft, confident fingers gently handled Gertie. The woman's sharp glance snared her like a rabbit. She bit her lip.

"It's a prolapse."

"A prolapse, what does that mean? Can you help her? Please can you help?" Minnie looked at the vet. "You can, right?"

"I need to take her to the operation room and see what I can do. You do know this might cost you more than the fowl is worth?"

"I don't care!" Minnie felt like screaming. "I just want Gertie to live, money isn't the problem."

"Fine. Wait in the reception area, and the nurse will let you know the procedure."

Minnie scrunched her nose. Nurse bull. I want this vet to tell me. I'm paying for it. "Why can't you tell me?"

There was a definite look of consternation on the vet's face. "I'll be busy fixing the problem."

"That works. Please help her." Minnie relented and cooed at Gertie, then reluctantly left the room and entered the reception area. It was empty.

Collapsing in a chair, she pulled out her phone and began to text Rita.

†

Ava contemplated the fowl in front of her and wondered at the logic of someone spending a hundred bucks minimum for a damn chicken. You could buy a replacement for a tenth of the cost.

"You can do this; it's a cinch." Jackie said.

Ava scrunched her nose. "Hmm, when did you become a vet? The chances are this fowl..."

"Gertie."

"Right. Gertie will die. The odds are against us."

"Yeah, but they can be with us. Positive vibes, Doc, positive vibes. Works every time."

Ava shook her head. "You've worked too long with my uncle."

"Absolutely. He's wonderful and has a great way of looking at life ...and death. Do you two ever talk?"

"Do you ever not talk? I'm trying to save...Gertie."

"Go for it. All life needs a chance. Some need a second one. That's your uncle's philosophy. What's yours?"

Ava wanted to disregard this woman's words, but the question niggled her. Even in college, people had wondered at her empathy level. *I have one, yes, I do.* She puffed out her flat chest. "I took an oath to help, and that's what I'm going to do."

Jackie winked. "Good answer."

"Let's get on with this." Ava said.

†

Jackie approached Minnie; whose expression appeared far away. Suspicion confirmed. Minnie jumped when she spoke. "Hey, Gertie is going to be just fine. The doc did a great job. Why not go for a coffee in town and come back in an hour? Gertie should be ready to go home."

"Aren't you closed? That means someone stays behind. I'll pay for the inconvenience." Minnie frantically rummaged in her purse.

"Not necessary. We're here to help." Jackie smiled. Minnie gave her a weak smile, then stood and looked around the reception area.

"Thank you, Jackie, and the vet too. I'm really sorry I was horrible to her." Minnie wandered out the door.

Jackie looked around and caught the time on the wall clock. "Going to be in big trouble again for being late." She rolled her eyes and went into the recovery room.

CHAPTER THREE

Sean Seymour looked at the land plan on his wall. Blue pins marked numerous parcels, showing the spread of his company holdings. Walking closer to the map, he smiled. His upper lip curled, and his moustache tickled his nose, which wrinkled at the invasion. His gaze travelled over the many farms he'd gobbled up in cheap deals in the last three years. The economy had been harsh for many in the community, even the Amish struggled on the edge of the property belt he was interested in. His eyes stopped at the two properties still unmarked by the prized blue pin.

"Damn that Barrington woman. At least the mayor is fixing the Reynolds property for me." He stuck a pin in the property next to the Barrington farm.

He turned away and, seconds later, entered the reception office. "Judy, get me that idiot, Paul Findlay, on the line. I need the Barrington farm details." He returned to his office.

A collection of pictures made a wall between him and anyone on the opposite side of the desk. His new bride, Delsey, was a beautiful and voluptuous blonde. She was twenty years younger than he and as intelligent as the blue pins he stuck in the map. Worked out well. His eyes traveled to the picture of a couple with three small children. Everyone looked happy. His finger gently traced over the woman and the two teenage boys in the picture, then hesitated over the female toddler.

The door opened.

"The files you wanted. Anything else?"

Sean snatched the folder, "Just the call to that fool, Findlay."

"It's going to voice mail. I've left a message."

Sean looked at his watch, it was 1:00 p.m. "Who the hell is he banging now? I know you're tight, find him."

"But I—"

"Do as I say. Now, get out of here." Sean pointed to the door. Alone again, he looked at the photo of a pedigree Dalmatian. "Blue, you are the best thing that's happened to me since the accident."

His phone line buzzed.

†

Joyce Reynolds watched her youngest son slouch toward the homestead. Usually, he loved working at Doc Lawrence's. She knew he struggled with the doc being away. *Damn, something has happened that he can't cope with.*

Wiping her hands on the apron she wore tightly around her waist, she quickly headed for the door and opened it for her son.

"Hey how was your day, baby?" She pulled Jerry into a hug and held him close. His body felt rigid, as he dropped his head on her shoulder. "Oh, come on now, Jerry, it can't have been that bad. You love working with the animals."

His head shot up, and fawn eyes stared into hers. He was as naïve as a new-born in certain circumstances, and those usually surrounded his interactions with people. Tears shimmered, and her heart ached. If only he was like his brothers. He wasn't. But that hadn't stopped her loving him more fiercely. "Come on, Jerry, what's wrong? Do I need to call the doc's?"

"No." His great moan split the air and could be heard across the paddocks.

"Tell me what's wrong."

Jerry stepped out of her hold and hung his head. "I got in trouble with the lady doc. Lawrence. Pam said I might lose my job."

The sombre words twisted her gut. "What happened?"

Jerry shuffled on the spot for several seconds. The wood began to protest.

Lifting her son's chin, she smiled. "It's never that bad, son, I promise. Tell me."

Jerry gave a weak smile. "I let Rock Rush off his lead, he normally stays right at my side. He sniffed the air and went to the cat area. Knocked over her cage and she got out then chased Misty Blaine around the room. I caught him before he.... Pam said Doc's going to get rid of me cuz I wasn't capable of looking after the animals. I can Mama, I can."

15

Joyce wanted to strangle Pam Dawber. She was such a cynical woman, had been since they were in school together, and never changed an iota over the years.

She pulled Jerry close again. "I know you can, Jerry, it's a misunderstanding. Accidents happen all the time, and this was an accident. Now come on inside. We have meatloaf tonight."

Jerry grinned. "I love meatloaf." He pushed open the screen door and entered the house. Joyce held back. Moments later, she heard her son laughing.

"Sinbad calm down. I'm home now. I'll take you for a walk. Did you miss me?" There were several chuckles, then she heard no more.

Her hands over her mouth, she smoothed back the skin as though the action would remove the strain. Jerry's brief explanation was enough to worry her. *Damn, I wish Doc Lawrence were still here.*

†

Minnie smiled, as she tucked Gertie into a large cage she had for sick chickens. She found the heat lamp and set it up. "You're going to like the next twenty-four hours, Gertie. Extra warmth, no hen pecking, and treats just for you." She reached across for the container that held sweetcorn and deposited a few kernels in the cage. Gertie stared at her for a second or two, then devoured the tasty treat. "Now I know you're going to be ok, Gertie." She threw in a few more kernels of corn and left the utility room.

Walking into the kitchen, she looked at the clock and then at her phone. No messages. She sighed heavily.

"Damn, Rita, I could really do with talking to you right now."

†

Jackie bit her lip, as she inserted her key in the lock. An abysmal silence greeted her, on entering the house. This was her afternoon off, and they'd made plans. She dropped her bag next to the doorstop and went ahead into the lounge. She should have known that Sue-Ann wouldn't wait. *Another argument tonight I guess.*

Her eyes drifted to a photo on the dresser, two women laughing and hugging each other close. God, that was ten years ago, fresh out of college. Would we look that happy in a photo now? Debatable.

She headed to the bedroom and could think of nothing more relaxing than settling down with a good book and just chilling. Instead, she headed for the bathroom to get ready for an evening in Allenstown, fifty miles away.

†

"Elizabeth Fiona Blaine, get the hell down here now!"

Her father's angry tone rolled Lizzy's eyes to the back of her head. She'd expected him to be mad once he knew about the visit to the vet's. Although, she had hoped to, at least, get through until after the weekend. He and her mom were usually at the golf club. *Obviously not tonight.* Misty calmly licked her paws, curled up on top of her quilt. "It's all your fault, you know. If you hadn't tried to claw out Rock Rush's eyes, he wouldn't have chased you, and I wouldn't be in this

17

mess... I hope Jerry isn't in trouble." Lizzy picked Misty up and headed downstairs. As she hit the ground floor, her mother came out of the kitchen side door.

"Hi Lizzy, have a good day?" Sheena Blaine came close enough to flick her well-manicured fingers through Misty's neck fur.

Misty hissed.

"Mom, you know she hates that." Lizzy held Misty tighter, as the cat squirmed to get away. "Dad requested my presence. He sounded angry. Why aren't you at the golf club?"

"Oh, some renovations or other in the dining area. Your dad has that red-cheek expression when he's upset. Wouldn't tell me why, though he was concerned about Misty. Anyway, dinner is in an hour." Her mom kissed her cheek and winked. "Don't let him bully you," she said, then went upstairs.

Lizzy sucked in a breath and walked toward her father's study and rapped on the door. When he barked "Enter," she opened the door with a fake smile caressing her lips.

"Hey Dad, what can I do for you?" She lifted Misty to her lips and whispered, "Go do your magic." As if on cue, the Savannah began to purr incessantly, padding over to the desk and climbed on top of it.

"Ah my little treasure, Daddy has missed you." He stroked Misty's ears, and she responded by curling around him.

Under her breath, Lizzy said, "Never, ever said that to me. Go figure."

Mayor Robert Blaine glanced up sharply. "You have something to say?"

"No... You wanted to see me." Lizzy walked over to the old armchair in the corner of the room and plonked down.

"I did, I do. You're friends with the Reynolds family, right?"

"Yes, why?" Lizzy frowned.

"Don't frown, it makes you look like a shrew."

That stung, I know I'm plain. Why he keeps reminding me every damn day of my life is a real kicker. "Dad, what do you want?"

"Do you have any influence over them?"

"No, why would I? I'm friends with Joyce from the charity meetings and...." Lizzy shuffled in the chair.

"Well, friends take advice from their betters, right? And you are better than them. Don't scowl, you are."

"Dad, that's atrocious. I am not. What world do you live in, for god's sake!"

"A practical one. I want you to talk to Joyce Reynolds and get her pliable toward selling the farm. They barely farm it, and the money they will be offered is generous, more than generous."

Lizzy felt her body grow rigid, but the blood flowing through her veins was moving so fast she swore it created sparks as she jumped out of the chair. "I will do no such a thing. Dad, what century do you think we live in? That's obscene." She walked toward the door.

"Your answer is no?"

"Yes, of course it is." She moved toward the door.

"I'll have that boy, Jerry, made a spectacle of. He's a menace to animals."

Lizzy slowly turned and watched, as her father held Misty close to his face. "You know he isn't." She curled her fingers into her palm. "He loves all creatures. Why is it so important? Better yet, who is the buyer?"

Her dad flicked away Misty who gave him an affronted look. "You don't need to know that."

Lizzy ground her teeth. "I do if you want me to persuade Joyce to sell."

"I knew you would come around to my way of thinking. It's in the blood. Seymour, the developer, needs that final parcel of land to reinvigorate the area. Well, that and another piece of land. He's taking care of that one."

Lizzy hated her father at that moment. She'd hated him for lots of moments throughout her life, but this was one of the lowest. "I'll talk to Joyce." She turned back to the door and opened it.

"Ah Misty, just you and me. Daddy has treats." He opened a desk drawer and rattled a bag.

Lizzy softly called, "Come Misty."

Misty didn't hesitate. She leapt off the desk and walked out of the room.

"What the hell? Come back here, you devil cat, I pay the bills."

Lizzy shut the door and picked up Misty, who purred as she nuzzled her neck. "Good girl. Now we need to save Jerry."

✝

Ava entered her uncle's house cautiously. The housekeeper usually pounced on her when she was halfway through the door. *Maybe today....*

"Ah, Miss Ava, at last. A little later than normal. I have a late lunch or early dinner set for you on the side porch."

Ava didn't have time to say hello, thanks, or anything. The whirlwind called Mrs. Dank had gone. Closing the door behind her, Ava wondered if she ever did anything at what most would call a normal pace. It wasn't as if she was a young thing either, probably in her mid-sixties. Ava walked down the maple-boarded hallway to the staircase and sighed. *What I wouldn't give for a nice bath, but oh no, Mrs. Dank has spoken, and I'll do as I'm told.* "I'm such a wuss."

Ten minutes later, she sat at the table on the side porch. *Sure enough, laid out splendidly, as always.* Cutlery in its place and napkins at the ready. Ava didn't have time to formulate another thought. Mrs Dank appeared, pushing a trolley laden down with so much food it could feed an army.

"Oh, that looks nice. Am I expecting visitors?"

Mrs Dank shook her head. "Silly girl, you probably haven't eaten since breakfast at six this morning. Plenty for later, or wonderful snacking for the evening."

Ava opened her mouth to speak.

"I'm off, my dear. My eldest son is visiting for the weekend. I must have everything ready. It's been ten years since I last saw him."

Ava saw a rare opportunity. "Why not take the weekend off and visit?" Mrs Dank's swarthy complexion seemed to grow deeper. *Crap, what did I say?*

"Why thank you, Miss Ava, but I promised your uncle I would take care of you...and well...you would be all alone. I know I'm not here all the time, but at least you see someone."

Ava stood and smiled. "To be honest, Mrs. Dank, I don't mind my own company. If I feel lonely, I'll call you. I promise."

Mrs Dank's forehead furrowed so much Ava thought something could be cultivated there.

"Now sit and eat. You need the sustenance. How do you do a full day at work when you are such a thin thing beats me." She rested her arms over her ample bosom.

Ava didn't bother to reply. Mrs Dank was gone, and Ava inspected the food. Hunks of fresh bread, pickles, and thick slices of ham would have been enough. Olives dotted on each of at least three alternative meats. Fortunately, chicken, her favorite, was there.

She drew her fork and snared half a chicken breast for her plate, then the phone rang.

CHAPTER FOUR

Rita Temple gave a half smile, the one she used to placate a troublesome client. And hey presto, Mrs. Clarise Jester nodded. Mrs. Jester finally put pen to paper and signed her divorce settlement. Rita noticed droplets of tears landing on the paper, fortunately not obscuring the ink. She snatched the document away.

"Clarise, you are going to be financially taken care of and live in the house you love for the rest of your life. I call that a good result." Rita watched, as the older woman—who wasn't that much older than herself—began to cry. Rita frowned. *Damn, wasn't expecting that.* "I'm sorry, Clarise. What's the matter?"

Through the woman's incoherent sobs, Rita tried to decipher words but couldn't. This had happened before, of course. Rita figured this woman had a great result out of a failed marriage. The husband had left her after thirty years marriage, for a twentysomething. At least there weren't any kids. Even adult ones could be a nightmare.

"I love him, and I would have taken him back...." The sobs increased.

Rita bit on her lower lip and flexed her fingers. "How about I get you something to drink? Tea, coffee, name your poison."

Clarise shook her head. She stood and left the room, the door crashing shut behind her.

Rita sat back in her leather chair and contemplated her client's reaction. *I'd never fall apart for anyone, especially if they cheated on me. Damn, why are these women so gullible?*

She stood and looked at the wooden clock on the wall opposite her. It was five fifteen. "Well, that's me for the day. I need a drink." Picking up her purse, she opened the door and entered the outer office where her assistant worked.

"Serena, did you get me a new phone?"

"Yep. Sorry it took so long. I had to have it couriered to Allenstown."

A phone slimmer than her previous was placed in her hand. "This is different?"

"Yeah, but it's still an iPhone. Yours was like ancient!"

Rita glared at her assistant. Serena was in her early twenties and as perceptive as a non-functioning homing beacon. "Are you saying I'm old?"

Serena threw her hands in the air and winked. "Your call."

Rita shrugged with a grin. "Yeah, I feel it sometimes." Pressing the power button, she waited for the screen to switch on and began the laborious task of initial setup. Five minutes later, alerts came through for several emails and five texts. Two from Minnie. *Oh crap.* "See you Monday, Serena." Rita left the office and pressed Minnie's number. With the phone stuck to her ear, she entered the empty elevator. "Hey Min, darling, sorry it's taken me so long to reply. My phone died…"

†

Ava wandered over to the corral and absently watched the miniature donkeys that were her uncle's hobby. In this area alone, he had ten. Over the whole of the property, he'd confidently boasted that he had at least eighty. The donkeys were interesting and friendly, in a nonobtrusive way. Not that she would know, really. Her interaction with animals had been limited in the last five years. Except for now at the "best vet surgery for miles." It wasn't that she disliked animals. She loved them. Losing Molly broke her heart. That's when she had abandoned her five years of field work and decided to concentrate on research projects, one in particular.

Although, being a vet was in the blood and expected in her family. A wet nose nuzzled her hand hanging over the fence. The donkey was barely able to reach it and she smiled. "Ah, it's you again. I told you I don't have treats every day." She gazed at the grey creature with the signature black and brown cross going down its back. The nose nudged her again, and she shook her head then reached inside her pocket and withdrew a small apple. The creature seemed to smile, ridiculous of course. "Here you go, Theo, don't tell your friends." She heard a ferocious crunch, as she turned away and the animal began to devour the apple.

Walking toward the house, she looked at the white painted woodwork of the two-story property. The style was a classic for the region. Why on earth her uncle thought it a good thing to buy such a humongous house for one widower, she'd never know. A better fit for a family, and a big one at that. Her thoughts wandered to the short conversation she'd had with her uncle earlier that day.

"Hey, Uncle Gerry I wasn't expecting you to call today. It's usually a Sunday."

He laughed. "Don't be impertinent, Ava, I'm not that predictable. Or am I?"

Ava chuckled. "Sometimes. How is the cruise, and what have you seen this week?" There was, she thought, a moment's hesitation.

"Cruise is luxurious as I expected and continues to live up to the hype. We are in Hong Kong, and I have never experienced so many people in one place in my lifetime. Incredibly bustling, energetic, and disruptive—"

"You want to come home to your peace and tranquillity, right?"

"You never let me finish. It was invigorating in a way. I thought I was getting old, and I guess I am, but now I feel like a teenager again… maybe early forties. I'll put the videos in the Dropbox for you. Ava, all I can say is thank you. Thank you so much for taking care of my home, my work, and my animals. You are going over to talk to my babies in front of the house as I asked?"

"Of course, I am. There's this donkey…"

"Sorry, Ava, I'm out of time. I need to reset my credits, must be more expensive here than the last call I made. Everything all good at work?"

"Yes, nothing to worry about. Take care, and I'm glad."

"Glad...oh I have to go, love you."

He was gone before Ava could reply. "I love you too."

She glanced back at the corral and nodded. I'm being sociable, Uncle, or as much as I know how these days. Hey, my best friend is a grey donkey I've named Theo. You would love the irony Uncle Gerry.

†

Minnie sat in the wicker chair next to a small pine table on the porch. Placing the dish of chili in front of her, along with a glass of water, she glanced around her property. Chickens everywhere!

She grinned and picked up her spoon, inhaling the aroma of the meal she'd prepared in the slow cooker that morning. After the adventures of the day, she was glad to just sit and take some time out. She grabbed a nacho chip, scooped more chili on, and relished the taste.

Fifteen minutes later, replete from her meal, she sank back in the chair and looked over her domain, or at least the part she could see with the naked eye. "I love living here, thank you ancestors." She giggled at the absurd words. "I'm going crazy, but what the hell, people think that of me anyway. My nephew and niece think I'm the mad chicken aunty already, and they're only ten." She stood.

A feline slinked out through the cat flap. At nineteen, it seemed her darling girl was even older than time itself. The cat glanced at her, stretched, and walked over. Her look said, *it's me, Mom, and you owe me my time.*

Minnie tapped the side of her chair. Ginger scrambled up, landing on her knee. She purred incessantly for several minutes, then simply closed her eyes and began to snore.

"Guess I'm here until you decide it's time for your wandering hour before bed. Works for me." She stroked Ginger's black ears and felt that tactile bond she loved with her first-ever pet. Closing her eyes, she recalled their first meeting…

"I can't keep her!"

Minnie overheard Mrs. Ratchet from next door 'shouting,' If that's what you could call it. Her voice from the other side of the wooden fence was actually quiet.

"She's beautiful, Mom, totally black, and she's only a few months old. You can't not keep her."

There was silence, and Minnie felt like her lungs would burst at the unconscious breath she held while waiting for a reply.

"We have five cats already, love. We can take her to the animal shelter. I'm sure they'll find—"

"Oh no, that means she'll be put down. Only last week, *The Star* mentioned they were overrun."

Minnie sucked in a deep breath and shouted. "I'll take her, Mrs. Ratchet."

The length of time before a reply made Minnie's heart work overtime.

"Is that you, Minnie?"

"Yes, Mrs Ratchet.

"Your mother isn't home, is she?"

"No."

The side gate allowing entrance to the Ratchet property opened. That had never happened in all the years Minnie had lived there.

Tiny Mrs. Ratchet entered the yard and smiled at her. "Minnie, unless your mom agrees, I can't hand her over."

"Oh, but I already have a name for her." Minnie folded her arms.

"You do? And what would that be, considering you haven't seen her yet."

At that moment, Susan Ratchet—sixteen and secretly Minnie's heroine; she was so good at all the sports and hot in every way imaginable—entered with a tiny black fluff ball in her hand.

"Whacha gonna call her Minnie?" Susan asked.

Minnie almost wet myself when her heroine spoke to her. She was in love. Lifting her head, she announced, "Ginger."

Mrs Ratchet shook her head, as Minnie turned her attention on Susan.

"Great name, why?" Susan grinned.

"Cuz, I loved Ginger in *Chicken Run*. Everyone deserves a chance." She moved closer to the animal she'd already adopted in mind and soul, and prayed her mom wouldn't say no.

"Want to hold her?"

"Susan don't, what if her mother doesn't agree?"

"Doesn't agree about what?"

Unbeknownst to Minnie, her mom had entered the yard.

"Mom look, this is Ginger. She's ours."

A slender hand touched the feline's ears and the purrs increased exponentially. "She is? You forget one thing. You didn't ask me first."

Minnie looked up into her mom's eyes. Sometimes they were that sparkly blue because she was happy, mostly it was tears since Minnie's dad died. "I'm sorry if I upset you, Mom." She turned to Susan and reluctantly held out the black fur ball.

Ginger was taken from Minnie's hold, but not by Susan. "She'll be a great addition to the family, and we'll need her for the mice."

"We don't have mice, Mom," Minnie frowned.

"Not yet we don't, but in three weeks we're leaving for the country. I'm sure …Ginger will be worth her weight in gold."

Minnie didn't understand the reference but didn't care. Her heart was full to the brim with happiness. Ginger was her first-ever pet.

"Mrs Ratchet, Susan, want to join us for a snack and a drink to celebrate Ginger's new home?"

That afternoon I remember with total clarity. It was one of the most wonderful I'd had since Dad died of prostate cancer, six months before. That day began my introduction to country life, my love of chickens, and Ginger of course.

She stroked Ginger's ears and listed to her purr, just as she remembered from when Ginger was a kitten. She bent and kissed her cat's head. "I don't know what my life would be without you, Ginger. Don't ever die." Ginger looked up for a moment, then jumped down and ambled off toward the barn on her nightly ritual.

"I wonder whatever happened to Susan? She was so damn hot." Minnie smiled to herself, then headed off to shut up the chickens for the evening.

CHAPTER FIVE

Daniel Barrington stepped down from the bus and looked around. The town was much as he remembered from arriving there as a kid, almost nineteen years earlier. He shifted his backpack and contemplated the three-mile hike to the farm. Keeping this visit a surprise from his elder sister had been Mom's idea, not his. At first it had been okay, but now, not such a good idea.

A blast from a car horn had him jumping out of the way of an oncoming truck. He tipped his cap at the several unsavoury words and finger gestures, cursing under his breath. Daniel glanced at his watch, six thirty. The walk to the farm would take at least an hour twenty. Fortunately, it wasn't winter and there would be plenty of light. "Sis should still be up until eight. Besides, who the hell goes to bed before midnight on the weekend?"

The welcoming sign and music from the local inn were tempting. "What the hell, she'll still let me in if I'm a bit later." He headed for the entrance and entered the establishment.

†

Jackie looked toward the bar area. Sue Anne arrived at the far end, talking animatedly with a buxom blonde. Sue-Ann's face told it all—she was happy. How many times had Jackie been given that smile in the last year—zero. Looking down at her club soda, she sighed. In the early days, her mom had told her Sue Anne wasn't for her. Jackie's friends had said the same. Years later, as much as she hated to admit it, the truth was staring her in the face—the relationship was over. The big question, did she love Sue-Ann enough to fight for her? Worse still, put up with her affairs.

"I guess it's up to me, take them or not."

"What?" Jackie looked into amused, deep-green eyes.

"I asked if these stools were free? I guess, on reflection, they could have owners. There is another drink here."

"My girlfriend's. And yes, well no, the others are free." Jackie frowned.

The woman's low chuckle resonated inside Jackie, and she gave her full attention to the woman.

"Then I'll borrow one for the table over there, if that's okay?"

Jackie gazed at the woman, whom she figured was in her mid-forties, gesturing toward a table that didn't have any seating. "Sure." She admired the strong arms that lifted the stool. *It has to weigh a ton, easily.* Jackie watched the woman easily carry the stool over to her table. *Wow she's alone.* Her deduction was authenticated when the woman sat and sipped her red wine.

"Who are you ogling?"

Jackie shifted her gaze to the speaker and gave a false smile. "No one. Can I say the same of you?"

"Oh, you are so jealous. It was nothing. She was fun to talk too."

"Does that mean I'm not?" Jackie clenched her teeth for the answer. Would it be the usual lie or finally the truth? A thin arm snaked over her shoulders. "Of course you're fun, but..."

"But?"

"You are so serious. Jacks, you need to find a life outside that damned job. You were late again."

Jackie tried to compose her emotions and let the hurtful comments go. Her eyes moved anywhere but Sue-Ann, and they landed on the stranger who'd asked for a stool. She looked intense as she stared at her glass of wine. *I wonder if you are at a crossroads too.*

"Sue-Ann, I need to work whatever hours are needed. Remember, we need the money to pay for the mortgage. Unless you have a new job?"

"Don't be ridiculous. I'm too good for the menial tasks that are available in Sterling. Anyway, you earn enough for both of us. I don't like it when you're pissed. I'm going for a dance."

Jackie cringed, as she watched Sue-Ann walk away and hook up on the dance floor with the blonde who had been at the bar.

"I'm such an idiot. Who puts up with this crap?" She reached for the glass of beer and downed it in one. Her eyes moved back to the strong stranger, and her heart sank. She watched a slim built woman with a fresh, young complexion approach and kiss the woman on the cheek. Her intense stare vanished, as she became animated at the contact and smiled. For a few moments, Jackie basked in the glow of that smile; it was genuine, filled with love and happiness. "Guess I'm the only one in the doldrums tonight." She slid off the stool and headed for the bar. There would be the odd, decent conversation, even if only fleeting.

†

Judy Seymour glanced at the board that held a multitude of pins mapping properties her father had acquired, most illegitimately as far as she was concerned. Damn, farming life was hard enough without a predator like her father taking advantage of circumstances. Only yesterday, Pastor Jacob sold his land. She'd hung her head, mirroring the tears falling slowly down the old man's cheeks. He had no close relatives to leave the small fam to, and he wanted to help a distant relative in Johnson County keep his farm.

To all intents and purposes, except blood, she wasn't related to her father. He had given up that connection when the rest of the family died in a car accident. She hadn't understood her father's aloofness. As the years progressed, she knew all too well the reason. He blamed her for being alive. Other fathers would have been grateful and happy— not hers. His new wife sucked him dry for money, and Blue…didn't matter that the dog had replaced her in his father's affections. Blue was beautiful and a great catalyst for her healing. She was sure Blue loved her more than her dad, but she wasn't going to push that envelope. She'd lost so much affection in her life, losing Blue would be horrible.

The sound of a door opening had her jump back from the board. Judy surreptitiously left her father's office and went back to her desk. She picked up her pocketbook and overcoat. Glancing one more time at her father's office, she sighed heavily and headed out the door. *Tonight, I need a glass of wine or two.*

†

Ava basked in the serene peace which sank into every one of her sensory receptors and smiled. *This I can work with.* She glanced around at the trees flanking her, taking in their natural beauty. The fact that she had left the main road at least ten minutes before helped her feel that she was alone again with her own thoughts, and not manipulated into someone else's drama. That was what a vet practitioner's life was like, as far as she was concerned. The day had been classic. *Who the hell cares if a chicken dies? There are millions on the planet, and for goodness sake we eat most of them.* The woman who paid all that money, for a non-laying hen, was stupid at worst, and at best eccentric.

Ava walked toward a dense stretch of trees, as the dimming light of the day gave a kaleidoscope of rainbow light through the limbs. Smiling, she headed in that direction. She came across a large, neatly trimmed thicket hedge over six feet high and considered her options. Go back home or see what was over the hedge—a conundrum if ever there was one. She walked closer to the hedge. "I wonder what's on the other side?" Throwing caution to the wind, she nervously touched the greenery—it didn't bite back. Taking stock of her situation, she figured her six-foot-three height gave a certain advantage. "I can do this," she challenged the hedge.

Moving back several paces, she made a run for it and dived toward the top.

✝

Daniel walked unsteadily toward home. His backpack shifted again, beginning to feel like a ton of bricks. *Shouldn't have had that last drink. Hmm it was worth it, that chick was gorgeous.* They knew each other, so she said. Minnie would know. *Maybe I'll call that girl tomorrow and ask if she wants to go out for a drink sometime.* He grabbed his crotch. *Damn, I need a leak.* He headed toward the trees at the side of the road and relieved himself against the first out of sight of the road.

Looking around him, he grinned. Of course, the short cut over the hedge. Minnie loved the feature and hated it being restrained. Sure enough, she'd allowed it to get out of hand, height wise at least, but in a neat way. *Ah Sis, you never change.*

"Guess I can make it over, used to roll right over it when I was a kid. Might need a bit more effort." He shifted the backpack to the center of his back and walked back far enough, he figured, to take the dive over. Then he ran.

As he vaulted over the hedge, he heard what sounded like a pathetic cry for help. He was already committed and dismissed the sound immediately as his befuddled mind. Daniel crossed his arms over his head and landed on the ground, rolling away from the hedge. The alcohol he'd drunk helped his body to relax. Dusting himself off, he was about to head to the homestead he could just see in the distance. He heard the sound again.

Turning he saw a body tucked, no tangled in the hedge.

"Whoa, are you okay?" He ran to check.

There was no response. He saw a woman suspended in the hedge, at least a foot off the ground, in an awkward position.

"I'll help." Daniel slipped off his backpack and knelt next to the stranger. "Are you hurt?"

"My left foot is caught, and I can't work out how to free it. I've been trying for hours. Please help me."

"I will, no worries, trust me." He looked over the problem, and although alcohol fuddled his brain, he could figure this out. He withdrew a multitool from his backpack and used the knife to disengage the final root that was holding its prey.

The woman fell gently to the ground.

"How do you feel?" Daniel asked, as the woman tried to stand. Her left leg gave way, and she wailed in pain.

"Not good. Take my arm. Let's get you to a safe place, and we can call a doctor."

"I'm sorry to bother you."

The brightest blue eyes he'd ever seen gazed at him. *Wow, two beautiful women I have met in the last few hours. Must be my lucky day.* Daniel grinned. "Never, I love taking care of people and animals in distress. It's my calling." He grinned. "Ten minutes at fast pace or twenty at slow. What will work for you?" He pulled the woman closer and saw pain etched on her flawless, milky white skin.

"We'll try for the ten."

"Brave, I like it. My family would be devastated if I didn't introduce myself. I'm Daniel, pleased to meet you."

"Ava, thank you again."

Daniel grinned. "Let's do this, Ava. Anytime you feel uncomfortable, we'll slowdown. " Perfect, thank you, Daniel."

CHAPTER SIX

Minnie checked for the third time. Gertie was comfortable in her makeshift box and seemed quite affronted when the laundry light went on and Minnie peeped in to see if her injured hen was asleep. "Sorry Gertie, I'll leave you alone now, I promise."

Tiptoeing out of the laundry, though she knew the hen would have no appreciation for the effort, Minnie headed for the kitchen and pressed the button on the kettle. A nice cup of hot chocolate would complement her time with Ginger. She glanced at the clock on the wall; it was eight thirty. A bit early to go to bed on a Friday by most people's standards, but she had cat duty at five thirty. No way would Ginger leave her alone until she'd been suitably fed breakfast. It was reasonably light at 6.00 am, and that meant the chickens would be clucking away at the top of their voices in a chorus of, "Let us out, it's light." And of course, they'd want breakfast.

She locked the doors and checked the windows of the main rooms and heard the kettle switch off. A few minutes later, steaming hot chocolate in tow, she headed for her bedroom. Placing the mug on her side table, she went into the bathroom and had a much-needed, refreshing shower. Half an hour later, happily ensconced in bed and flicking the screen of her iPad to find her favorite game, she heard a scuffling on the porch below her window.

What the heck is that? Minnie nimbly climbed out of bed and peered down, though she knew the chances of seeing anything were remote. The green metal roof blocked any observations. The door handle rattled, and she frowned.

What do I do? Her eyes flicked to the bedroom door. There was a gun safe in the hall, not that she'd ever used a gun, or wanted too. However, it could be a preventative measure. She didn't need to load it. She quickly dragged on her robe and ran down the stairs. Fortunately, the gun cabinet was just to the left of the stairwell, rather than close to the door.

Where the hell did Mom and the boys keep the key? She looked inside the dresser drawer, and a cluster of keys greeted her. She grabbed them manically. More scuffling on the porch was joined by muffled voices. *Oh crap.* After three attempts, she found the right key and opened the cabinet. She took the largest of the rifles, mentally groaning at the weight. Walking slowly to the door she drew in a deep breath. *There's no way the sheriff could get here if I called.* "Who is out there?"

The noise became louder, with the sound of a chair scraping on the porch.

Should I open the door? No stupid, that would be worse.
Heaving the gun higher, she said, "I've got a gun, so if you
think you can intimidate me, I've got news for you."

She thought her voice was strong, but the laughter
outside the door made her bristle. "This is my property, and I
haven't invited anyone over, so go away." As soon as the
words were out of her mouth, she realized the stupidity of
them. It was too late to take them back.

The door handle rattled again, and an amused male voice
spoke.

"Well actually, it's mine too. Are you going to let me
in?"

Minnie frowned. "Damn you, Sean Seymour, you might
think you can own my land, but that isn't happening in my
lifetime." She placed the gun to the side of the door and
opened it wide. "I'll have you know that—" The words
stopped, as she stared into the grinning face of her kid
brother. "Danny! Why didn't you tell me you were coming
home? You scared me, idiot." She threw her arms around his
stocky frame, hugging hard, then kissed his cheek.

Danny lifted her off the ground and squeezed tight. "I
thought no one scares you, Minnie. It was supposed to be a
surprise. I didn't think you'd be scared. And who the hell is
Sean Seymour?"

"Oh, I'll tell you later. Get inside, you must be hungry."

Danny placed her gently down. "I am. First, we have a
casualty of the monster hedge you refuse to tame." He
pointed to a figure in the dark resting on one of the cane
chairs.

"What happened?" Minnie moved toward the stranger
and had the second shock of the evening, as she came face to
face with the dour vet who had saved Gertie. "Ms. Lawrence,
what's the problem?"

Pale features turned to her, startling her with the vulnerability that replaced the previously sharp gaze. "I'm sorry to bother you, but I think I've twisted my ankle." The voice was different, no longer cold but pleading. Minnie knelt to look at the injured body part. She couldn't fathom much out. "Let's get inside, and I can look it over for you. Danny, will you help Ms. Lawrence?"

Danny grinned. "Oh so formal, this is Ava. Need another shoulder, Ava?" He didn't wait for the answer. Minnie watched, as he deftly, with care, helped the vet out of the chair and virtually transported her into the house. She watched her brother in fascination. Shaking her head, she followed them inside.

†

Danny sat back in the easy chair in the parlor. His eyes wandered over to the chair opposite, where Minnie sat. Though older by four years, he considered her the younger of the three siblings. Their elder brother, Samuel, lived in Chicago, with a woman who was his opposite. Sam had always been studious, preferring to spend most of his time in the library or in his bedroom reading. Not surprising, he ended up as a personal injury lawyer. How he had managed to snare crazy, outgoing Annie baffled Daniel. Love, he'd heard, saw no boundaries.

"You look deep in thought; penny for them?"

Danny grinned and winked. "I was thinking about Sam and Annie and how well they're matched."

Minnie chuckled. "Yeah, it still amazes me every time I see them at Thanksgiving. Love follows them. The twins are like clones of their parents."

Danny laughed, and Minnie raised a finger to her lips.

"Sorry, the patient first, and she's sleeping. Thanks for putting her up for the night. I didn't relish driving her home on a night like this. I would have lost my license if a cop stopped me." The pitter patter of rain on the corrugated roof grew to a ferocious pounding as he spoke.

"I wouldn't put a cat out in this weather. She was lucky you found her. Can you imagine what state she might have been in, spending the night in the hedge? I shudder to think."

Danny watched his sister frown and bite her lip. "What do you think, just a sprain?"

Minnie sighed heavily. "I think it's a bit more serious than that."

"You never said. She thinks it's just a twist."

"Yeah well, all that bruising, and her ankle is the size of a football. I'm not a doctor, but she needs one. That's why I insisted she stay the night. Tomorrow, I'll have Doctor Jackson call by. Anyway, as much as I love having you home, I thought you had final exams soon. Mom never mentioned you were coming over. You know she's in Chicago with Samuel, right?"

Danny threaded his fingers through his hair and thought about how to tell his sister he was flunking the course.

"Hey buddy, you have the spike look. What's going on? You only ever mess up your hair when you're nervous or struggling to come to terms with something."

Moving forward in the chair, he clasped his hands together. "I don't think I'm cut out to take the final exams." He held up his hand before his sister could speak. "Not everyone is cut out to be an academic like Samuel. I bit off more than I can chew. My lecturers have said, unless I find a miracle, I'm done for." He winced at the defeatist tone in his own voice. *Men are supposed to do better than give up. What does this make me?*

Minnie got out of her chair and knelt beside him. "It's what you always wanted to do from the first time I showed you Ginger, and then when we came to live at the farm. Danny, it's in your blood. Forget what the stuffy profs say; you can do it."

Danny placed his hands around Minnie's face. "That's why I came home, Sis. You always make me feel good, even when I lose faith in myself. Why are you still on your own? You'd make the perfect wife, certainly for a guy, but women must be even more blind." He kissed her cheek.

"I like being on my own. This is not about me. I'm off to bed. This time, if anyone shows up, you can deal with them. The blunderbuss is on the floor in the hall. Love you, little brother, sleep well."

"I love you too, Min. Want me to make breakfast?"

Minnie softly laughed. "Knowing you, breakfast would be dinner. I'll take care of it. Good night."

The door shut behind Minnie and he pursed his lips. Minnie was the best. She had a natural way of looking at problems and made you feel easier about the conflicts that invaded your mind. As he rose from the chair, he reached inside his pocket and drew out a beer coaster. Neat script recorded *Judy 01050186, call me.* Coming home to Sterling wasn't such a bad thing, and he'd even helped someone, all in the space of twenty-four hours since leaving campus. He headed toward his room, a smile of satisfaction creasing his lips. *I love being home.*

CHAPTER SEVEN

Ava opened her eyes, closing them abruptly as rays of sunshine filtering through flimsy bedroom curtains blinded her. She slowly opened one eye, then the other, becoming acclimated to the glare and allowing the warmth of the sun to permeate her face. She sighed, wondering why Mrs. Dank had chosen not to wake her before the sun came up. The woman was a very early riser and expected others to be the same. *This bedding doesn't seem familiar.* Ava realized that she was still partially clothed. For sure, she wasn't wearing her negligee. As she peered under the bedclothes, her eyebrows raised. She was still wearing her shirt and jeans. The only thing missing was her boots. Her mind went into overdrive, as the predicament of the previous evening dawned on her. Gingerly, she wriggled the toes of her left foot, and all seemed to be pain free. Pulling back the coverlet, she swung her legs out of bed and placed her right foot on the ground. *Hunky-dory, must be just a sprain.* The bandage administered the night before had done the business. As she placed her left foot down, there was no protest. Ava smiled and stood. Blinding pain shot up her calf from her ankle. She pitched forward and gave a cry worthy of a banshee. She clutched onto the dresser, preventing a freefall out the window.

The door to the room swung open, and that woman rushed to her side. Ava was sure she knew her from somewhere. *Who is she?*

"Hey, you shouldn't have gotten up. I was coming to check on you and see how you felt. I guess now I know."

Ava clutched the woman's arm and accepted gentle help back onto the bed. She shuffled to sit with her left leg raised on the cover. "I'm sorry to be such a nuisance. I'm sure, with a little help, I can get back home. Do they have a taxi service in Sterling?"

Ava was astonished at the pained expression her question aroused.

"You are a guest in my house and injured. I'd never let you go home in a taxi in this state. Besides, there is only one, and Kevin goes fishing on Saturday mornings. I'm calling Doc Jackson to look at your ankle. I think it's more than twisted." She turned to leave.

"I don't need a doctor. A lift home would be good. If that can be arranged. Perhaps Daniel will take me?"

The woman's expression was tight lipped, as she went to the door.

"Is that a yes?" Ava waited. For the life of her, she couldn't remember the woman's name, no matter how kind she had been. The young man, on the other hand, she recalled with clarity. Frowning, she figured the only place she might have met this woman was at work, then the penny dropped. "Gertie, I'd just appreciate being in my own home."

There was an outraged glare.

"My name is not Gertie. That's my chicken's name. I think you are the most ungrateful woman I've ever met. Regardless of what I think, I'm calling the doctor. You can ask him for a ride home. Daniel is busy." She stormed out, slamming the door after her.

Frowning, Ava staring at the green wooden door. What did I say that was ungrateful? Surely, she doesn't want a stranger in her home. I will never understand women and their moods. She lay back on the bed, as a sharp pain throbbed at her ankle. Balling her fist to her mouth prevented her crying out in pain.

†

The vet's words smarted. Obnoxious. "How could she not remember my name?" Her hand trembled when she clutched the phone to contact the doctor's office. Composing herself, she gave a summary of the situation to the receptionist. A few minutes later, she placed the phone on the bench and looked at the clock. The doctor would be at least three hours. Apparently, the doctor's office was short staffed. The choice was to wait until the office closed or go to the emergency room at the local hospital.

Minnie eyed the eggs, bacon, and hash browns beside the range and pursed her lips. "I don't know why I'm bothering; she won't appreciate it." As soon as the words were out, she regretted them. No matter what, the woman was in pain, and breakfast might help. It can't have been fun stuck in a hedge for a couple of hours. "Maybe I should cut it back…" a smirk traced her lips for a few seconds.

"Cut what back?"

Minnie's mood lifted, as she turned and she smiled at her brother. His tousled brown hair made him look even more loveable than he already was. Danny was her favorite brother, though she'd never say that. Everyone who met him thought the same. Clearly. the vet was smitten. Minnie curled her upper lip at that thought.

"Any chance of one of your wonderful breakfast treats?" He grinned, moving closer, then dragging her into a hug with a kiss to her cheek. "Morning sunshine."

Minnie held him tight. He was thinner than the last time he was home from Madison. She could distinctly feel the bones. "For you, anything. I've got bacon, eggs and hash browns, but if you ask nicely, I can flip a pancake or two with maple syrup. Your call."

Danny's chuckle was a deep, rich sound. *I've missed that.* "Anything you have will be great. You always were a better cook than Mom. What about our injured patient, is she joining us? I can go get her if she's struggling to walk?"

Minnie moved out of the hug and shook her head.

"Not awake yet. I'd understand that after her ordeal."

Minnie turned to the range. Closing her eyes, she sucked in a deep breath and turned back to her brother. "Danny, she is awake I was a bit mean to her earlier, to be honest." Danny looked bewildered, as the skin pinched between his eyes. "I know what you might be thinking. In fact, I feel terrible, really."

Danny took a seat opposite her. "Exactly why do you think you were mean? The woman that is my little sis doesn't have a mean bone in her body. Unless of course all those sci-fi movies you love have finally transpired and you are really an alien in disguise." He chuckled.

Minnie laughed, "What do you mean by that?" She knew already, one of her all time favs was *Invasion of the Body Snatchers*.

"Do I need to explain?" Danny winked. "Want me to fetch our new best friend?"

"Sure, I think the new best friend is aimed at you not me. She can't even remember my name. Thought I was called Gertie!"

"Gertie the chicken, different sure." Danny laughed. "I'll go check? Or you won't eat breakfast, because you'll worry about her." Danny left the room.

It was true; she would, already was. "Damn that woman." She turned back to the range and began preparations for the meal for three. *The vet likes him. She'll join us for breakfast to be with him. Pity I didn't get that charisma in my genes.*

†

Ava watched the gentle ribaldry between the two siblings and her insides warmed. An only child, she had never experienced this part of family life. Daniel had mentioned that his sister was called Minnie, and still, the only name Ava had recalled was the damn chicken's. She'd apologized on entering the kitchen, and Minnie appeared to accept that. At least she must have. The food she'd cajoled Ava into eating had been delicious. She settled back with a black coffee, listening to the conversation between the siblings. Something about a crook in town trying to take over the farm. Even in this small town there were the evil doers, it seemed.

"Sorry, I'm sure you're not interested in the family problems. How does the ankle feel?" Minnie asked.

Ava glanced at the offending limb and shrugged. "Perfectly fine at the moment."

"Yeah well, you're not moving around. I'm going into town in half an hour. Want me to go to your practice and let them know you're incapacitated for the moment?" Daniel gave her a huge smile.

"Thanks. I called when I woke up this morning. So far, no emergencies. Jackie will take care of things until I get there."

"Won't that be a bit late? The doctor isn't due for at least another two hours." Minnie said.

Ava frowned. "What time is it?"

"Ten thirty. Are you open all day?" Minnie asked.

"Until four. The staff aren't keen doing the extra hours on a Saturday. Once I came here, I felt it's better to have the place open six days instead of five, as my uncle prefers."

"Makes sense." Daniel picked up a slice of toast and headed for the door. "See you around three Min. And Ava, it was a pleasure to meet you. I hope the ankle is just a twist."

"Thank you, Daniel, me too." She smiled as he left the room, then turned to Minnie. "Your brother is very kind. What does he do for a living?"

Minnie picked up her teacup and drank before speaking. "You'll never believe this, but he's in the last semester of his veterinary course at Madison in Wisconsin. Takes his finals in six months."

"Really, how interesting. I can see how he would be good with animals and people. Does it run in the family? Well of course, the animal part is a given after yesterday." Ava tried to give a friendly spin on the words but wasn't sure she'd managed it with Minnie's bland expression.

"I don't know what you mean?"

There was a distinct chill in the air and Ava frowned. "I meant you bringing in a chicken that was sick. Most people would have wrung its neck."

The look of horror that flashed over the woman's face had Ava biting her lip. *I'm not a people person, never have been. Damn, I need to learn to be subtle instead of saying it how it is.*

Minnie scraped back her chair. "I have to clean up the dishes and check on my chickens afterwards. You can read this until the doctor gets here."

The local newspaper thrown across the table landed in her lap. "Thanks. I'd help if I could."

A terse comment followed. "You've done enough."

The sound of running water at speed indicated the conversation was ended.

†

Minnie walked slowly over to Gertie's nursery cage. She looked perky and clucked loudly when Minnie drew back the wire net cover. "Hey there old girl, bet you have a tall tale to tell the girls later, not to mention Mr. Pip. Who is going to be over the moon to see you again." She reached inside her pocket and withdrew several corn kernels and held out her hand. Gertie, dived for the treats and gobbled them up, giving her a beady-eyed look when they had gone. "Sorry Gertie, maybe later." She slid back the cover and looked around. There were several clusters of chickens either scratching around or sunbathing. Some lay on their sides and soaked up the sun. To a chicken novice, they'd look half dead. A small, ginger and black rooster strutted around near

50

the cage. He eyed her carefully. "Don't worry, Mr. Pip, your favorite wife is coming home to you soon."

She checked the water dispensers, filling those that needed it, and inspected the three main houses. "Hmm I'm gonna have to clean them out tomorrow, or Monday at the latest." She crinkled her nose. Her gaze traveled to the house and her unexpected guest. *Unwanted too, with her lack of empathy. I should go back; it's only polite. She might need help, not that I think I can do much. She's a giant compared to me.* Her mind had been fragmented and upset when she took Gertie to the vet's. She hadn't really noticed anything about Ava Lawrence other than she was tall. Minnie was at least a foot shorter and would be no match for helping the Amazonian to a more comfortable chair.

A few minutes later, she was on the porch and about to head inside when she heard a voice. It wasn't familiar, at least... *Wow.* She edged silently to the open kitchen window and peeked inside.

"Puss, you've been on my knee for fifteen minutes now. As much as that's great for you, I need to move, but slowly. Do you think we can do that?"

Minnie smiled, as Ava tried unsuccessfully to push Ginger off her knee, who adamantly refused to move. *That's my girl.*

"Will please work?" Ginger snuggled deeper into Ava's lap. "Guess not." Ava's head bent, and she scratched her forehead. "Well, if you are here for the duration, I guess we can talk. You do know I'm not much of an in-your-face people person..."

Minnie turned away and snuck off the porch. When she knew for sure she was out of ear shot, she let herself laugh. *So, she is human. Ginger, you can charm the pants off everyone— go girl.*

She looked toward the giant hedge and headed out. "Maybe it's time I brought it down to a manageable level." With a spring in her step, she entered the main field.

CHAPTER EIGHT

Jackie grimaced, as Pam whined incessantly about the fact that the vet wasn't in attendance.

"Well Miss high and mighty Lawrence is good at making us work more hours, but look, she doesn't even turn up. I've had to apologize to at least two customers today that we have no vet. It isn't good enough Jackie, and I'll tell her so."

Jackie nodded. Sure it wasn't good that the vet hadn't turned up, but she had phoned to say that something had come up and she would get there as soon as possible. "I hope it's a better hangover than I have."

"What did you say?"

"Oh, I'm sure the doc will be here as soon as possible. It's only midday."

"Why do you always believe the best in people, and where is the dumb boy? Isn't it his turn for the afternoon shift? I tell you, things aren't what they used to be, that's for sure. The sooner Doc Lawrence is home the better."

Jackie's eyes rolled skyward. *Not sure I don't agree, but I'm not going to tell this shrew.* "Jerry has this Saturday off. It's his mom's birthday, and he wanted to do something special with her."

Pam snorted. "What's that simpleton going to do, take her out for dinner? Not likely."

Jackie's fingers flexed claw like at the words and was about to respond, when the door opened, and she shifted her attention to the entrance. "Doc, what happened?"

Ava hobbled in on crutches, with her ankle and calf encased in a yellow cast. "A misadventure with a hedge. Any patients for me?"

Jackie saw the normally pale skin turn three shades lighter—*not good.* "No. Pam, what about the two customers you mentioned. Are they coming back?"

Pam shuffled papers on her desk, not making eye contact with her. "Nothing important, they just wanted to buy some food for their dogs."

Jackie wanted to strangle the woman. This was how things got blown out of proportion with a person like Pam at the wheel. *Why on earth does Doc Lawrence keep her?*

"Great." Ava said.

"Why not take the rest of the day off Doc? You look pale." Jackie noted the pinched cheeks and tight-lipped response.

"She always looks pale." Pam announced.

"I do?"

Jackie sighed. "Well yes, but you have pale skin, that's all." Jackie walked over to Ava and smiled. "What's the verdict?" She pointed at the ankle.

"The doctor thinks it's a transverse fracture and needs an X-ray, which can't be done until Tuesday."

"I thought you needed to rest up with something like that." The glare she received had her back tracking. "Conscientious, I get it."

Ava frowned. "I'm the only vet here. I can't let my employees run the business."

Jackie digested those words of wisdom and clenched her teeth. "You don't think we're good enough to keep the place open in your absence?"

"Tell me if I'm wrong, but you are not a qualified vet, and this is a vet practice."

The totally placid answer had Jackie on the back foot. Crap, this woman has absolutely no social skills whatsoever. Oh my god. Doc Lawrence the elder, you might not have a practice to come back to.

"True. I'm sure Pam will bring you a coffee in your office shortly. Will that work for you?"

"Yes, thank you." Ava slowly made her way to the door marked *Dr. Lawrence* and entered.

"I'm not her maid. You can take the coffee. I'm going home early." Pam snarled as the door shut behind Ava.

Jackie drew in a deep breath and turned to the receptionist. "You will be nice. You will take her a coffee, and you will stay until four."

"Oh yeah, and who put you in charge?"

"I did." Jackie was about to face off against Pam when the outer door opened again.

"My cat needs something for hairballs have you got anything?"

†

Ava settled into the oversized, black leather armchair that sat in the corner of her uncle's office. Air exhaled from the cushion as she sat, pretty much how she felt, deflated. Her gaze dipped to the cast on her foot, *Damn this is the last thing I want. God help me when Mrs. Dank finds out. She'll never leave my side.* Her eyes traveled to the certificates on the wall to her right, mostly professional, but there was something different about the one furthest away. Even squinting, she couldn't make it out. It was more a picture of an animal and a large, red wax emblem at the bottom, with what was probably a signature.

The door opened without anyone knocking, and Pam bustled in.

"She said you might want a coffee. If you want anything else, I'll be at my desk." Pam thumped the cup on the desk, and the pens in the holder rattled.

"Thanks, and who is she?" Ava was perplexed and a tad angry. This woman was the sullenest receptionist she had ever met in her life.

Pam snarled over her shoulder. "Jackie."

Ava smiled as the door shut and contemplated getting out of the chair and walking the few yards to the desk. Right now, she was more comfortable sitting than walking. *Jackie huh. Pam is a piece of work, for sure.* Her uncle seemed to find, or wanted to, see the best in everyone. Her thoughts traveled to the woman who had surprised her in the last twenty-four hours. Minnie Barrington was feisty but gentle. Though not a chocolate-box beauty, there was something arresting about her. Ava smiled thinking of the curve of Minnie's lips. *Kissable.* There was a brief knock before Jackie opened the door.

"Can I come inside?"

"Sure," Ava nodded.

Jackie glanced around. "Damn, that woman didn't even place the coffee close to you. I sometimes wonder about her brains."

"Why does my uncle keep her around? She isn't exactly a good fit to be the first person who greets the customers." Ava studied the frown on Jackie's face as she sighed before perching on the side of the desk.

"Doc Lawrence is her godfather. Her father was best man at Doc's wedding. When Pam's husband left her six years ago, Doc offered her work. There isn't much of that around here for someone who has never worked before. Being a permanent housewife doesn't qualify you for much these days."

Ava stroked her chin. "I guess my uncle is an all-round do-gooder, a bit like my dad." She realized she'd said the tender words aloud. "Well if it was up to me, I'd replace her and have someone who could at least manage a smile when the client comes in. It's a business after all." She emphasized the gruffness in her voice.

Jackie chuckled and stood. "Me too. Then again, I'm not as attuned to life as the doc is. He's the best. Have you heard from him recently?"

"Yes." Ava was surprised at the question.

"Good, just want to know the old dog is having fun. He is, isn't he?" Jackie retrieved the coffee cup and walked closer to Ava.

For a few moments, Ava wasn't sure how to answer. "He called yesterday, wanted to know how the donkeys were. I believe he's enjoying his vacation."

Jackie grinned. "Ah that's Doc. Those darned donkeys are his babies since Megan died— he sure loved that woman."

"I never met her." Ava could barely hear her own voice and became perplexed at the shocked expression on Jackie's face.

"Never, wow. You missed out big time. She was a lovely, gracious woman but had a strong will—wouldn't allow people to take advantage of the doc. She did it in a nice way. Her funeral was the biggest I've ever witnessed in these parts."

Ava watched a sadness etch over the normally cheerful expression of her senior vet nurse and wondered why. Her brow furrowed. *Now why would I care? I hardly know this woman.*

"I'm sure she was. Are you going to give me that coffee or drink it yourself?"

Jackie looked down at the cup in her hand and smiled. "Not likely, and you're not either. It's stone cold. Unless you like it that way." They both looked at the cup.

"No, I'm good, thank you. Do we have any clients?" Ava asked and looked down at her leg.

"Nope. I haven't heard Pam arguing with anyone, so I doubt she has turned anyone away. Out of interest, why do we open on Saturdays, at least why a full day? We haven't had a single person come through the door past one o'clock since you started this." Jackie held up her hand. "I'm not judging, just asking."

Ava was ready with a reprimand, but Jackie's smile mitigated that. "I thought it good business practice. I've been here a few weeks now, and I agree. We don't get the traffic I thought we might. Early days maybe?"

"Not the big city and people around here know who is available and not. Does the doc know you changed the hours?"

"Is that any of your business?" Ava bristled.

"Nope, none. Need anything else?" Jackie asked, as she opened the door.

"No, no. I'm going home. You can all go home." Ava shouted, angry at all kinds of things but not sure which was the one that triggered her temper tantrum. Things had never pushed her tolerance rate in the past. Yet here, in the space of a few hours, she desperately wanted to reach out and grasp what was annoying her the most and throw it as far away as possible. Throw it where it belonged, out of her life.

"Are you sure?" Jackie asked.

"Yes, I'll see you Monday, bright and early." Ava looked away toward the certificate on the wall.

"I was wondering if—"

"Just go, Jackie, or I might change my mind." Ava snapped. Jackie had left, but the door was slightly ajar. Ava listened intently for Pam's reaction, knowing the woman could not keep her excitement to herself. *Sure enough.*

"About time," Pam huffed.

Ten minutes later, Jackie shouted have a good weekend and the building settled into silence. *I like silence and my own company.* Then it dawned on her that she didn't know who to call to get her home. Minnie had mentioned a taxi service, but it wasn't regular. *Crap what do I do now?* She unsteadily stood and headed slowly for the door.

†

Jackie walked toward her car twirling her key fob between her fingers and pressed the unlock. A beep and the unmistakable whirling of the lock mechanism greeted her. Her cherry-red Honda Civic looked good for being fifteen. Her foster mom had bought it for her, second-hand, when she was twenty-one. *God, that was eleven years ago.* It was her final year in college, the year she'd met Sue-Ann. Jackie leant against the door and stared over the top of the car roof. The first thing she saw was the pub, its walled garden facing her. She heard, rather than saw, that there were several people enjoying a beverage in the outdoor beer garden. *I should go home; Sue-Ann might be home.* Sighing, she glanced back at the surgery and wondered about Doc Lawrence's niece. *She's a piece of work. One minute appearing sociable, and the next completely anti-social.*

"Well, speak of the devil." Jackie whispered. Ava Lawrence stood outside the front door. "She looks lost. Must be waiting for someone, she said she was going home."

Jackie was about to open the car door and leave, then made what she hoped wasn't a foolish decision. Locking the car, she walked over to her boss. "Hi, are you waiting for a lift?"

Ava arched her eyebrows then frowned. Jackie damped down the desire to laugh. This woman needed to smile more often. The sour puss expressions wouldn't help her at all in this town.

Raising her hands. "Not my business." Jackie turned away.

"No, please stay. I'm sorry for being angry with you before. To be honest..."

Jackie waited and saw a brooding expression on the porcelain skin. *How on earth does anyone keep such a skin tone during summer?* "To be honest?"

"Oh," Ava's eyes became downcast. "I've had a hell of a twenty-four hours. Well, not exactly twenty-four. Mrs. Dank is going to kill me."

Jackie laughed. "Ah Mrs. Dank. Lovely woman would give you the shirt off her back, but very intense. Your uncle

loves her, and she was great for him when his wife died."
Whoa, there is someone who can ruffle her feathers.

"Yes, intense is a good word. I said I could take care of myself and forced her to have the weekend off. Her son is home." Ava waved at her foot. "I guess I can't."

The forlorn tone had Jackie feeling sorry for the vet. *This will likely backfire on me. What the hell.* "Have you organized a lift home?"

"Minnie told me there was a taxi service, but I forgot to note the number. I was trying to figure out what to do. Walking any distance is out of the question." Ava scowled at her foot. "Dumb huh?"

Jackie smiled. "No, as you said, it's been a hell of a time. How about I give you a lift home? I know the way."

"I couldn't possibly take you out of your way. Besides, why would you? I wasn't exactly nice to you earlier."

"Sure, you were. You gave me the rest of the afternoon off, and not having to listen to Pam witter on about how unfair life was being to her was the icing on the cake. I owe you."

"Thank you, I'd appreciate the ride."

"It's a hot one today." Jackie grinned. "Want a drink first, then you can tell me how you managed to hurt your ankle and who Minnie is?" She sucked in a silent breath, hoping she hadn't taken the thank you too far, then heard the most delightful laugh and shot a glance at Ava. S*exy.*

"I could do with a drink. It isn't far is it? I'm pretty beat."

Jackie pointed to the building across the street. "You can't get any closer."

Ava smiled, and this time Jackie's heart did a triple somersault. What hot blooded lesbian wouldn't have the flutters? that smile was gorgeous.

"Sounds good, let's go."

Jackie hesitated, then held out her arm. At the look of confusion from Ava, she smiled. "You said you were beat. For the record, I remember having a leg injury as a kid."

"Lead on. By the way, you know Minnie. Ms. Barrington, with the chicken." Ava nodded and reached out, and Jackie clutched her outstretched arm.

She chuckled as they waited for the vehicles to pass to cross the road. "This is one story I'm dying to hear. Minnie is a wonderful person."

"Yes, she is. Her brother, Daniel, is wonderful. He saved me from spending the night in a hedge."

Jackie's heart plummeted at the vigorous response. *Guess I have no chance with this one, even if I were in the market, and I'm not.* They crossed the road and entered the pub.

"Hedge huh, now I really am interested."

CHAPTER NINE

Minnie watched Gertie wander slowly to a cluster of chickens. A couple of them gave her a wide birth. Others allowed Gertie into their inner sanctum. Within minutes, she was back to scratching in the dirt for a tasty morsel or two, clucking happily.

Thoughts turned to the vet who had saved Gertie. Ava Lawrence was a paradox, for sure. One-minute cold and aloof, the next congenial. Hearing the woman talk to Ginger had melted Minnie's resolve to be as indifferent to situations as the vet obviously was. On her return to the house, she'd attempted to be casual. Ginger afforded her an icebreaker, and she told Ava the story of how Ginger had been named. The vet's blue eyes lit up like a neon sign when she smiled, and there was only one thing to call them, hypnotic. It hadn't been long afterward when the doctor arrived and agreed that she might have more than a sprain. He'd dutifully taken Ava to the clinic to put a cast on her ankle until the X-ray department opened on Tuesday.

Ava had been polite in her thanks and seemed to hesitate before leaving but didn't say anything more.

"I'm sure she has plenty of people to take care of her. She seems the capable type." Ginger appeared at her feet and wound his silky body around her legs, purring. "You are one insistent cat." Minnie bent and picked up her girl, snuggling her close to her shoulder. "Maybe I'll call the vet's on Monday and check how she is. Yeah, that's what I'll do." Her phone rang, and she wrestled it out of her pocket. "Hi."

"Min, what are you doing tomorrow for lunch?"

The rapid question had Minnie pondering the question longer than she should.

"Are you there, Min? Look, I know its short notice. I thought it was time we caught up. I miss you."

"I'm free, Rita. Are you coming here, or do you want me to travel to the city?"

"I'll come to you, be there around eleven. You can choose where we have lunch. Got to go, Krissie is staying over tonight, and she wants to go out on the town."

Minnie laughed. "Krissie never changes. See you tomorrow around eleven. Enjoy."

Ginger licked her face, then climbed down her body and landed on the ground. With the flick of a tail, she was off toward the hay barn. Minnie put her phone back in her pocket and checked her watch. It was two, and she'd had no word from Danny on his plans. "Guess I'm on my own again. Who knows? One day I might meet someone who wants to share all this with me." She chuckled. *Fat chance.*

†

Lizzy sat opposite Joyce Reynolds, feeling like a Judas. Her dad was predictable in an obnoxious way. His idea of using Jerry as a scapegoat to have her do his dirty dealings was just the tip of the iceberg. If it hadn't been for her mom's connections, he'd never have been Mayor.

"You look pensive child. What's wrong?" Joyce pushed the plate of ham sandwiches closer to her.

"Sorry, Joyce, I was thinking." She absently picked up a sandwich.

"Not good thoughts by the look of that serious expression."

Lizzy sighed heavily and placed the sandwich on the side plate. "It's about…" She closed her eyes, then started again. "Jerry is…" Lizzy bent her head.

"You don't have to explain. Your father is going to have Jerry replaced at Doc Lawrence's, because he made a mistake with Rush's dog." Joyce's tone was factual.

"No, no Joyce. Well at least not for that reason, it's complicated." Lizzy scowled. "I hate my father." Joyce laughed, and Lizzy shot her a surprised look. "You think it's funny? Jerry could be in big trouble."

Joyce moved out of her chair and crossed the distance between them to sit beside Lizzy on the sofa, taking her hand. "Tell me first why you hate your father. Most only children, and daughters at that, are the apple of their father's eye. I'm sure it isn't as bad as you think."

Lizzy gave Joyce a tearful look and sniffled away the emotion that was clogging her throat. "Why are you so nice about everything Joyce, even when someone is planning on hurting one of your own?"

"Well that's easy, in this instance."

"It is?" Lizzy blinked rapidly. "I don't understand."

Joyce grinned and pulled her close. Lizzy smelt fresh earthy tones, clasped close to the older woman. Her mom, in contrast, had smelt like expensive perfume. *I wonder if they ever met.*

"You care about people, Lizzy. You care about my boy, and I know you won't do anything to harm him. So, I guess what we need to do now is find a way that prevents this. Any suggestions? Because of course, I don't know what it is your father wants."

"He wants you to sell your farm to Seymour the realtor." Lizzy blurted out and watched Joyce's normally gentle expression showed dramatic change. Her hold went rigid; her face contorted into a sneer.

"Of course, Sean Seymour has your father in his pocket. I always suspected." She pulled away and stood to walk over to the window. "What are you here to do?"

Lizzy gulped down the distress she felt in the room from them both. "I'm supposed to make you sell, then Dad won't have Jerry lose his job or take a court action on the Vet's for his irresponsibility."

There was silence for a few moments. Joyce turned and shook her head. "That isn't his choice; it's the Lawrence's', unless he has Doc Lawrence in his pocket as well, and I doubt it. Gerry Lawrence is solid gold."

Lizzy squeaked out. "He's not here, though his niece is. She isn't like her uncle. Pam said she's a cold fish and very business-like."

"You believe Pam Dawber? Lizzy, she's a troll. God forgive me for saying that about a person. Pam has no compassion. Have you talked to Ms. Lawrence?"

Lizzy shook her head.

"Mamma, I'm home."

Lizzy sucked in a deep breath, hearing Jerry's voice.

"Hello there, son. Are your brothers still working in the corn field?" Joyce's face became beatific, as she shouted her reply to the closed door.

Jerry entered the room and grinned at Lizzy. Her heart fluttered, as it always did whenever she saw him. Was she mad to like him in a sexual way, she tried not to. Except he made her heart soar.

"Sam and Al said they would do a couple more hours, then go to the bar. Said not to wait for them at dinner. Hi Miss Lizzy."

"Hi Jerry."

"Lizzy and I have some business to take care of, Jerry. Give us half an hour, then maybe Lizzy will go with you and Sinbad on a walk." Joyce winked at her son. "Your favorite peanut butter jelly sandwich is in the refrigerator."

He grinned at Lizzy, who went weak at the knees, thankful she was sitting.

"Love peanut butter jelly sandwiches, thank you Mamma. See you on the porch in half an hour, Lizzy." He grinned and left the room.

"Right, Lizzy Blaine. We need a plan to save Jerry and any stupid court case against the Vet's and, I hope, my farm. I think speaking with Doc Lawrence's niece is our priority."

Lizzy's heart finally stopped fluttering, and she nodded automatically. "I agree. We could ask her out to lunch tomorrow. I know a great BBQ place."

†

Judy Seymour peered at her appearance in the bathroom mirror of the Ray's bar. She had recklessly accepted a call from Daniel Barrington to meet him there at noon. Giving out her phone number after too many drinks the night before was rash. She'd never done that before. Daniel was different; she'd had a crush on him since the first day he arrived in school. A seven-year-old tyke with tousled hair had the most gorgeous smile she had ever encountered, then and now. He was good looking, at least to her. He had a prominent crooked nose, like the rest of the Barrington clan, which made him less classically handsome. She smiled. *My version of Mr. Darcy, and he doesn't need to take his shirt off to make my blood pressure rise.* She giggled, partly snorted, as she placed a hand over her mouth to mask the sound. A woman came out of the stall behind her.

"Hey, it's only one-thirty and you're in the party mood. Go girl." The stranger approached the basins and took soap from the dispenser to wash her hands.

"Well not exactly, but things are looking up." Judy flicked back her auburn bangs.

"Looking up is great too. Who is he, or maybe she?" The stranger winked, as she dried her hands under the air drier.

"It's a he, and it isn't like that. Just nice to connect again. I'd better go. He's waiting for me at the bar."

"Can't let him wait, though occasionally it helps. Good luck."

Judy nodded. "Thanks, you too." She left the bathroom and headed for the lone figure at the bar. He must have had a radar on her, as he turned with a wide grin on his face.

"Thought the toilet bowl had taken you prisoner." He pushed a beer toward her, and she sat next to him.

"Not quite, thanks for the beer." Picking up the schooner, she took a deep drink. "So, Daniel Barrington, you still haven't told me why you're home. I thought university semesters were similar to schools, and there are no holidays for at least three months. What gives?"

"Oh, just needed to catch up with the family. Don't you do that when you're at a crossroads?" He picked up his beer and began to drink.

Judy had limited knowledge of family interactions, especially when she needed help in the decision-making process. She glanced at Daniel. He looked pensive, as he lowered the glass to the bar. "My mom died when I was twelve. My dad isn't the best confidant, and he remarried recently. We don't exactly gel. Anyway, this isn't about me, why are you at a crossroads?"

Daniel frowned, then shrugged. "The truth. I don't think I'm up to the level required, education wise, that will enable me to pass the final exams."

Judy saw the dejected expression and felt deeply for him. If anything made him more loveable to her this disclosure had. "Why do you think that? Have they told you that's the case?"

"I've been informed that I must get better grades, or I'm not eligible to take the finals." He turned to her with a pained expression on his face. "I so want to be a vet. I love animals and want to work with them. It's the only thing I've ever wanted to do. If I fail, what will I do with my life?"

The solemn words echoed in Judy's head. How often had she suffered this self-doubt and ended up manipulated by her father? Too often. "You have…" *Damn I almost let him know I remember him.* "Your sister, if you trust her judgement, then I'm sure it will all work out." She placed a hand on top of his, and he smiled. Her insides lit up like a fireworks display.

"My sister will like you. What are you doing tomorrow for lunch?"

Judy sucked in a deep breath. "Nothing, absolutely nothing."

"Great, want to come over to my place and have lunch with me and my big sis?"

"Sure, sounds good. What time and where?" She already knew where and hoped against hope that Minnie wouldn't hold her father against her.

†

Ava glanced around the dark interior. There were a couple of people with their backs to her, sitting at the bar, otherwise the place was empty.

"Let's get you settled in a booth. I'll order the drinks. What would you like?"

"I don't drink much during the day. Right now, with all that's transpired.... What the hell, even if it is just after midday. I'll have a chardonnay, let me pay."

"I'll set up a tab. We can work it out later. Sit here. You can watch who comes and goes, a great pastime." Jackie grinned and turned away, heading for the bar.

"Sounds good." Ava settled into the booth, at least the outer side of it, allowing her injured leg to stick out. She could trip someone if they didn't notice her. At this time of day and for the short time they'd be there, it wasn't an issue. Her gaze wandered over black-and-white photos that adorned the walls. No real continuity in the subject matter, but they did look interesting. The one in front of her showed a cityscape, with a young girl holding a loaf of bread outside a bakery. In itself, the scene wasn't anything but average. Except the girl's smile lit up the picture. She was obviously pleased with herself. Ava sat back and mused over what the girl must have been thinking at that moment.

"You look preoccupied." Jackie slid onto the bench seat opposite her and slid Ava's drink forward.

"Oh, just looking at the pictures on the wall." She picked up the glass of wine. "Thanks." She took a sip. The liquid was cool and fresh, as she swirled the contents in her mouth.

"Welcome." Jackie picked up her schooner of beer. "Yeah a cheap way of decorating, I always thought."

"I don't know. I find old photos like these can be remarkably interesting." Ava glanced once more at the smiling child in the photo.

"Each to their own, I guess. You were going to tell me what happened to you and how the Barrington's helped."

"I was, yes. Well, I decided to take a walk..."

Five minutes later, Jackie swigged back half of her beer. "That's a neat story. Danny's at the bar with a friend. Want me to call them over and you can thank him again?"

Ava turned her head swiftly. *What? I never saw him.* "Where?"

"At the bar." Jackie pointed to the two people Ava had given a cursory look at their backs.

"Oh, I'm sure they don't want to join us. They look...close."

"He's with Judy Seymour. Probably doesn't know that family is like the devil in these parts nowadays. He's probably being nice and could do with a break."

"What do you mean?" Ava glanced at the two at the bar, not sure Jackie was right in her assumption.

"Her father is Sean Seymour, the property developer. I think his goal in life is to buy every property around here for the next hundred miles. He doesn't play fair either, and worms his way into deals by nefarious means."

"That's a bit inflammatory, isn't it? Do you have proof?" Ava frowned. "You really can't say things like that Jackie, you could get in deep trouble."

Jackie leant back on the bench and finished the rest of her beer. "Everyone around here says the same. He'd have to take a lawsuit out against us all. Except Judy, Delsey...hmm Mayor Blaine, that's it I'd warrant."

Ava took another sip of her wine and wondered how someone could be loathed in a relatively small town and still live there. "What's his daughter like?"

"From all accounts, the opposite to her father. But that could be just a ruse to get the gullible in front of her dad to make a deal. From what I've heard, she's done that a few times."

"Whoa, I thought I was pretty negative about people. Jackie, you win hands down here."

Jackie chuckled. "Sorry. If you lived here, you'd have a pretty bad opinion of him too, I'm pretty darn sure."

"Forgetting the Seymour character for a moment, why did you take pity on me?"

Jackie set her glass on the table and shrugged. "I told you, you saved me from Pam for the afternoon."

"Is that all? I figured you had plans. It is Saturday. Do you have a significant other?" Ava saw a conflict on Jackie's expression.

"Yes."

The curt answer said a multitude of things to Ava, none of which she felt qualified to challenge. "Have you been together long?"

"A decade or more. What does it matter?" Jackie picked up their glasses, and before Ava could say she hadn't finished, she was gone. "I guess something isn't going well in that relationship," she whispered. Her gaze traveled to her rescuer and his friend. Jackie walked up and spoke to the bartender, then engaged in conversation with the couple. A few minutes later, Daniel Barrington turned and raised his glass to Ava. She automatically reached to raise her own glass, but there wasn't one. Frowning, she lifted a feeble hand to wave. *Damn Jackie, she'd better not…too late.* The couple was headed her way.

"Hey, how are you feeling? He looked at her leg and shrugged. "Sorry, can't be good. I hope Minnie gave you the lecture on what not to do." Daniel chuckled. "This is Judy. Do you mind if we join you?"

"No, no take a seat." Ava smiled at the younger woman, who returned the smile and sat opposite her.

"You must be new in town?" Judy asked.

†

Lizzy Blaine couldn't think of anything more relaxing than walking with Jerry and his beloved dog, Sinbad. Well she could, that he was holding her hand and they were in love. She saw Jerry as similar to one of her favorite movie characters, Forest Gump. Question was, how could she move forward and make it more than a simple friendship? She had no way of knowing if he felt the same as she did.

"Missy Lizzy, I might not work at Doc Lawrence's soon." He frowned. "I will always love Misty." He sighed heavily. "She doesn't like dogs though, and that's a problem."

Lizzy frowned. "What do you mean, Jerry?" She placed a gentle hand on his arm, and he looked hard at her.

"You and I won't see each other if I have to leave Doc Lawrence's." His solemn explanation touched her deeply.

She reached for his hand, as he smiled at her and squeezed it. *God he is so handsome.*

"I don't think that will happen, Jerry. Besides, I can always come visit you, and we can take Sinbad for a walk." She watched his eyebrows net together, staring hard. Her pulse took the Olympic long jump.

"I walk Sinbad twice a day and three times on the weekend. Are you sure?"

His surprised expression and answer warmed her heart.

"We can work out a schedule when I'm not working. How does that sound? In fact, why don't we do that anyway, because I sure don't think you will lose your job." His beaming smile had her grinning right along.

His hand didn't release hers, and they walked amicably. Sinbad dashed here, there, and everywhere, especially when Jerry threw his ball.

I think I just found out how to thaw the gentle giant. Now to stop my dad taking the farm.

CHAPTER TEN

Jackie stifled an all-out laugh, listening to her boss tell them about one of the donkeys on Doc's property. Ava was oblivious to the fact that her calm explanation was quite funny. Danny Barrington was listening to Ava but diverting his eyes more toward Judy Seymour. *Hmm, that could be a kettle of fish better left on the boat.* Danny caught her eyes.

"Jackie, had any similar experiences?" Shrugging, she gave him a nod.

"Not with donkeys. Although it obviously runs in the family. Doc Lawrence's hobby must be rubbing off on Ava." She was given a glare from her boss. "Or not. I don't have any pets."

"Really? I always thought anyone who worked in veterinary had a gazillion pets," Judy said.

Jackie frowned, about to find some good reason, when Ava saved her.

"I don't have any pets. I live in an exclusive apartment in a gated community. Pets are not allowed."

This helped not having to admit Sue-Ann's allergies prevented them having animals. Jackie did wonder why anyone who worked with animals would live in a place that didn't allow pets.

"Pity, maybe I should ship Minnie there. She might give up this insane collection of critters and get a life," Danny said. "Except it wouldn't be Minnie."

"Well dah, of course you would, Danny. I bet when you settle down, you'll end up like Minnie, with a small holding full of assorted animals."

Danny grinned, "Well for sure. I love saving the unwanted. Damn there are so many people who don't understand what having a pet entails."

"Judy, what's your fav pet?"

All eyes turned to Judy. Whose shocked expression made Jackie wish she hadn't asked.

"I…to be honest, I'm not sure."

Ava held up her hands. "Folks, simply not everyone is into keeping animals."

Jackie rolled her eyes at Ava. "Yeah and where would we be without the people that do?"

"Touché." Ava smiled and reached for her glass at the same time Jackie retrieved the empties. Their fingers touched briefly. Jackie pulled away at the electric shock she received.

"Another round everyone?"

"Hey, it's good, Jackie, we were going Dutch." Danny held on to his empty glass. She chuckled.

"I figure even the Dutch occasionally accept a drink from a friend." Jackie winked at him and headed for the bar. She was about to make the order when Danny turned up at her shoulder.

"Hey Jackie, thank you. I really can't afford to get into a round."

"Who said you had to? I've known you for years."

"I don't want to look a cheapskate with Judy. I haven't even bought her a drink. We have been going half and half."

"Ah that Dutch stuff again." Jackie chuckled and cuffed his chin. "Then you can say you bought this round, simple."

"It wouldn't be right. I can't accept the offer."

"Anyone going to order? I haven't all day." The bartender wiped the bar in front of them.

"Yes, same again for the four of us." Jackie said.

"Damn what is it with you women? I never get a say. Minnie is just the same."

Jackie laughed. "Ah Danny, we love you. Let it happen and remember it well. Women are no longer the second best. We are equal and can afford to buy the drinks without wanting anything in return. Just accept it." Danny shook his head and dropped a kiss on her cheek.

"Thank you."

"You are welcome."

†

Minnie sank down on the porch chair that afforded the best view of the yard. Poppies and lots of other colorful wildflowers covered the area, until you hit the hedge. *Ah, that hedge had a lot to answer for.* She heard a car coming up the drive; its throaty exhaust meant it wasn't Danny.

A silver-tinted Lexus screeched to a halt outside her home.

Hmm nothing like trying to make an impression.

A man about her height, five foot and a bit, as her mom used to say, exited the vehicle. He stretched before adjusting his clothes.

She stood and walked down the few steps to stand opposite the man.

"What can I do for you Mr. Seymour?"

He shuffled on the spot and gave her a hard stare. "Minnie, I need to speak to you about the farm."

"Sure, you do. I don't want that experience right now, so I suggest you leave."

"Why are you so adamant to ignore me?"

"Because you are the worst manipulator I've ever known. God, you used your own daughter to get people to sell up. Trust me, even if I'm the last woman standing, I will stop you making our town into an obscure backwater mall."

"Oh, you might be on your own after today. Then your property would be worth a third of what it is today. Have you asked your mother her opinion?"

Minnie watched, as Seymour appraised her family's property. "Not for sale. Now will you please leave my property, or do I need the police?" She enjoyed making Seymour frown. "I'm sure I can get a warrant to stop you entering my property again. I hate cold callers."

He sneered at her. "I'll look forward to taking the keys from you personally when the time is right. It will be soon. Count on it." He headed back to his car.

"Over my dead body." Minnie shouted, regretting her bravado almost at once. Who knew what the realtor was capable of?

Seymour turned back and grinned. "It can be arranged." He smirked and slid into the vehicle. Moments later, he was heading up the drive and leaving a puff of dust in his wake.

I guess I asked for that. The bigger question, in the grand scheme of things, is has he bought the Reynolds property? Is he about to? Surely, Joyce wouldn't give in to him. She loves her homestead. It gives the elder boys work and it's a home for Jerry. According to her watch, it was a quarter after five. "I think I'll go pay my neighbor a visit." She headed back to the house to pick up her purse and phone. Danny might call her.

†

Joyce Reynolds busied herself with preparations for dinner. Though it would be just her and Jerry, she'd made enough chicken salad for the whole family. The older boys would eat it tomorrow, or even when they arrived home in the early hours. They were good boys and deserved the downtime. When she heard a knock, she wiped her hands on her gingham apron and went to the door. She grinned. "Why Minnie, this is a surprise. Come along in."

"Thanks Joyce, I hope it's not inconvenient. I know it's almost dinner time."

Joyce waved away the suggestion. "Saturday night, Sam and Al are in town having their usual weekend beers and won't be home until the early hours. Jerry is walking Sinbad. Can I get you a lemonade, or perhaps something more potent?"

Minnie smiled and shook her head. "I'm good Joyce."

"Well let's go into the parlor. I haven't seen you for ages to have a good talk. I was wondering how your mom was keeping, and Daniel, he must be almost finished with his studies?" Joyce led Minnie into a room off the kitchen, motioning for her to sit in one of the easy chairs.

"Mom is typical mom, 'everything will be alright in the end.' I think she's happy traveling and doing stuff just for her. We think it's great—her time to have fun. She did an amazing job bringing us up alone for so long. Danny's home, he came back unexpectedly last night."

"Well that's good. I often think of you alone on the farm and wonder if it's good for you. Yes I know, silly me, your generation can take care of themselves. Though as a young woman you need to get out and about and find someone to share your life with. You can't do that holed up at the farm." She watched Minnie's resigned expression and thought of her middle child. Al wasn't meant to be a farmer. His aspirations had been to attend art college, until his dad died.

"Joyce, let's face it, who wants to take on my menagerie? We know I'll always put my animals first over any relationship. Guess I need to find someone who loves animals and farming like I do. A bit difficult around these parts."

Joyce chuckled. "What you need, Minnie, is simply for someone to love you. The rest will fall into place."

"Yeah, and it's meager pickings in Sterling for sure, especially for me."

"Well, I heard Jackie Cochran, Doc Lawrence's vet nurse, might be free soon. She loves critters, all of them, and my son thinks she's goddess-like. Let me tell you, if Jerry gives his agreement , she's top notch." Joyce smiled at Minnie's shocked expression.

"How do you know this? I haven't heard anything on the grapevine."

"Nothing is secret in town, if you go to the right place. Anyone who is good to Jerry is excellent in my book. Sue-Ann is the opposite—toxic."

"What!" Minnie threw up her hands and grinned. "Wow, I'm really out on a limb. I never hear these things. Are you sure you're not a lesbian in the closet?" They both laughed.

"You don't travel the circles I do." Joyce winked.

"Maybe I should. What are they?"

Joyce chuckled. "You're not old enough."

"I feel a century old some days, believe me Joyce. Look, the reason I came over was I had a visit this afternoon from our less-than-friendly realtor, Sean Seymour. He said something that didn't sit right with me."

"That would be?" Joyce knew the answer. For it to have traveled to her nearest neighbor so quickly was disturbing.

"He implied you were about to sell and that I'd be the last farm standing. Frankly Joyce, I think he lied to me to make me consider a sale." Minnie shrugged.

Threading her fingers together, Joyce considered how to answer Minnie. "Lizzy Blaine came over today. She broached the subject of selling." Joyce saw Minnie close her eyes. *Damn I've seen that expression of defeat too much in this area since Seymour began gobbling up properties for his mall enterprise.*

"I'm not selling to that creep, Seymour, and not for some damn mall that will be an eyesore in the area. Might have to sell in the future, if that's what my kids want. Right now, other than Al, they want this life. Does that answer your question?"

Minnie sighed. "That's a relief. My mom calls me obstinate, and I can be. Would be about selling up. It would have been hard though, holding on with everyone else gone."

Joyce reached out and took Minnie's hand and held it in a light clasp.

"I figure, as long as we stick together, we can beat that scoundrel, Seymour. In fact, I said the same to Lizzy, and she's going to help. We're going to invite Doc Lawrence's niece to lunch tomorrow at Baker's BBQ. Why not join us? The more the merrier." Joyce smiled and released Minnie's hand.

"I can't, I have a date."

Joyce chuckled and winked. "Really, and who would that be?"

"Not what you're thinking. It's a good friend of mine. We met years ago. She's a high-powered lawyer in Allenstown, and this is a rarity that she comes to see me." Minnie shrugged.

"My, she could be just the ally we need in our battle against Seymour. Right, you ask your lawyer friend if there's anything legal we can do. I'll work on the vet. I think we deserve a decent drink. Besides, it is Saturday. What's your poison Minnie?"

CHAPTER ELEVEN

Jackie arrived home, having left her car in the bar's parking lot and been dropped off by Kevin, the local taxi driver, who was taking Ava home. She glanced at her watch. "Damn, late again. I wonder what Sue-Ann will say tonight. Nothing good, that's for sure." She unlocked the door and stepped inside. The first thing she noticed was the silence. Music usually bounced off every wall. She placed her keys on the hall table and walked toward their bedroom and opened the door. The bed unmade, normal. Glancing around, there was something just not right. Though she was unable to put a finger on what. She then checked all the rooms in the house. Her partner wasn't at home. Taking a seat next to the kitchen bench, she punched in Sue's number and waited for it to connect. "Hi, you've reached Sue-Ann. I'm out partying. Leave a message. If it's urgent, I'll get back to you when I'm sober. Don't hold your breath." Jackie cringed. The first time she'd heard this message, she'd reprimanded her lover for its obnoxious overtone. Of course, the words fell on deaf ears. Sue thought it was funny and cool. "Give me a call when you finally do sober up. Oh, it's Jackie, if you happened to forget what my voice sounds like." Sure, the words were sarcastic, but apt. She placed her phone of the bench and smiled as she recalled her afternoon. For the first time in ages, maybe years, she'd enjoyed being in company, without the need to constantly apologize for Sue-Ann having to be the center of attention. Her phone rang and she grabbed it. "Where are you?"

There was a moment of silence. Jackie closed her eyes at the next words.

"Home safe, and as dictated to, I'm calling you. Kevin helped me to the door. I'm sure if I'd given him a sign he'd have come inside and helped me to bed. Not my type. Enjoy your evening, Jackie, I shall see you on Monday. Good night."

Jackie scrunched her face. "No, no please, sorry Ava. I was expecting another call."

"Not a welcome one I take it. Anyway, have a nice evening."

"Ava, are you doing anything tonight?" Jackie heard the desperation in her voice and wished it gone.

"No, I'm exhausted. Thankfully, I can just crash at whatever time I want. After the wine, I probably will be in bed early tonight. What are you doing?"

"Oh, clubbing probably, just waiting for Sue-Ann to come home. See you Monday. Sleep well." Jackie desperately wanted to say something different.

"Thanks, you too. Oh, and thank you for taking pity on me. I will remember your kindness."

Before Jackie could reply, the call ended. She contemplated the phone in hand as she would a puzzle, then returned it to the bench and walked over to the refrigerator. *Guess it's going to be warmed up pizza for dinner.* For the first time in years she didn't feel depressed. The conversations and company of Ava, Danny, and surprisingly, Judy Seymour, had made her happy. In her heart, she knew what needed to happen. *Am I brave enough for that conversation?*

†

Minnie wobbled, as she crossed the final field and saw her house in the distance. Joyce's version of a Moscow mule had more vodka than ginger ale. Minnie found it delicious, though after two she decided it was best to make the call and go home. Chuckling to herself, she recalled Joyce's choice of a whiskey sour. Her late husband had always said Saturday evening was a time to relax from the strain of the farm and enjoy a decent cocktail. Samuel Reynolds had been a bartender during college, to make money before heading back to the family farm. Even after his death, Joyce kept up the tradition. She'd enjoyed not drinking alone this week, especially as the boys went out and Jerry didn't drink.

As Minnie entered the gate leading to the main farmhouse drive, several chickens arrived out of nowhere, flocking around her. "Hey kids, I haven't set foot for a second and you want food. Let me get in the house and see if I have any treats for you. Maybe cheese might be on the menu tonight." She chuckled at her foolish pander to the fowl and headed for the house.

Stepping on the porch, she looked around her. "Not happening, Seymour. Definitely over my dead body." She entered the house.

†

Lizzy slowly made her way up to her room, knowing her mom and dad would be together at some function or other. She would be alone except…Misty appeared and meowed for attention. "Hey, my little princess. I've got a story for you tonight." She picked up Misty, hugging her close. "I'm going to have to find a way for you to like Sinbad, especially after your bad experience with Rock Rush. It's important, Misty." A deep purring against her neck appeared to acknowledge the request.

"Right Misty, first I'll get changed, then how about some chicken for dinner? I can tell you all about Jerry and Sinbad. You're going to love them…just like I do."

†

Ava hobbled toward the kitchen bench and held on to the countertop, this was not going to be easy. She needed to keep her balance, while opening the refrigerator to retrieve something to eat. "Why the hell am I so stubborn? I should have organized a takeout at the bar, as Jackie suggested." Her vet nurse was nice, not chocolate-box attractive; her nose was way too long. It gave Cyrano de Bergerac a run for his money. Ava chuckled and looked intensely at the refrigerator. Jackie's voice and smile were her biggest assets,

86

the voice melodically soft, and a smile that melted the most anxious. *And she cared, even about me, a stranger really.*

"Okay monster machine, please be gentle with me." Ava pulled open the large door and held it open, so that she could balance against it. She spied the tuna sandwich and reached for it. "Why was I so scared? This is a piece of cake." As she shifted her position, the door began to shut. Her arm was caught in the door, with her body at an awkward angle. "Damnit." *I can work this out for sure.* She sucked in a deep breath and maneuvered enough to reopen the door. She snatched the sandwich and threw it at the countertop, hoping it wouldn't slide off the edge. It didn't.

After a couple minutes of more shuffling, she retrieved her sandwich and relaxed into the nearest chair. *Pretty sure my body was yelling, "For god's sake, about time."* She glanced down at her leg and shook her head. "You'd better not be broken or anything serious. I can't afford to be out of action. It doesn't fit in with my plans, do you hear me?" She took a bite form the tuna sandwich and looked around. Her uncle and aunt had good taste. The kitchen was traditional, with all the modern conveniences streamlined to fit the concept of the property. The weeks she'd been there had taken a mental toll. Being a proper vet again, as her uncle called it. Her uncle had seen sense when he asked her to take over for his trip, while the larger farm animals were taken care of by another practice. That chicken of Minnie Barrington's had been a challenge. *I guess the chicken got its revenge, I'm as incapacitated as it was, right now. The irony of it all.*

Ava considered making tea, but fatigue wrapped around her like a cloak. "Time for bed. Tomorrow, I can simply lay in bed all day. Who would care?" She smiled and stood, then hobbled out of the kitchen. It was going to be a major accomplishment to take the stairs to her room. As she was about to take the first step, the phone rang in the hall. Her body sagged. She reluctantly made her way back to the phone. "Lawrence residence."

"Ms. Lawrence, I'm Joyce Reynolds. You don't know me—"

"Jerry Lawrence's mother I presume. How can I help you?" *I hope she isn't going to give me a hard time over disciplining him. It's work—stuff happens.*

"Yes, yes Jerry's mom. He loves working for Doc Lawrence, and he adores all the animals." Ava rolled her eyes. *Get on with it.*

"We need your help—"

"I don't discuss situations that happen at work in my leisure time. Perhaps if you make an appointment with my receptionist."

"No, you don't understand. It isn't just about Jerry being sacked."

Ava frowned. "Who said he was being let go?"

"Well, not in so many words, but the mayor said if I didn't sell my farm to Seymour, Jerry would lose his job. My son loves working with you and the animals. We all know he isn't the full dollar, but that doesn't mean he should be used in this way."

The impassioned words hit Ava hard. *Why are people so unkind? Reminds me why I chose to live in the sterile world of a laboratory.* "What do you need me to do?"

"Will you please meet me and the mayor's daughter, Lizzie, for lunch tomorrow? There is a great BBQ place in town. If you like BBQ that is,"

Ava smiled. "Yes, I like BBQ."

"Great. We will give you all the background you need over lunch."

"Someone will have to pick me up. I have a cast on my leg and can't drive."

"Of course. Thank you so much. I will be there at your place eleven thirty. Again, thank you, Ms. Lawrence."

Ava rolled her eyes. "If we are having lunch, I think Ava sounds better."

"Lovely name. Ava, have a nice evening. I look forward to meeting you tomorrow. Good night." The phone call ended.

So much for staying in bed all day tomorrow.

CHAPTER TWELVE

A rooster crowing off key made Minnie smile. "Ah right on time Mr. Pip. Thank you for waking me up to such a wonderful morning." She climbed out of bed and drew back the curtains, filling the room with light and heat. Pulling back the bedclothes to air the bed, she entered her en-suite bathroom, a luxury she'd added several years ago. No more waiting for the family bathroom to be free meant she could take her time without a constant 'aren't you done yet.' Not that it had been as bad in the last four years, once Danny went to college. Dragging on her work clothes, she wondered when Danny arrived home. *He wasn't in before I went to bed.* She needed to feed the animals and check the property before leaving to meet Rita in town. "I'm so looking forward to this lunch. Something must be up for her visit." She left her room and descended the stairs, noting Danny's boots at angles on the floor next to the coat rack. "He came home, and some things never change. He never could put his shoes in order." She laughed, rearranging the shoes, then headed out the door, her priority to check on Gertie.

†

Judy Seymour carefully opened her eyes, shutting them quickly as the stream of sunlight blistered her eyes. "How much did I drink last night?" she moaned and tried again to open her eyes. This time, there was less of a protest. Nonetheless, she placed a hand to strategically shield her eyes. Memories surfaced, and she shot out of bed. *Crap, is this my bedroom?*

A gigantic Dalmatian canvas filled her vision, and her rapidly beating heart slowed. "Hey Blue, how are you today?" She heaved a sigh of relief. She was home. She'd have to wait till breakfast to know exactly how Blue was. Her love of photography had captured the dog when he was a year old. He looked like he was laughing.

She swore her dad's dog meant more to him than his new wife, certainly more than his daughter. She'd spent one week's wages on having the image transferred onto a gigantic canvas. When she'd brought the portrait home and showed her dad, he sneered and said she was stupid spending time on something irrelevant, like photography. The next day, she was about to mount the canvas in the lounge.

"We don't want it in the main room," her dad protested. "Dogs aren't everyone's preference. I think it needs to go in a room where there will be more a personal appreciation."

Her dad shoved his hands in his pockets, while Blue ran around their legs, wagging his tail.

"Are you saying that my photo of Blue isn't good enough to go on show in our home?"

"Think what you want. It's my birthday next week. I'll take it as my present, rather than the boring present you usually give me. It will look great in my study." Sean Seymour moved closer to the canvas on the floor.

Judy had given in to her father forever, in the hope that he might actually see her as a person in need of love and reassurance from her only living parent. This performance proved, as on many occasions, it was not going to happen.

"Sorry," she picked up the canvas and headed for the stairs. "I paid for this. It's mine to do with what I want, and I want it where I can see it."

"What about my birthday present?" Sean shouted.

"I guess it's the boring old twenty-year-old Scotch malt whiskey you said you liked." She left him standing with his mouth open.

It had been the first time she had ever defied her dad. There had been others over the last eight years, but nothing significant. He was like a vampire who drained her lifeblood until she lost the will to fight back.

She picked up her phone and saw an unopened text timed at fifteen after midnight.

Hi, remember me, Danny. I'm the guy who invited you to lunch Sunday, as in today. Hope you are still interested. It's late sure. I had a great time, hope you did too, text me if there's a problem. Otherwise I'll pick you up as arranged? Danny xx

The xx at the end of his name meant more to her than the message.

†

"Mom, why aren't you having breakfast? Are you sick?" Jerry's usually cheery face held a frown.

"No darling, I'm perfectly fine. I'm going out to lunch with Lizzy and another friend. It's a treat." Joyce smiled at her youngest and watched as he took a few seconds to register what she'd said, then she saw that handsome smile of his.

"I love treats, can I come?" Jerry grinned, and her heart melted.

"You need to walk Sinbad. Your brothers will expect you to take care of the small animals on the farm for the day as usual." Joyce busied herself with the breakfasts for the elder boys, wrapping the plates in tin foil and depositing them in the oven. When they woke, they'd need sustenance.

"Mom."

"Darling?" Joyce turned and faced her son. He looked just like her late husband, with that tender furrow above his eyes. "I will be back to make dinner, don't worry." She wiped her hands on her apron and went to the kitchen table. She rested a hand on his shoulder.

"I was wondering if it would be okay for Lizzie to walk with me and Sinbad every day—not today though, she is with you." He grinned. "Her dad doesn't like me. I know that. Don't want her in trouble, she's special." He shrugged.

Joyce had always hoped that her son would one day find that special someone. He was just a little slower than most. His heart was tender, and when he did learn, he never forgot.

You couldn't say that about a lot of people. "I think that's a great idea. Did Lizzy say she'd like that as well?"

"Oh yeah." He grinned. "We held hands. I liked that, Mom. It reminded me of you and Dad and when you smiled all the time."

Joyce struggled to prevent the tears forming with the memories of her late husband and the times they'd walked hand in hand. "That's nice, love. Why not take Sinbad for a walk after you've finished eating breakfast as an extra treat?"

Jerry grinned and tucked into his bacon, nodding vigorously.

Well Lizzy Blaine, you and I will need a little chat. She grinned and carried on with the task in hand.

†

Jackie walked into the bedroom and growled. When she'd left at seven, Sue-Ann wasn't home. She pushed at the body in the bed. Her partner groaned, giving her a bleary, bloodshot look, and dragged the covers over her head.

"We need to talk. Get up and have it out here or go somewhere public, your choice."

"I'm not getting up before two. What's wrong with you, Jackie? You know that it's Sunday." The words didn't deter Jackie, and she pulled back the covers.

"I'm not waiting any longer. Either get up and discuss things like an adult or get out of my house." Though she said the words, it hurt her more than it did Sue-Ann.

Sue-Ann glared at her. "I hate you Jackie." She climbed out of bed and headed for the bathroom. "I want a BBQ lunch at Baker's for this." She muttered other incoherent words, as the door slammed shut.

"Great, now I get to stump up for a breakup lunch." Jackie shook her head and left the room to get a coffee.

CHAPTER THIRTEEN

"This place we are going too does have cutlery, right?"

"Sure it does, and you will not be pulling a face like you did when I mentioned Baker's BBQ. Seriously, they even have napkins." Minnie chuckled, relishing the wind through her hair as they headed toward the venue. Rita's blood-red Mazda MX-5 was a luxury Minnie couldn't afford. Her serviceable, ten-year-old Chevy Colorado was no contest with a beautiful morning like this. Nope, the sun on your face and the breeze in your hair was a match made in heaven.

"Hmm, so what's with Danny being home? Thought you said he had a few months to go before taking the finals?"

"Cold feet I guess. He thinks he can't make the grade." A snort and flick of eyes had Minnie on the defensive. "He can, you know he loves animals."

"Loving doesn't necessarily mean he's academically capable to make the grade. You sacrificed a great career for Danny to go to college. He'd better not let you down."

"Don't be so mean, Rita. I love my life."

"Sure, you do. You have no love life though. We've known each other for years, and I can count on one hand the number of dates you've had since you came back home. None of them serious."

"Oh that's like the pot calling the kettle black. Since I've known you, you've been through the phone book on dates and still not found your "Ms. Perfect." Unless this visit is because you have?" Minnie half expected the usual no-chance response, but there was no reply. Before she could ask more, Rita pulled into the half full parking lot.

"And here we are. Kinda rustic looking." Rita said.

"Let's go in and eat, and you can tell me what's going on. I've known you ten years, and something for sure is."

Rita's stare was disconcerting, causing a maelstrom of emotions Minnie didn't equate to her best friend. She climbed out of the convertible.

†

Ava looked around the basic eatery. Posters of local "heroes" adorned most of the wall space, along with some weird looking fish portraits. Joyce was fussing over the BBQ they had ordered, ensuring everything was as it should be before they ate. Smiling, Ava wondered if Joyce would insist on grace before they ate; it was Sunday. Lizzy Blaine was quiet, a bit too much. They were not acquainted, and Ava understood the need for personal privacy.

"I need to get more pickles. This is not enough. What were they thinking?" Joyce returned to the order line.

"Does she do this often?" Ava asked the reticent third member of their lunch party.

"I have no idea. This is our first time out together." Lizzy didn't meet her eyes as she spoke.

"A first for us all then. What do you do for a living, Lizzy?" The woman still didn't look directly at her when she replied, more interested in the complimentary package of mustard which she twirled in her fingers.

"I help my mom with her charity work."

"Very noble of you. Which charity?" Ava didn't think a town this size could accommodate a major charity, certainly not one that could afford to employ at least two people.

"Oh, church stuff mainly. My mom likes helping people."

The forlorn words had Ava musing. Perhaps the woman's own daughter needed some help. She didn't appear confident at all. *Not my problem.*

"You obviously don't agree with your father's views on the Reynolds's property." Grey eyes caught hers, reminding Ava of a rabbit caught in headlights. "Nothing wrong with that. We all disagree with our parents from time to time. Believe me, mine are not happy with some of my choices."

"Really?" Lizzy gave a serious look.

"Oh yeah, they wanted me to be a proper vet, as they call it. Research was a cop out, according to them." Ava shrugged and took a sip of her water.

"You must be really clever. I managed a third in college. My dad was upset. My mom said she figured I'd be a late bloomer." Lizzy shrugged. "I'm thirty; I guess she's still waiting."

"Does it matter that much? You are her daughter, and she loves you no matter what."

Lizzy was very attractive when she smiled. "What about your parents? Did they forgive you?"

Ava lapsed into her thoughts, then shrugged them off. "My parents love me. They accept that I needed to go my own way. Although, they will be hoping, after my stint here, I'll join the family practice."

"Will you?"

"Will she what? Sorry I've taken so long. Our meal will be getting cold, and I see you haven't started without me." Joyce plonked down on the seat next to Lizzy.

Ava smiled. "We were just chatting, generally. It's a very busy spot. Is everyone in town here?"

Joyce grinned. "No, but it certainly looks like it. I met Minnie Barrington. She's with a friend from out of town."

Lizzy didn't reply, but Ava saw she dropped her gaze to the food and began to help herself to brisket and pickles.

"I'll have to say hello. She helped me big time when I injured my leg, a very generous woman."

"Minnie is gold. A tender heart for everything, and I mean that. Those chickens rule her life, I swear." Joyce snagged some chicken and pickles, along with a slice of bread.

From her position, Ava saw Minnie and her friend enter the room with their food package, looking around for a seat. A part of her wanted them to find a seat as far away as possible. Another part said there were seats at their table. Minnie caught her gaze and smiled tentatively, as they headed in their direction.

"Hi, okay to sit here?"

"Why of course, Minnie." Joyce replied pointing to the seats directly next to them, although there were others at the far end of the long picnic table.

"Great, good to see you all. I didn't know Baker's would be this busy." Minnie grinned, taking a seat next to Joyce. "This is my best friend, Rita. She lives in Allenstown, doesn't come this way often. Thought I'd treat her to some great small-town BBQ."

"Hi Rita, welcome. You won't find anything better for a thousand miles." Joyce announced with a grin.

"Hi, it's a little different to what I normally eat on a Sunday, but for Minnie here I'll try anything." Rita sat next to Ava.

"What do you normally eat on a Sunday?" Lizzy timidly asked. Her hands clutched the piece of bread she held, and Ava was sure she would make it into breadcrumbs.

Rita laughed. "Honestly?"

Lizzy nodded her head.

"I'm a lawyer. I go to lunches and dinner so often during the week that on a Sunday, which is my only day off I might add, I sleep late. I have a bacon buttie at lunch, and a cheeseburger from Sonic for dinner. Bliss." Rita chuckled.

"She's done that for years. I said she needs to find a partner." Minnie grinned, opening their food parcel.

Ava had to stop herself laughing at the astonished expression on Lizzy and Joyce's faces. "Where do you practice? Not that I'm in need of professional help."

"Allenstown, I'm a city girl. Can't get my head around Minnie's fascination with the country." She winked at Minnie.

"I live in Allenstown. I'm here doing vacation relief for my uncle."

An affectionate roll of the eyes accompanied Rita's smile. "Be very careful, you could end up a permanent resident." Rita winked at Minnie. "I hear the town grows on you."

"I've never lived anyplace else." Lizzy blurted out.

"Let's eat, or our meal will be stone cold." Joyce said. "Ava, you asked for the ribs. I must admit they look succulent."

Ava smiled. "Yes, they do."

She snagged some and was about to take a bite, when Lizzy said, "Wow you were right, Ava, the whole town is out today; Jackie Cochrane is here." Ava almost put her neck in traction, as she turned to look where Lizzy pointed. Sure enough, Jackie was looking for seating. Ava glanced at the woman with her, a skinny blonde with a sullen expression. Though she was chocolate-box pretty.

Joyce stood up and waived. "Hey Jackie, we have room on our table. Come join us."

Jackie shook her head, but the woman with her dragged her forward and they headed to the table.

"Wow, it's busier than I thought it would be. I was expecting it to be quiet at this time. Is everyone in town here today?" Jackie sat next to Minnie.

"I said the same thing." Ava replied, caught by Jackie's intense hazel eyes.

"Why Doc how nice to see you. How is the leg today?"

"It's still attached." Ava muttered and looked at the injured appendage.

"Good, we need you."

Ava looked at Jackie, unsure if there was another meaning to her words. A hand was thrust forward. "I'm Sue-Ann, Jackie's partner." Ava gave the hand a swift shake. "Pleased to meet you."

"You won't know my friend, Rita, she lives in Allenstown."

Ava saw a distinct disengagement from the named women.

"We know each other." Rita muttered. Sue-Ann didn't meet Rita's gaze.

"You look familiar I have to say. Darned if I know where I've seen you." Jackie said.

Rita shrugged. "If you go to certain clubs in Allenstown, we might have seen each other. That's where I know Sue-Ann."

Sue-Ann took a slug of her beer. "Jackie wants to have a serious talk. Stupid woman thought Baker's was going to be empty, no chance."

Ava cringed for Jackie. No love lost in that relationship.

"Eat, Sue-Ann," Jackie ground out and dropped her gaze to the food in front of her.

"Yes, a good idea." Ava returned to her spare rib.

Twenty minutes later, the meal consumed and the debris taken away, Ava began the conversation she was there for.

"You wanted to have a chat about the mayor's plans for your farm and Jerry's involvement, Joyce. I guess now is as good a time as any, as we've eaten." Ava gave her a serious look.

"Yes, I was hoping it would be quieter."

"Sorry to interrupt; I think it's shocking what that man is trying to do, using Jerry like that. Shame on him." Minnie declared. "Sorry Lizzy."

"No reason to be that's why I'm here. I don't agree with his tactics either." Lizzy shyly said.

Jackie leaned closer to the table. "What's going on?"

"None of our business, Jackie. I thought you wanted to talk to me." Sue-Ann pouted.

Jackie turned. "Not everything is about you!"

"Apparently, Seymour, the realtor, is using the mayor's influence to try to persuade me to sell the farm." Joyce said.

"What? Tell him to stick it where the sun does not shine. Where does Jerry come into all this?"

"There was an altercation recently, and Jerry thinks he's going to lose his job. The mayor backs that up with some ridiculous accusation about the incident at work."

Jackie turned narrowed eyes toward Ava. "You haven't let him go for that accident with Misty and Rock Rush?" The incriminating words hung in the air over the table. All eyes speared Jackie, all but Sue-Ann, who was watching the women at the table in front of her.

"No. If I had, it has nothing to do with the issue in hand." Ava retorted her nostrils flaring.

"Damn right it does. I was really getting to like you after yesterday." Jackie sighed into a sullen slump.

"What do you mean yesterday?" Sue-Ann glared at Jackie, then Ava. "Are you having an affair? Was that why you were late again? I call that the pot calling the kettle black, and you come on so self-righteous." Sue-Ann stood. "I'm leaving. Are you coming?"

"I'm staying until I find out what's happening here." Jackie decisively replied.

"I'm going home." Sue-Ann shook her head, snarling. "Don't expect me to wait around for you." She left the building without a goodbye or backward glance.

"Perhaps you might need to calm her down, Jackie." Joyce said.

Silence settled around the table. Jackie didn't respond

"You might not want my input, but I'm fascinated with this story." Rita offered a tentative smile. "Of course, I'll understand if you don't want a stranger knowing your business."

"Rita, it's a mystery why he thinks he can use my son. The more heads around the problem, the easier we can solve it. My husband used to say that, and he was usually right. Besides, you're a lawyer, so you might give us some useful advice." Joyce smiled.

Minnie chuckled. "This is just up her alley. Rita and I met ten years ago; she was one of my lecturers at college. A really great one, I have to say. Then I joined a murder mystery group at the same time she did. As the two newbies, they teamed us up together. We were unstoppable. I think they banned us after three months." Minnie grinned. "Rita knew what was going on after the first half an hour. Trust me, never go to a movie with this woman if you don't want to know the end at the beginning."

"I'm not that bad, Min." Rita winked at her friend.

"Was it a good movie?" Ava asked. The light banter diffused the emotional charge around the table and deflected attention away from Jackie.

"Oh yeah, Ben Affleck was one of the stars. He reminds me of…"

"Well enough of this social chitchat. What's the problem with Jerry?" Jackie ground out.

"Well it appears Mayor Blaine is blackmailing Joyce, using Jerry as a pawn." Minnie replied.

The chicken woman had been less than confident at their first meeting. Ava gave her a second glance, she was different in this setting. "What I want to know is how someone can think they can influence my decision about an employee. I've never met Mayor Blaine." Ava nodded in Lizzy's direction. "I make my own decisions."

Jackie snorted. "Sure, you do. We all do…not."

A serious frown creased Ava's forehead. "Are you saying that if the mayor approached me to terminate one of our employees, I'd agree without just cause?"

Jackie looked directly at Ava, then took a deep breath. "No, at least from what I know about you, no you wouldn't."

"Good." Ava looked at the rest around the table. "I might not be as influential in town as my uncle. Believe me, if I think something is unjust, I will support the victim. Joyce, Lizzy, please let us know what you need."

An hour and lots of soft drinks later, Ava was clenching her jaw. She desperately needed the bathroom and had no clue where it was. If she waited much longer, she'd pee her pants. That would not be a good look.

"I need a bathroom break." Jackie stood.

"Actually, me too." Ava struggled to stand on her crutches. Lizzy held her firm as she did. "Thanks Lizzy."

The younger woman shyly smiled. "Want me to help you?"

"Oh no, I'm good." Ava held up a hand.

"Lizzy, I'll take the doc. I have the experience, I'm a nurse remember?" Jackie winked at Lizzy, who chuckled. Jackie took Ava's arm. If she hadn't been so desperate for the bathroom, there would have been a protest.

One of the two-bathroom stalls was out of action and the other taken. Ava leant against one of the basins. "So, what do you think?"

Jackie stroked her chin down to her throat. "I think it's cruel and illegal, but the lawyer thinks there are no grounds to call it that."

Ava was about to speak, when Jackie began an impassioned rant. "How can anyone use such a great guy like Jerry for monetary gain? People do stuff wrong all the time. Believe me, I know first-hand. Just because he isn't as quick as the people around him means he's the scapegoat. I hate people."

The vehement shock waves hit Ava like a physical blow. "You don't hate people. Some perhaps, don't we all? Maybe you should go and make up with Sue-Ann."

A stranger's voice from the stall interrupted them. "Oh I wouldn't bother, if you're talking about Sue-Ann Locket. She's a skank and a player. That woman has the morals of an alley cat, and I hate to say that because I love my cats."

Ava watched a scarlet stain cover her vet nurse's cheeks. This was not a good day for Jackie.

"How would you know that?" Jackie's words, spoken quietly, alerted Ava. She'd seen her fair share of smouldering fires about to explode.

"She asked me out on a date a few months ago at a bar in Allenstown."

"Did you go?"

Ava placed a hand on Jackie's arm, which was shrugged away.

"No."

This woman was taking an inordinately long time to get out of the cubicle, and Ava desperately needed to go. "Have you nearly finished? Not that I want to rush you."

"Sorry, I had a curry last night, and it's going through me."

Ava placed a hand to her forehead and shook her head. *Way too much information.*

"Why didn't you go out with Sue-Ann?" Jackie badgered.

"Not my type. I heard she was in a long-term relationship. I respect that. Wish she did. I feel sorry for her partner." The toilet flushed and the woman came out. "Oh god, sorry I'm such a chatterbox."

Ava could feel Jackie relax a little. "Hey, you go. You'll be quicker than me." Ava pointed at her leg. She pushed Jackie forward and heaved a silent sigh of relief when Jackie closed the stall door.

"Do you both know Sue-Ann?" The chatterbox was washing her hands.

"Yes. How was your food?"

The petite blonde gave Ava an engaging smile. "Good. This place is renowned in the county for their BBQ. I wish I hadn't been persuaded to have that curry last night. I'd have enjoyed the BBQ more." The woman rubbed her hands under the drier, then left with a cheery smile.

Ava leant back against the basin and wished she hadn't. Her bladder had decided it had waited long enough, and she peed her pants. She peered down at the dark stain between the legs of her wheat-colored pants, allowing the embarrassment to wash over her. The door to the stall opened, and Jackie stepped out.

"All yours. I'll watch the door. It will be hard for you to work the space in there." Jackie stood at the next basin and began washing her hands.

Ava didn't move, sure that if she did, there would be a puddle along with the stain on her clothes.

"Want some help?" Jackie asked, shooting her a concerned look.

Ava squared her shoulders. "You know that we've had a pretty intense few hour? Maybe for you more than me."

"Yes and?" Jackie frowned.

"Want a laugh?"

"Sure, go for it."

"I'm not sure I can go to the stall and not make a puddle. I've already peed my pants."

Ava wasn't sure what she expected at her words, but the raucous laugh was probably not so bad in the circumstances.

"Well Doc I guess the damage is done. We can always say the faucet went wild." Jackie chuckled. Although it was at her expense, Ava was glad. This was the Jackie she preferred, not the intense angry one.

"You have to promise me that you will never divulge this to anyone." Ava gave her a serious look. Secretly, she was glad Jackie had forgotten her own problems for a moment.

"My lips are sealed." Jackie nodded. "Come on, let me help." Jackie took her arm and shut the door behind her in the stall.

Ava wondered how Jackie would get over her partner's betrayal. It was certainly not something she hoped would ever happen to her. "Better not to get involved in other people's relationships I always say." She quietly whispered.

"What was that?"

"Nothing Jackie. I'll be out in a few moments."

CHAPTER FOURTEEN

Ava sat in the wicker chair on the porch and looked over to the donkey field. Sure enough, Theo was there. Unfortunately, there was no way she could give him a treat. Her leg was hurting like hell, after spending half an hour getting out of her soiled clothes. Thankfully Jackie had made a plausible excuse and brought her home. They'd left immediately after the embarrassing event. *What a day.*

Her phone rang, she answered.

"Why hello, how is my favorite niece doing?"

Ava chuckled. "I'm your only one and not too bad. More to the point, what about you?"

"Oh, nothing exciting…"

"Yeah right, and this call out of our planned schedule?"

Her uncle laughed. "You and your schedules. I know I asked you to help me for three months. Any chance you can extend the term?"

Ava shook her head. He'd been speaking to her parents, for sure. "I have a job. Taking a three-month sabbatical was fine because it was basically accumulated leave. What are you talking about, another week or more?"

There was a distinct silence at the other end of the line. She almost fell off her chair at his next words.

"I'm getting married tomorrow, and I promised my new wife a trip to the Galapagos Islands. There's an extension to this cruise that leaves in a week. It's another month."

Ava opened her mouth to speak several times but found no words. "Who is this woman?"

"Gail joined the ship a month ago, and we fell in love."

This is a weird place. I've spent years doing the same thing in the same place without any major distractions. Now all hell lets loose when I leave my routine.

"I need to call my company and find out if I can do that." There was a loud beep in the background.

"Sorry to be a pain, but I need to go Ava. The emergency test signal has just gone off. Thank you." The call ended.

"I never said yes yet, and who the hell is this woman called Gail?" Ava rolled her eyes, then looked out at the natural vista. *Another month, what's the worst that can happen? They let me go?* She struggled to get out of the chair. A sharp pain had her settling back in the seat. "I guess I can call them from here." Withdrawing her phone, she dialed a familiar number.

"Hi, this is the voice mail for S Parkinson. Leave a message at the tone."

"Susan, it's Ava Lawrence. I need another month sabbatical. Let me know if it's approved."

Before Ava ended the call, a breathless voice answered. "Hey Ava, we've missed you. I've missed you." Ava rolled her eyes. "You want more time? We were hoping that you'd be back early."

"Sorry, my uncle has announced he's getting married again. He needs me to take on the load for another month. Can you let me know if it's approved?" Ava was ready to end the call but added, "Sorry I interrupted your weekend, Susan." *Mistake.*

"No, no I was waiting...hoping. How is it going?"

"Better than I thought. I'm actually enjoying life as a hands-on vet again. I have met lots of good people."

"You never liked that part of the business, you always said."

"Maybe I've changed. I need to go, Susan."

"Does this mean we might never see you again?"

"Why do you say that?"

"Because you might do what your folks want."

Ava bit her upper lip. "I might, would that be so bad?"

"I won't see you again."

"Susan, we might not have worked out romantically, but we remained friends. I don't forget my friends." There was a definite catch of breath from the other end of the line.

"I'll talk to the board." Susan abruptly ended the call.

"I don't know what she's worried about. Research is so much easier than the front line." Chuckling, she tried to get up again and managed to stay upright without too much pain. "Ok Theo, tomorrow for sure."

†

Minnie reflected on the lunch date catch up with her friend, as they neared the farm. Rita had been quiet most of the lunch. Her only interaction was to give sage advice to Joyce about her predicament. *Something must be wrong, big time.*

"We haven't had a good conversation yet. How about we chill out on the porch. I'll let you have some of my wonderful homemade lemonade." Rita didn't reply, as they negotiated the bend that led them to the same hedge Ava had landed in. "Did I tell you? Ava, the vet, fell into the hedge. That's why she has the cast. Danny found her, and she stayed the night. A bit of a cold fish at first, she thawed and is nice." Minnie smiled.

"Thawed, yeah, sure she would. She had you taking care of her. It's a no brainer."

Minnie laughed. "Why thank you, my dear friend." She buffed her nails against her sweater.

"Will Danny be there when we get back?" Rita asked.

"I'm not sure. I left a note for him that I was going out for lunch. I didn't see him last night or this morning. Does it matter?"

"No."

Minnie wasn't sure what was going on, but something certainly didn't track. "Are you ?"

Rita gave her a sharp glance for a second before returning her attention to the road. "Yes."

Minnie settled back into the leather of the seat. "Great, lemonade it is then."

†

Jackie drove home, half expecting or hoping Sue-Ann wouldn't be there. She climbed the few steps onto the porch, where Sue-Ann glared at her from the swing seat. She was, and held a glass of something, definitely alcoholic.

"You owe me an apology, big time."

Jackie watched her partner take a long swig of the drink. *Probably bourbon and Coke, her favorite.*

"For what?" Jackie moved closer and took the wicker chair next to Sue-Ann.

"Leaving me."

"You left, not me!"

"Semantics." Sue-Ann finished her drink and tried to stand. She wobbled.

"For goodness sake, Sue-Ann, how many have you had? It's barely been an hour since you left Barker's."

She looked at her glass. "I need a refill, and it's been two hours."

"Oh, now we are counting time. Oh of course, it isn't all about you for a change. Look, I'm over this relationship, and I know you are." Jackie closed her eyes at the finality of what she'd said.

Sue-Ann's cheeks flamed. "Don't tell me you've fallen for the boss and you want to ditch me. Classic." Sue-Ann pitched forward and fell against the screen door.

Jackie stopped herself getting up to help. *No, no, this time I have to stay strong.* "Think what you like, but you are not welcome here in my home anymore."

"It's my home too!"

"Sure, it was five years ago. Until you lost your job and had me pay you out of the mortgage. I own this place, at least the mortgage. Get real, Sue-Ann, what the hell has happened to you?"

"I hate you." Sue snarled.

"Well that's twice in a day. I guess we really are over." Jackie's stomach churned. "Time for us to both move on."

"You'll regret this and beg to have me back."

Jackie stroked her nose. "Nope, never going to happen in my lifetime."

Sue-Ann scowled. "It won't work out with that vet. She's not into you. Her eyes were all over Minnie Barrington. Your loss."

Jackie balled her fingers. "Go away Sue-Ann, and please don't leave anything behind. It will end up in the trash if you do. I never want to see you again."

†

Joyce sighed as she dropped Lizzy at the top of her drive.

"Thanks Joyce. I know we didn't accomplish much today, though I think Ava will help us. She seems nice, and Minnie's lawyer friend gave us good advice. Didn't she?"

"Yes, to both. Still, we don't have a plan on what I must do to save my farm and Jerry. He will be upset if he knows that he's responsible for this. Not that he is, of course." Joyce sighed heavily. "I wish my husband was still alive."

"Would he know what to do?" Lizzy frowned.

Joyce shook her head. "Nope, but sometimes it's just nice to have someone who loves you beside you as support. You'd better go, Lizzy. Your dad would hate to see my beat-up truck outside his house."

Lizzy rolled her eyes. "Never going to happen on a Sunday. He and Mom go to the golf club for lunch and dinner after a couple of rounds. I doubt I'll see them until tomorrow."

"I didn't know that. Do you want to come back and have dinner with me and the boys?" Joyce had always liked Lizzy. Even as a child, she was very caring.

"I wish I could. I'd love to have dinner at your house with...the boys."

The smile spreading over Lizzy's face told Joyce it was one boy.

"Misty needs feeding, and she'll want some company," Lizzy continued. "Unfortunately, she isn't a dog. I can't exactly bring her with me."

Joyce pondered that for a few moments. "Is this a regular occurrence for your parents on a Sunday?"

"Every week, without fail."

"Well, Lizzy Blaine, from next week you are making your own regular commitment. I'm inviting you over every Sunday, for lunch with me and my boys. You don't have to come every week, but you are invited." Joyce watched an astonished expression change to one of joy, as the biggest smile she'd ever seen from Lizzy beamed out at her.

"Thank you, Joyce, I'll be there." Lizzy skipped out of the vehicle and headed up the drive with a wave.

I've often wondered what life is like with lots of money. Now I know. You ignore your children once they reach the so-called adult age. Damn. My kids will always be a priority, no matter how old they are. Lizzy now comes under that umbrella. Joyce set the Jeep in motion and headed home.

†

Minnie lifted Gertie in her arms. The chicken was doing great, healing far better than she'd expected. "Mr Pip is going to be so glad you can be with him again." She ruffled the ginger and black feathers and placed Gertie in the compound where Mr Pip was watching. Minnie waited as Gertie did a 360-degree turn, shaking her body and made a sound you could only assume meant "Right, I'm back." Minnie watched Mr Pip, as he rushed over to Gertie, who was coy for a few minutes before she allowed him to give her a worm.

"All is right in that world." Minnie smiled, then looked over to the porch and Rita sitting there. She loved her friend, did love her, but had always known that their lives were poles apart. Rita was the city girl. Striding towards the house, she noticed Danny's car had gone. She had not expected her brother to be at home, especially with Judy Seymour in the picture.

As she took the steps to the porch and looked at Rita, her heart swelled. *If only.*

"Hey, did you miss me?" Minnie took the seat next to her friend.

"Absolutely. I have to ask, why do you like chickens and so many?" Rita sipped her drink.

"Oh, they grow on you. Did you know that they are prejudiced?"

"What?"

"Yeah, color coded for sure. Though with chicks it's a bit different. They take them all in, no matter what color. I find that fascinating." Minnie poured a glass of lemonade.

"Are you kidding me? Chickens have pea brains."

"Yeah and that means what? We have a massive brain in comparison, and believe me, we don't always make better decisions."

"Of course, we do." Rita frowned.

"What's wrong Rita? You've been less than yourself today."

There was a lull over the area. If you dropped a pin, it would have sounded like an explosion.

"Minnie, I'm forty-five, have a good career, can support a family. I'm not there, nowhere nearing achieving my utopia."

"Utopia?" Minnie frowned, when did Rita talk like this?

"Yeah. Surely it must have crossed your mind that there are things missing in your life. If you had them, wouldn't you have your version of utopia?" Rita leant forward and gazed over the gravel area toward the barn. "Unless you already call this"—Rita pointed around the yard—"your idea of utopia?"

"Well yes, I guess it is. I could do with winning a million dollars on the lottery to make it easy for the upkeep of the farm, but where is this coming from? I've never heard you speak like this, and we've known each other for over a decade." Minnie shuffled forward in her chair and took Rita's hand. "You know you can talk to me if it's sensitive."

Rita stiffened. "I thought that's what I was doing?"

Minnie shrugged. "Well yes, but this is different.... Come on Rita. Utopia. When do you say things like that? You are the most practical person I know, and you've often told me so over the years. What's changed?"

Rita sighed. Minnie watched her friend gaze out on the yard.

"Why don't I make up the spare room and you can stay the night?"

"I can't do that. I have an appointment at 8:00 AM with a client."

Minnie laughed. "Well that's the Rita I'm used to. Dare I ask what your utopia is?" Rita turned, and the look she gave caught Minnie's breath in the back of her throat.

"I'm sick of being single. I want someone to come home to every night, who loves me warts and all. It's pretty simple, don't you think?"

Minnie managed a tight smile. "Yeah, yeah it is. Have you thought that going to the clubs you do might be a problem?" Rita frowned, but Minnie persisted. "I mean, from what I recall when I was last in town with you, it was all happy-go-lucky places, no real commitment, if you know what I mean."

"A shag for the night and dump the phone number in the trash."

Minnie's cheeks flamed. "Well…yes I suppose."

"Krissie said the same when we met up this week. She said I needed to look at online dating."

Minnie gasped. "She's only twenty. The younger ones do that a lot these days." Rita shook her head. "I feel sorry for the Jackie person I met today."

"Why?" Minnie was intrigued.

"Minnie, her partner is a skank and a cheat. She's into anyone's pants who will buy her drinks for the night. Trust me, I know. She tried to work that number on me, at least a year ago. Glad I wasn't tempted, now that I've met her partner." Rita picked up her lemonade and drank thirstily from the highball glass.

"Jackie is really nice. She doesn't deserve that. To be honest, no one does. I'm glad I have all the animals and the farm to look after. Not to mention Mom and now Danny when they come home." Minnie smiled.

"Yeah, I guess you have the life you want." Rita hesitated. "Do you regret giving up everything and maybe a chance to find someone to share your life with for this place?"

Minnie grinned. "Rita, I do it for love, and I do love my life. Doesn't mean I can't meet someone who would be happy to share this life. I guess you'd call that my utopia."

Rita nodded and clutched Minnie's hand tight. "I noticed that vet was looking at you at lunch. Maybe that would be a perfect match."

Minnie gave a small smile. "Maybe. Hey, we could have a double date, because Jackie obviously is a settling down girl! After today, I think things will change in her personal life. A free agent again"

"Yeah, she's attractive in a country girl kind of way." Rita winked.

Minnie shook her head, laughing as she stood. "Well that's settled then."

"Minnie…"

A car appeared at the top of the drive, and they both watched as dust encompassed the vehicle. Moments later, it skidded to a halt in front of the house.

"Do you know the car?" Rita asked.

"Nope." Minnie went down the steps of the porch. Her smile disappeared when Danny stumbled out of the passenger side. Looking at the driver, she closed her eyes. *Not welcome any day of the week.*

CHAPTER FIFTEEN

Ava grasped the handle of the door to the surgery and sighed. With the brightest smile she could muster, she entered the lion's den. Confrontation was not an option. A few nice, simple cases would be right up her street.

The first person she saw was Pam at the reception desk, who gave her a tight smile. The waiting room had only a couple of people, both with cat carriers. Giving a nod, Ava entered her office and closed the door behind her. Beads of sweat dripped down her face. *That was hard.* Her leg hurt like hell, had done for a day now and the X-ray wasn't until tomorrow afternoon. Her uncle expected her to keep things going, and she would. Though god only knew how in her present condition. The door to her office opened, as she reached inside her trouser pocket for another pain killer.

"Hi Doc. How's the leg?" Jackie breezed in. Her natural smile was as good as any drug. *What the hell am I thinking?*

"Truth or lie?"

Jackie sauntered in and sat on the edge of the desk facing her. "Between you and me, Doc, always the truth." Jackie looked at the cast on her leg. "Hurts like hell, huh?"

"Damn yes. I never got any sleep last night. Couldn't get into the right position. Do we have a lot of patients today?"

Jackie stroked her sharp chin. "Maybe if you had a significant other to help at night that might work." Ava's nostrils flared. "However, to answer your question, just basic small animals for their yearly inoculations."

"Thank god, I can do that." Ava let out a huge sigh.

"Hmm that bad. As a vet, you could always use the jargon you'd say to an animal patient's family, to help ease their pets' discomfort."

"Jesus, Jackie, I'm not stupid. I've tried everything I know."

Jackie raised her hands. "Sorry just trying to help.

"I know, thank you. Look, I had a call from Minnie Barrington. She asked me out." Ava frowned. "I guess I should go. According to your philosophy, she could help me with my pain relief."

Jackie jumped off the desk and walked toward the door. With hand on handle, she replied. "Might work, Minnie is a keeper. Bear that in mind." Jackie's tone was sharp as she left the office.

Ava felt deflated even more than she was. Picking up the phone, she dialed Minnie's number.

†

Minnie glared at her brother. Bloodshot eyes and general intolerance to any loud noises testified to the fact he was hungover.

"What's for breakfast?" Danny whispered.

"Eggs, bacon, a round of toast. Basically, the usual." Minnie shook her head. Certain she saw several shades of green traverse his face.

"I'll just have coffee."

"Really. Did I say that was on the menu?" Minnie walked over to the counter and deposited a mug of coffee on the hard surface. "Enjoy. I have work to do." She left by the side door and headed for the barn.

Halfway toward the barn, she felt a tinge of guilt at how she had treated Danny. She steeled her thoughts. He was under the influence of the bitter enemy, the Seymour family. Damn, he was so stupid. Her phone rang as she was about to turn back. She frowned at the unfamiliar number.

"Hi."

"Hello Minnie, this is Ava Lawrence."

"Oh. Ava it's good to hear from you. Is it about Jerry or the Reynolds in general?" There was a significant silence at the end of the line. "Or maybe something else?"

"You called me last night and asked me out."

Minnie clasped a hand to her temple. *Crap, I did too.*

"I thought that, after I get my leg fixed...how about dinner?"

"Dinner, yes. I'm sorry, how is your leg?"

"Hurts like hell. Tomorrow, I hope they can fix me up."

Minnie smiled. "If you need anything, please call me. After all, I feel responsible."

"Oh no, it was all on me. I just wanted..." A voice in the background said the first patient was ready. "Sorry, I have to go."

"Yeah, take care of yourself." There was a quick response of thanks, and the call ended.

Minnie gazed at her phone. *This is all your fault, Rita. Why did you persuade me to call Ava and ask her out?* She pulled a face and headed with determination to the barn.

✝

Ava leant against the window frame of her office and looked out onto the backyard, which housed the exercise area for recuperating dogs and slightly larger animals, donkeys she figured. Jerry was talking animatedly to Trigger. The Labrador was being obstinate, hunched down and glaring at Jerry. The cast covering the stitches on the hind leg and traveling halfway up the back weren't helping. Although on meds, Trigger had decided he'd had enough of the vet world. Ava hobbled to the side door and painfully made her way down the five steps to reach the ground. With gritted teeth, she walked unsteadily toward the pair.

"Ain't gonna hurt you, Trigger. Doc has fixed you up good and proper. Let's just do the poo thing, and you can go back and settle on your bed." Ava smiled at Jerry's explanation. "I might find you a treat. Your mom said you love treats." Jerry spoke gently.

Ava looked at the dog, his tail wagged for a second. Progress. Its brown, soulful eyes looked at her.

Jerry turned. "Oh sorry, Doc Ava. He doesn't want to poo, but I'll keep trying." His expression fearful.

"You're doing great, Jerry. Sometimes we can't perform to a schedule. I'm sure he'll eventually realize it's something he needs to do." Ava heard a curse from a familiar voice and turned to the outbuilding that housed the stores.

123

"Does this mean I can keep my job, Doc Ava?"

"Sure it does, Jerry." His beaming smile even had her take a second look. He certainly was handsome. "Keep up the good work." She headed the short distance to the stores building and opened the door. She found Jackie hugging one of the benches; she was crying. The prudent thing was to leave. Ava turned around so fast, she lost her balance and shrieked out in pain as she landed on the floor.

"What the hell? Oh for goodness sake. Doc, you need a nanny. What the hell are you doing here?" Jackie scrubbed at her eyes, then grasped Ava's arm, helping her up.

"A nanny? I'm not a child." Ava bit out. Jackie would not want sympathy she knew that.

"Right at this moment that is exactly what you need. You shouldn't even be at work. Although, I applaud you for that." Jackie shrugged.

As they stood close together, Ava saw the lines of strain on Jackie's face. "I could say the same about you...the not being at work thing that is."

"Touché," Jackie gave a tight smile. "What would have happened to the practice if we had both not turned up today? Jerry and Pam in charge. Hardly a good idea." They both laughed.

"I guess we make a good team to balance it out. I wonder how my uncle does it." Ava smiled.

"Your uncle is ace." Jackie grinned. "He has a generous heart and extends it to more than his patients."

"I don't understand?" Ava frowned.

Jackie laughed. It was good to hear.

"Jerry, Pam, and even me. We adore him. He sees things in people that others ignore. Your uncle believes anyone can attain their dreams, even the trivial ones." Jackie took the curve of her left arm. "Time to take you back to your office and something more comfortable than the floor of the storeroom."

Ava shook her head and shrugged off Jackie's arm. *I'm not an invalid.*

"What? You don't want to go back for the afternoon practice? Can't say I blame you, and we'd understand. At least Jerry and I would. Pam will probably throw a hissy fit."

"No, no. I'm good. I can do this on my own." Ava waspishly replied, then left the room with gritted teeth. As she slowly made her way back to her office, she let out a painful groan. *Jackie was being nice. Why was I such a jerk?* Ava settled into the chair at the desk and sighed at the relief of sitting down. Before she could decipher her feelings, the phone buzzed. Pam announced her next patient. A rabbit called Bingo was stuck in a bingo wheel.

"Now I've heard everything." Ava muttered, as the door opened. A woman with the worst blue-rinse hair she'd ever seen entered and placed the wheel on Ava's table.

"I know it was foolish. I put him in the wheel for my knitting group's bingo evening as a treat. I thought it would be fun having a rabbit called Bingo actually kicking out the numbers." The woman gave a sob. "You can help Bingo, can't you? He hasn't eaten all day, and he loves his shredded carrot."

Ava now recognized others had far worse problems than she did. An owner like this, no mattered how remorseful, should not be allowed to own a pet. She gave a tight smile, though she wanted to take this rabbit from the woman for cruelty. "I'm sure we can work this out."

CHAPTER SIXTEEN

Judy Seymour clasped her hands together, waiting for an audience with her father. She figured even the Pope didn't leave people waiting this long. After all, she'd been requested for the audience at least three hours ago. She couldn't blame her stepmother, who hovered incessantly asking if she wanted a coffee or something to eat. Judy didn't want either. She sighed. She'd decided just to accept what was, meaning their marriage, and hope that her new stepmother would uplift her father and make him happy again. In Judy's eyes, at least, it hadn't.

The door to her father's study opened, and he gave her his best impression of a smile. *Yeah even a mime has more emotion.*

"Judy, sorry for the delay. Business never stops." He waved his hand inside the room.

Judy entered and sat in the chair furthest from her father. She watched, as he took his seat in a polished brown leather recliner and steepled his hands.

"What news?"

"What news?" Judy asked.

"Girl, I heard you were cosying up to the Barrington boy over the weekend. I call that a great strategy."

"Are you spying on me?" She held up her hands. "Hell no, I'm of little significance. For your information what I do after the office hours isn't about you or any of your business." Judy heard her voice move up an octave.

"You live under my roof. Everything you do, I pay for. Never forget that."

"How the hell can I? You always bring it up, Dad..." He raised his hand.

"The news, what is it?" The tone told her everything she needed to know. She was a ghost to him, fitting really, in the family circumstances.

"Mr. Seymour, I resign from the company. I'll leave your house within the next forty-eight hours. I think we are done here." The shackles that had bound Judy since the accident disappeared. She walked towards the door and turned back. Her father genuinely looked shocked. *About time.*

†

Joyce Reynolds watched her two elder sons laugh and joke, as they pitched hay from the barn into the pigsty. Two years apart in age, they were best buddies and did everything together, always had. You would think they were twins, in looks too. They took after her husband, with heavy-set dark features along with the best smile in the world that softened all the edges. The phone ringing in the hall had her turning back to the house.

"Hello, Reynolds residence."

"Joyce, my dear, how are you?" There was no disguising that voice.

"Mayor Blaine, this is a surprise. What can I do for you?"

There was a cough at the other end of the line, and Joyce knew exactly what he wanted. Let the weasel ask himself instead of sending his child.

"I was wondering if you'd have lunch or maybe dinner with me at the golf club this evening? There's a delicate matter I wish to discuss with you." He replied.

"Delicate, as in you threatened to have my boy sacked from his job. It didn't work!" Joyce balled her left fist, dearly wanting to punch the man for his underhanded tactics.

The mayor cleared his throat. "Perhaps I was a little presumptive. Let's talk. Seymour's project is important for the whole community."

"I can't make it today. I have plans. I'll call you before the weekend to set a meeting." She didn't wait for a reply and replaced the handset on the cradle. "Damn, now what do I do?" Frowning she went to the kitchen and began to set up a fresh pot of coffee. She certainly needed one. She chuckled. "Why the lawyer, of course. She said she'd help. Now, where did I put her card?" She rushed up the stairs to her room.

†

Rita stroked her chin. *Hmm gonna have to get rid of those hairs before I go out again.* She glanced at the number scribbled on her note pad and twirled the Mont Blanc fountain pen her dad had given her when she passed the bar. Since then, she'd bought ten at the last count. This one was her favorite. It held her dad's belief in her. When she signed her major papers, it was always the one she used "What the hell." She dialed a number, then glanced at the time. It was 8:15 PM.

"Hi."

Composing herself, Rita pursed her lips. "Hi Jackie, it's Rita Temple. We met yesterday at the BBQ place."

"Oh, right, yes. How can I help you?"

"This might be rather presumptive of me. Would you consider going out to dinner one evening?" The silence seemed to stretch forever. "Sorry, look I'm out of order. I'm sorry. You have a partner." About to end the call, she heard a quiet "…no significant other."

"Great. Look tell me when you're free and where you'd like to go."

"Can I take your number? I'll give you a call, and we can figure out the details."

"That would be great…yes that would be great. Take your time. Have a great evening talk to you soon, bye." Rita ended the call and sat in her chair. She clasped her hands around her head. "I'm an idiot, hitting on a woman who might have lost the love of her life. What the hell am I doing?" She sighed heavily and walking over to the cabinet that showcased her awards from college and the odd nod from the legal board. She opened the door and took out a strong box that she brought back to her desk. She opened her purse and withdrew a key to open the box. Photos and letters, along with various trinkets were snuggled in the box. They were monetarily worthless but worth an irreplaceable fortune to her. She picked up a photo of a young graduate, her smile captivating. "I love you." She kissed the photo and put it in her pocketbook.

CHAPTER SEVENTEEN

The verdict was in on Ava's injured ankle. In fact, it had been for two days, though she hadn't mentioned it to anyone, not even her parents. Doctor Jackson had said the best solution would be screws, meaning surgery. "The sooner the better," he'd said. The doctor was going to find out when the operation could be done and call her. It hadn't taken long. She'd just come off the phone. The surgery was booked. *Tomorrow.* Dragging a hand though her hair, she sighed heavily. *Who is going to take over here? I can't let my uncle down.* She chewed the inside of her lip, crying out as she drew blood. There was a rapid knock on the door. It opened and Jackie stood there.

"We have a rather feisty bull mastiff, called Pitch, in the owner's vehicle and refusing to leave. Even Jed can't persuade him to come out."

"Who the hell is Jed, and I need to know this why?"

"Doc, Pitch is on your list for a castration. I guess he knows somehow. Jed Simon is the owner." Jackie shrugged.

I'd be doing the god damn same in his shoes. Ava struggled to get up from her chair and reached for the crutches. "How do you think I can help, exactly?"

"I don't know, doctor patient interaction. Not your style, I know. We need something new. I'm just a vet nurse, remember? You're the boss." Jackie held the door open. Brushing past, Ava glanced at her senior vet nurse, whose expression was nondescript. She shook her head and concentrated on the task at hand, making it to the car park. The pain in her ankle had been getting worse as each hour went by, not that she was going to say so.

Ten minutes later and no joy, Ava leant against the Ford truck. "This isn't working. Frankly Mr. Simon, when you can control your animal, we will do our job." Clasping her crutches, she began to walk away.

"That's a mistake."

Ava carefully turned and narrowed her gaze at the speaker. "Really, and what makes you such an expert?"

"We have Jerry." Jackie seemed to grow in stature as she spoke, and her gaze never wavered when they connected.

Ava closed her eyes, partially in pain, but really discomforted that Jackie was right. "Maybe you should have thought of that first. I need to see my next patient." With determination, she slowly made her way back to her office, ignoring Pam's stare. Inside her office, she settled into her chair. *Damn I hurt.*

†

Jackie frowned at Ava's retreat. *Does she really care? I just don't understand her at all.* Jed Simon's face wore a bemused expression, as he continued to try cajoling his dog. Jackie made a call and smiled at the response.

"Hey Jed, trust me. If there is anyone who can talk to animals, this is your man. Our very own Doctor Doolittle."

"He talks to animals?" Jed frowned.

"All I know is that if Jerry talks to an animal, particularly dogs and cats, they become best buddies." She grinned as Jerry arrived. Without any direction, he began talking to Pitch. At once, the dog's tail wagged.

"This replacement vet isn't nice, doesn't give a damn. I'll be telling Doc Lawrence when he returns. I'll take Pitch to see the vet practice in Ralphstown. They will fix my boy."

"Jed don't be so hasty. Ava is a great vet. I agree her manner today was a bit sharp."

"A bit, I wouldn't want to go home to her every night." Jed snorted.

"She's having a hard time being incapacitated with a broken ankle. It happened at the weekend. She wouldn't take time off, even though she's in pain. I can tell you, she's a better surgeon than Doc Lawrence. Not that I'd tell him so myself." Jackie replied with a wink followed by a smile. She watched Jed stroke his dark stubbled chin.

"My youngest broke his ankle. He was in pain for days until he had screws fitted. Right as rain now though. He's even taken up baseball again." The anger left Jed's voice. "I'll be back at four to take Pitch home."

Jackie placed a hand on his arm, "You won't be disappointed, Jed. I promise he is in good hands." They both looked, as Jerry had Pitch doing tricks in the drive. *That boy is a genius. No way would this practice survive without him.*

Ava looked over the patients she'd operated on in the hospital wing. Dolly the chihuahua, the longest stayer, wagged her tail and began doing cartwheels. "Hey Dolly, don't make all my hard work on the hernia become unstitched." She chuckled softly and moved to Pitch. As she got closer to the much larger dog, he eyed her suspiciously then settled back down. "Don't worry, Pitch, you and your dad are going to be out doing all the things you did, and maybe more, within a short time." She opened the cage and ruffled his ears.

"See, I told you Jed. Pitch is in good hands." Jackie's eyes caught hers, and Ava received a very confusing message.

"There's my boy." Jed Simon grinned, as Jackie brought him out of the cage.

"Is Pitch ready to go home?"

"Yes. We need a check-up in a couple of weeks and any problems..."

Jackie held up her hand and smiled. "Got it, Doc. I can take it from here."

"Yes, yes of course you can." Ava slowly turned away, then stopped at the next words.

"When's the surgery on your ankle, Doc? My boy had a similar injury. Hurts like hell I bet. Jackie said you weren't usually that grumpy." Jed Simon was engulfed, in a subdued way, by his dog.

"Tomorrow as it turns out..." She left the room and headed for her office. She'd cut short the day's normal hours and was closing at five. Even Pam gave her a smile, as she slowly passed by the reception desk.

She sat down and made a call to the vets her uncle had suggested if she needed extra help. Ten minutes later, she'd secured a qualified vet who could help in emergencies. She pulled out the papers she'd printed off from the hospital for her own surgery. Mrs. Dank was the only one she could put down as a person who would care for her after the surgery. The office door opened like a dramatic gesture in a play.

"Did you even knock?" Ava looked at Jackie, who looked annoyed.

"Knock? When were you going to tell me you were up for surgery tomorrow?" Jackie glowered, placing her hands on the desk.

"I didn't think it was your business. I've arranged a replacement for the time I'm unavailable."

"Of course, you have!" Jackie walked to the window that looked onto the yard and storehouse.

Ava watched her and wondered why she was so angry. Although a part of her was oddly pleased.

"Why didn't you tell me?" Jackie turned around and stared at her. "Who is going to look after you? You can't do this by yourself." The impassioned words were not lost on Ava.

"Because we've been busy, and I forgot." Jackie growled and Ava sighed. "To be honest, I was about to put Mrs. Dank down as my contact. After all, who else do I know here who can do that?"

"I would." Jackie whispered.

Ava wasn't sure she'd heard right, but as she looked closely Jackie's expression was honest. "You would?"

"Yes."

"Can I get that written in blood?" Ava gave a small smile.

Jackie laughed. "Your blood maybe. I hate the sight of my own blood, just for future reference."

"I've got that." Ava smiled. "Well then, you can help me fill in this form. Your full name for starters." Jackie laughed.

"Jackie Joan Cochran." Jackie walked back to the desk and dragged a chair to sit next to Ava.

For the first time since she'd suffered the injury, she felt better.

✝

Jackie flopped down on the sofa in her house, looking around at the serviceable furniture she'd bought over the last five years. Sue-Ann's expensive influence had long gone, after she'd sold her share of the house to Jackie six years ago. Her ex-partner had refused to put any money into the house for refurbishment or furniture. The buyout was supposed to be temporary, until Sue-Ann had a decent job, which never happened. Jackie basically ended up as Sue-Ann's keeper. She held her head in her hands, realizing that her relationship had ended way back then. On reflection, their sex life had only existed when Sue-Ann demanded it. In the last year, Jackie couldn't remember them ever having sex. They had become ships that passed in the night, no longer lovers, not even friends, just together for the sake of it.

Today felt different. Since Ava had taken over from her uncle, things had gone from loving a very predictable job to loving the job but never knowing what might happen next. *I love it.* Ava was a contrary person, sometimes aloof and darn right obnoxious to the patient's relatives, yet sincerely caring and doing the best she could for the animals in her care. Then there was her attitude toward Jerry.

"Yeah Jerry, he deserves a pay raise after today." Jackie shook her head and smiled. No way was Ava Lawrence a hardcase through and through, not after taking time out to help his mother take a stand against the mayor.

Her phone rang, and she reached for it in her shirt pocket. The caller ID was oh so familiar and not welcome. "Yes" she testily answered.

"Oh darling, don't be so annoyed. It isn't all my fault." Sue-Ann's voice was silky.

Jackie pursed her lips. "What do you want?"

"Who said I wanted anything?" The pout on her ex's lips was easy to "see."

"You are calling me. The last time we spoke, I said I never wanted to see you again, or something along those lines. I haven't changed my mind. I ask again, what do you want?" The background music indicated Sue-Ann was in a club or bar. *Nothing changes.*

"Darling, I know we had our ups and downs. I'll forgive you for throwing me out of our home."

"Hey, wait up there. This is my home. You haven't paid for anything, not even food, in the past five years."

"Technicalities Jacks. Look, I want to come home. The cab is waiting. Will you pay him when I get there? I've run out of funds." Sue-Ann's voice became a purr.

Jackie closed her eyes. *Less than a week and she's begging to come back.* A part of her, the young Jackie who fell in love with Sue-Ann, felt sorry for her ex-lover and almost…almost gave in. *I'm not that that person anymore.* In college, Sue-Ann was the woman who would always be the love of her life. *That was then, this is now.*

"Jacks, come on, you owe me for all those years."

Jackie's nostrils flared. "Why do I owe you? Don't you owe me?"

"Oh darling, I taught you everything about loving a woman. It must mean something. You were a naïve orphan girl. I did you a favor." Jackie felt physically sick. Had she been the only one in love in their partnership? Right then, it sounded like it.

"No." Jackie disconnected the call and turned off her phone. She looked around the room and felt the enormity of making the final break. She had no tears.

CHAPTER EIGHTEEN

"Are we home yet?" Jackie smiled, as Ava rambled on and on from her hospital bed, about a camping trip with her parents. The surgery had gone well, but Ava had hallucinogenic complications with the anaesthetic. Rare, but it would wear off.

"Not yet Ava, soon." Jackie took Ava's hand closest to her and held it. The skin was soft and warm.

"Mom, I don't want to see animals suffer again."

Jackie frowned. "Ava, you help animals, it's all good. Rest now." The clasp around her hand was so tight, Jackie thought blood flow would be cut off at the strength.

"Will you be here when I wake up, Mom? You know I hate the dark." Ava's voice was barely a whisper.

"Sure, I will." Jackie prised her hand away from the strong grip, as Ava fell asleep.

A nurse entered the room. "Ah you've settled her down. We were getting worried. Are you family?"

Jackie shook her head. "No, a work associate. She's one of our local vets."

"That explains it then." The nurse smiled and began her observations.

"Explains?"

"Apparently, she was very agitated about a cat who had a bug, and no one could help cure it. To be honest, I hope it wasn't a bad memory. She cried in the recovery room." The nurse smiled "Her obs are looking good." She left the room.

Jackie wasn't sure what she'd gleaned from that conversation. One thing for sure, Ava hated the dark. When she left, she switched on the side table light and told the nursing staff to keep it on during the night.

†

Minnie watched her brother. He appeared sheepish as he entered the house. She didn't say anything, and he took a seat at the kitchen table.

"Min, I'm sorry." She turned and he held up his index finger. "Not sure why though. Can you give me a clue?"

"I told you that Seymour was trying to buy everyone out for a ludicrous mall scheme. I'm sorry you didn't take it in that his daughter was part of that package." Minnie clenched her hands together. "Are you dense? Oh maybe you are, that's why you can't finish your vocational course."

"That's harsh, Min. I didn't know her family were villains. For the record, I don't think she is."

"What, your dick is speaking for your brain? Danny you have always been gullible, and right now it's exponentially exaggerated."

"Oh, big words. Yeah right, Rita's visit. You always did try to make a good impression when she's around. You do know that most lawyers are sleazebags or just out for the big buck. I bet you don't know the truth about her, as I didn't know Judy's background."

Minnie ground her teeth. "You have no right to judge. Take a look at yourself before you do. All I'm going to say is Judy Seymour is not welcome here. If you want to continue that relationship, it doesn't happen on Barrington land." Minnie growled and left the kitchen, slamming the door behind. "Damn, I hate arguing." She climbed the stairs to her room.

†

Ava woke, taking in her surroundings. For a brief moment, she panicked then remembered the surgery. Settling back on the pillow, she sighed as the door opened.

"That's a heavy sigh. Good morning Ms. Lawrence. I'm Staff Nurse Row. How are you feeling?"

Ava blinked a few times. "Alive, and I don't feel any pain. Got to be good right?"

"Great. We were worried about you for a time there, but you rallied. Your friend was a good leveler I think."

"Friend? What were you worried about?" A bleep went off on the pager attached to the nurse's uniform.

"Be back soon."

The room was empty. Friend? Who was she talking about? I have no recollection of seeing anyone familiar after

Jackie left me here at seven yesterday morning. She glanced at her leg encased in a new cast and wondered how she'd maneuver out of the bed. Turning to the side, table she saw it was seven thirty. Jackie wouldn't be coming to visit. She'd have her hands full at the practice. Ava had told no one else about the surgery, except Mrs. Dank, who had insisted that if Ava was detained at the hospital, she'd be there if needed. It was very nice of the woman, but peace and quiet would serve its purpose.

The door to the room opened and Nurse Row appeared again. "Sorry about that. What did you ask me?"

"You said I had a visitor and you were worried about me." Ava frowned.

"Yes, didn't catch the name, but she said she was a work colleague." The nurse smiled and began to check her pulse. "You had a bit of a reaction to the anesthetic, became a bit of a rambler. Your friend calmed you." She dropped Ava's wrist. "Great. You are looking good. The surgeon is due on his rounds in a couple of hours. If he gives the ok, you can probably go home. Assuming someone is there to take care of you for a while."

"Yes, I have a housekeeper." Ava whispered.

"Good. Take care of yourself. My shift finishes in an hour, so I probably won't be back. I'll have someone bring in your breakfast." The nurse gave her a cheery wave and left the room.

Jackie calmed me down? How the hell did she do that? She doesn't know the first thing about me. Ava balled her fingers into the palm of her hands and resisted the urge to call Jackie. Maybe it was better not to know.

The door sprung open, and small wiry woman with a lopsided smile entered with a trolley.

"Good morning, Ms. Lawrence. I have the breakfast you ordered yesterday, freshly squeezed orange juice, hot black tea, and scrambled eggs on rye." She pushed over the lap table and placed the items on the pine surface. "If you need anything else, please ring the bell. Enjoy." The woman left before Ava could say more than thank you.

Ava's stomach growled. *I didn't realize I was so hungry.* She began to inspect the eggs.

CHAPTER NINETEEN

The phone displayed a missed call from Rita. Minnie didn't usually take her phone with her when she mucked out the chicken house, fearing she'd drop it in the debris and clear it away, never to be seen again. A picture in her mind of Mr Pip or Gertie finding it and making a call amused her, feasible too with the likes of Siri. She dialed Rita's number and waited for the connection.

"Minnie darling, thanks for calling me back. Perfect timing, I've just finished with a client and can take a break. Who better to take a break with than my best friend?" Rita's voice was upbeat. *When has she ever called me darling?*

"I like the sound of that. I've just spent the last couple of hours mucking out the chickens and general housekeeping for them."

"Oh, smelly work, right? Do you need to go shower first?"

Minnie laughed. "Nope, I still have lots more chores to do before I take a shower. What's up?"

"Does there have to be anything up?" Rita's defensive reply surprised Minnie.

"Well sure. I haven't heard from you in months and now two weeks in a row, not that I'm complaining."

"Actually, that Reynolds woman we met on Sunday called me to ask for advice."

"Joyce Reynolds?"

"Yes."

"What did she want, or shouldn't I ask? All that client confidentiality stuff."

Rita chuckled. "You can ask, as it's partly to do with you, I guess. She wants to take this Seymour character down or at least stop his manipulating the situation illegally. I've arranged a meeting with her on Saturday around eleven. Oh, and I also took your advice."

Minnie frowned. "On what?"

"I asked Jackie Cochran out. She hasn't agreed yet, but I figured I'd tell her I'd be in town and Saturday night would be perfect. Can I stay the night? Maybe you and I can have lunch Sunday before I go home."

Minnie sucked in a sharp breath. "Sure, do you need me at the meeting on Saturday?" A phone rang in background.

"Sorry Min, I have my next client. No rest for the wicked. Saturday sure, talk with the Jane...Reynolds woman. See you Saturday, got to go, bye."

The call ended.

Minnie leant against the boot room door, her heart heavy. *Was Danny, right? Do I really know Rita at all?* Minnie placed another call. "Hi Ava, it's Minnie. I heard you had surgery. Want some company tomorrow for brunch? I have to go to town early, but on the way back I can get some of Ma Baker's apple pies."

"Thank you, Minnie. I'd like that. See you tomorrow."

Minnie placed the phone on the bench and went out to tackle some more chores. *Why did Rita call me darling? She has never done that before.*

†

"Where is the vet? I want to see Dr. Lawrence, not some untrained half-wit!"

Jackie blew out a breath at the words. "Sorry Mrs. Cross, our resident vet is unavailable. You know, of course, Doc Lawrence is on vacation. He would have told you personally, as he did all his important clients. His niece is taking over in his absence, but she had an accident over the weekend. I am qualified to give you diet advice for Violet. I have the training. If you want me to show you the certificate, I can." Jackie bit her bottom lip.

Sheila Cross was a senior member of the community, with connections to the older wealthy families in the area. Her patronage usually came with added benefits in that her friends followed. There were less beneficial side effects; she wanted only the best. In her eyes, that was Doc Lawrence senior. He was a magician with this woman.

"I want to see Doctor Lawrence, senior or junior, not someone unqualified." The woman crossed her arms with a belligerent expression.

Jackie nodded, "I'll work something out for you. Unfortunately, it will mean that you may have a long wait."

Mrs. Cross unfolded her arms. "Good, I can wait as long as it takes." She picked up the cat carrier and walked over to the designated waiting area.

Ah but can your cat?

"How are you going to fix that? The locum vet will only come out for emergencies." Pam hissed.

"Shut up, Pam, don't you think I know that?" Jackie threaded her fingers together. She walked out of the reception area and into the breakroom to call Ava.

"I have a problem." She went ahead to tell the story.

"You won't get a vet to come out for diet advice. What made you say that, Jackie?"

"Oh, so now you think I'm a half-wit too."

"No. Send a taxi for me."

"I can't ask you to do that."

"You didn't. As the resident vet it is my professional opinion to the solution, which you asked for. Make it happen, Jackie."

Jackie growled when the call ended.

†

"Damn—Minnie." Ava looked at the time. It was ten thirty. She hoped the woman's number was stored on her phone. It was.

"Please answer." The phone went to voice mail. "Hi Minnie, sorry there is an emergency at the practice, and I have to be there. How about we have lunch or dinner on Saturday? You can choose our venue. Text me and let me know."

Mrs. Dank had made temporary accommodation for Ava in a first-floor room, until she could climb the stairs ably again. Ava made her way slowly to the room. Changing clothes was a nightmare, at least the bottom half. Well a crisp white shirt would work. She looked at her tan half-cut trousers. *They're going to have to be okay.*

Her phone pinged.

No problem. Saturday evening dinner would be great. There are only two up market restaurants, the golf club and Ginger's. Which would you prefer?

Your call, you have the local knowledge. Let me know the destination, and I'll meet you there at seven. Sorry I can't pick you up.

No problem. Want me to pick you up?

Do you drink?

Hell, yeah but not when I drive.

Then don't. Get a taxi, my treat. Then you can have a drink. Does that work?

Cool. See you Saturday, Ava. Looking forward to it. Minnie

†

Jackie shook her head, as Ava entered the practice. *This really shouldn't be happening. I'm perfectly capable of organizing a diet for Violet.* Mrs. Cross wasn't their only client, though telling Ava the background on the woman had been incentive for her to appear, despite the fact she should be resting. Jackie swiftly walked toward her.

"Hi, how are you doing? Sorry I haven't been able to check on you personally."

Ava shrugged, leaning on her crutches. "You've sent emails on what's happening here and called me every evening, thank you. This Cross woman, where is she?" Jackie pointed to Mrs. Cross, who was animatedly talking on her phone. Ava turned her way.

"I thought we didn't allow phones in the practice for customers?" Ava frowned, as she turned to face Jackie.

"We do. Pam should have stopped this. Want me to have a word?" Jackie felt she was letting Ava down. She watched, as Ava switched her attention to the receptionist. Pam was laughing with someone on the phone, ignoring a client who was looking around nervously with three cat carriers near her feet.

"No." Ava slowly click, clicked across the wooden floor. She made her way toward the reception desk. Jackie followed close behind. "Hi, you have a handful here. Any emergency?"

"Oh no, just the usual yearly inoculation before they go into the cattery. Pete and I are going to visit my mom in Sacramento. She had a heart attack last night. I'm here on spec, only arrived in town a few weeks ago. I hadn't got around to organizing the details for the cats." Jackie saw a nervous smile cross the woman's weathered face, as she peered down at her charges.

"Why don't you follow me? We'll fix them up."

The woman's mouth dropped open. "I haven't checked in yet. The receptionist is busy on the phone. There are others before me."

Ava turned toward Mrs. Cross and nodded.

God help Pam, Jackie thought.

"Don't worry about that. I'll take care of it." Ava turned to Jackie. "Right, Jackie?"

Jackie nodded. "Absolutely Doc, you are in charge."

"You're the vet? Oh, this is awesome service. I'll tell all my friends." The woman picked up the first carrier.

"Let me," Jackie said as she lifted the two of the carriers. *Wow, who is going to be more pissed, Mrs. Cross or Pam?* She damped down a laugh. Ava gave her a sharp glance, and she arranged a more sober expression on her face, internally laughing like hell.

†

"You can't do this, circumventing my authority." Pam Dawber shouted at Ava.

"Really, who is the vet here, you or me?" Ava tried not to get angry with the woman—impossible! Pam gave what could only be described as a grapefruit expression. *I hate eating grapefruit, I always pull a face like that.*

"Your uncle would never have treated me this way. I organize the appointments, no one else."

Ava sucked in a deep breath. *I'm ready to go home, big time.*

"I bet Jackie said I wasn't capable?" Pam complained. "She has never liked me. I'm good at my job."

I don't have the energy for this confrontation, and I'm ready for my painkillers. "Jackie hasn't mentioned you in any detrimental way. I'm going on my experience today. A client was waiting inordinately long. You didn't even acknowledge her. Even when I intervened, you seemed oblivious except to whomever you were talking on the phone with. For the record, I'm not my uncle…"

"No, you are not. That's for sure. It shows."

"Really, how?"

"You gave priority to a client who wasn't even registered over Mrs. Cross."

Ava swiped a hand over her mouth, inside she felt like a raging bull. She had been advised by her uncle that she couldn't dismiss anyone while he was away, no matter how aggravating she might find the staff.

"Tell you what Pam, you leave your phone in the locker room when you work, and I'll say no more."

"I won't do that! It only applies to the clients."

Ava lifted her hands. "Precisely. Didn't work right? Mrs. Cross was on her phone when I came in the practice. Now I'm revoking it for everyone." Pam gave her a look that might have struck her dead if it was charged. "Pam, leave the personal stuff for your break or outside the practice. Is that all?" Ava watched several changes of color travel over Pam's face. *Have I gone too far? I really wanted to tell her she didn't need to come in tomorrow. Damn Uncle Gerald, he's going to get an earful when he next calls?*

"Yes." The hissed words reverberated in the room. Pam scowled and left, closing the door with a resounding thud.

Ava settled back in her chair, trying to decide if coming in to help out had been a good idea. She felt like shit. There was a solid knock on the door, and it opened.

"How are you doing?"

"Does feeling like crap work?" Ava closed her eyes, as she leant back in the chair.

"You shouldn't have done this Doc. Seriously, are you mad?" Jackie closed the gap and entered Ava's personal space.

151

"Since I've been here, Jackie, yes. I really think I'm going mad. Roll on the day when I can go back to a laboratory without all this personal stuff invading my space."

"Do you mean that?"

Ava considered the quietly spoken question. At this moment in time she did, big time. Before her foolhardy accident, she had begun to see another life outside the lab that tempted her.

"I guess that means yes." Jackie turned away, heading for the door.

"You want the truth?"

Jackie spun around and nodded.

"I was actually liking the change, then I did this stupid thing." Ava pointed to her leg. "Now I feel useless and crabby."

"Crabby works in the circumstances." Jackie smiled.

"For you maybe. I think Pam Dawber believes I've grown horns overnight. I banned all personal calls at work for everyone."

"Wow, I applaud your bravery. Pam, is a hostile enemy, trust me. I just give her a wide berth when she's in a mood."

"Why are you so nice all the time? You've just gone through an emotional trauma. I'd expect you to be a bit crabby too."

"Oh, thanks for reminding me of my single status." Jackie shrugged. "It hasn't been as traumatic as people might think. We've been drifting apart for a few years. I guess I finally engaged my brain instead of my heart. Have you ever experienced the same thing?" Jackie straddled the chair closest to her and gave Ava an intent stare.

"No, no I never have. I tend to keep relationships low key."

"Why?"

"Because...hell, just because. Not everyone wants the responsibility of another life." Ava scrunched up her face. *Did I really mean that? I loved Molly.*

Jackie sighed and unhooked herself from the chair. "It might be worth it with the right person."

"Yeah and you're the resident expert. I think I'll take a rain check." Ava regretted the words as soon as they were out of her mouth, seeing the change in the pallor of Jackie's face. "I'm sorry..."

"No. No, you are right. It didn't work this time. I think there is someone out there for everyone, and that includes me. The challenge is finding that right person. I hope you understand that one day." Jackie turned toward the door. With a hand on the doorknob, she said, "Living your life without someone to share it with will be very lonely. What people don't understand is that it doesn't have to be a lover. It can be the person or maybe the animal who simply makes you happy. Together, you make each other's world so much richer." Jackie exited the room.

Ava simply stared at the closing door.

CHAPTER TWENTY

"I have to admit that giving advice to country folk is a bit of a challenge. Min, how have you stood this kind of life for so long?"

Concern clouded Minnie's expression, as she and Rita entered the farmhouse. "Easy I was brought up here, at least during my formative teen years. What do you mean by challenging anyway?" Minnie kicked off her shoes in the hall and ignored the fact that they splayed across the wooden floor.

"They are just so darn…naïve. You could do so much more. Why put a chicken first before a six-figure salary? I've never understood that." Rita glanced toward the stairs. "Same room?"

Sucking in a breath, Minnie nodded. "Make yourself at home. I need to get ready for my date." She turned toward the kitchen. Danny might have left her a message on his comings and goings for the night.

"A date?"

"I guess you've forgotten." She turned back. "You don't think you're the only one who can snag a date in this town? Rita, silly you." To her friend's scowl, she explained. "Ava, the vet, said yes. I've booked a table at the golf club. Any more questions?"

"No, I remember now. You also mentioned a double date."

"Why would you want that? We country folk aren't exactly your idea of a good time. I'm surprised you even asked Jackie."

"Yeah me too!" Rita muttered under her breath.

"Hmm, not the right attitude. I hope you don't bore Jackie to death." Minnie delved in her pocket and withdrew a key. "Here, take this if you're later than me."

Rita snatched the key and her overnight bag and stomped up the stairs without another word.

Minnie watched and wondered why she cared. She knew why. Sighing heavily, she approached the kitchen.

†

Jackie looked at her wardrobe. Jeans of differing shades, plenty of pastel shirts and a couple of washed-out blue slacks. Nothing dapper. *Damn, what do I wear for this date?* Rita was attractive and very sophisticated. *Add wealth to the equation.* Her eyes settled on her work clothes, dark blue overalls with her name emblazed on the left-hand breast pocket. *I could always go in that garb. She might find it sexy.* She sat on the edge of her bed and sighed.

155

"I'm so goddamn out of practice for going on a date."
Threading her fingers through the coverlet on the bed, she
contemplated her predicament.

†

Joyce sat in the rocker on the porch, swirling her whiskey
sour in its glass, as her eyes went over the notes Lizzy had
taken during their meeting. Most of what the lawyer said had
gone over her head, lots of jargon which made little sense to
her. Fortunately, Minnie seemed well versed with the
language. *I'll have to ask her about that next time I see her.*
All that Joyce knew was that if they stood together Seymour
didn't have a hope in hell of achieving his plans. But could
they keep up the defenses indefinitely? The sound of laughter
brightened her heart. She looked up to see Jerry and Lizzy
walking with Sinbad between them. How innocent those two
were in their love of each other. They were, for sure, in love;
it shone like a beacon of light when they were in each other's
company. There were obstacles to them having a life
together, but it didn't have anything to do with the two of
them. Nope, the obstacles would come from peer
pressure…and the mayor. Joyce smiled, hoping Sheena
Blaine might be a bit more understanding. After all, the
Blaine money was Sheena's inheritance, not the mayor's.

"Hi mom." Jerry grinned and waved at her.

"Hi yourself. Have you had a good walk the both of you
and Sinbad?" Joyce smiled at Lizzy. Whose cheeks were
faintly pink as she nodded shyly.

"We did. Lizzy knows the names of all the pretty flowers
in the Barrington back meadow. That's clever, right mom?"

Jerry's words were directed at her, but his attention was squarely on the woman at his side.

"Oh, it's nothing. I always loved looking up the names of flowers and stuff as a kid."

"It is Lizzy. Don't say nothing, because it isn't. I don't know them. Do you, Mom?" Jerry's face showed he was perplexed.

"I do not, son, maybe one or two as you probably do."

Jerry chuckled. "Weeds, sure."

Lizzy smiled. "Weeds are flowers too, Jerry, just not as attractive to some people."

"I figure I'm a weed, especially to Mrs. Dawber. She only likes the flowers. Well maybe not Doc Ava. I think she's a weed like me, according to Mrs. Dawber."

Joyce supressed a belly laugh. Jerry might not be the sharpest tool in the box, but he sure got it right with the way people think about others. "Now why would you say that?"

Jerry shrugged and his cheeks went a shade redder.

"Come on you two, sit with me for a while and tell me why you think that, Jerry. For the record, you and Ava are attractive people in my eyes."

Lizzy grinned. "In my book too."

"I'll fetch some refreshments." Joyce was about to rise from her rocker, when a large yet gentle hand settled on her shoulder.

"I've got it, Mom. Shall I make you another drink?" Jerry pointed to the half-empty glass on the side table.

"Thank you, son. You know how I make a mean whiskey sour."

He winked and then turned to Lizzy.

"I'll have whatever you're having, Jerry." Jerry frowned.

Joyce wondered why Lizzy's reply was a problem for him. His explanation melted her heart into a shower of liquid. *I do love you son.*

"I can fix you a soda. If you want what Mom wants, or a beer, or wine, or tea…I'm good at tea too. Coffee is more difficult. I think the percolator hates me. For you, I'll make it though."

Joyce saw Lizzy had tears in her eyes. "Why don't I help you, then I'll decide."

Watching them leave the porch and enter the house, Joyce marvelled that life really was diverse in how it chose the people you love. Settling back, she picked up her drink. *I'm going to fight Seymour, come hell or high water, for as long as I can.*

†

Ava looked at the clock. It was four thirty, three hours until her date. Mrs. Dank had diligently helped her organize her wardrobe. A yellow cotton dress was laid out on the bed. The long sleeves would complement her lean physique, and the side slit would work with her injury. A thin, red belt lay by the dress. The last time she'd worn a dress, and this one in particular, had been at a fundraiser for research into respiratory cures for domestic dogs and cats. The event had been successful, due to her parents making a very generous contribution. The project was, after all, her nominated research program.

Sighing, she sat on the edge of the bed. Her gaze traveled to the oversized panties, plain white. She cringed and wished for her normal lingerie, flimsy and sexy. "At least I can wear a bra of my choosing." Her eyes rested on the pale-yellow uplifting garment.

"Have you everything you need, Miss Ava?"

Ava smiled. The oh-so-formal Mrs. Dank had been great. Not something Ava would normally say of a woman who had been draconian since the accident. There had been severe words from the housekeeper when she found out that Ava had gone to work. Except the emotion behind those words had been quite warming. This woman, who knew nothing about her other than she was the niece to her employer, had treated Ava, a relative stranger, with tenderness and dignity. It was the complexity of entering the realms of interaction with people again, Ava figured "I think you might be right..."

"Well of course I am. Are you looking forward to your date? She's a lovely woman, Minnie. I've known her since she arrived in Sterling, a caring beautiful child. Most of the town loves her, they would be upset if..., well it's early days." Mrs. Dank smiled and fussed with the coverlet on the bed.

Ava, for the first time, realized the enormity of going on a date with someone that this town thought was wonderful. *Crap.* Her uncle's words not to upset anyone pealed like bells in her head. "I'm looking forward to my date with Minnie. I'm sure it will be very enjoyable. What are your plans for the evening?"

Mrs. Dank regaled her with the family commitments for the evening. Ava tuned in and out, as she wondered if her rash decision to go on a date with Minnie Barrington had been a smart idea.

CHAPTER TWENTY-ONE

There had been no message from Danny on his plans. Obviously, their morning spat had been more painful for him than her. Still, Judy Seymour was not welcome in her home. She pouted a little. *I guess it's Danny's too, but he doesn't contribute anymore to the upkeep.* Sighing, she looked at the time. Rita was getting ready for her assignation with Jackie. A date, Rita called it. Her own idea in meeting up with Ava was more about getting to know her than anything sexual, though she had told Rita it was a date. *I should never have asked Ava out to dinner. She's been so good about the whole Mayor and Seymour situation. Then there's Jerry, and damn my hedge for causing her injury.* Minnie collapsed on the sofa, energy for her dinner with Ava dissipating with every second. *Dare I her call her and cancel? God no, that would be terrible. We can still have a good time. It doesn't have to be about sex. It can be friends, yes, we could be friends.* She stood quickly and became entangled in a black leather pocketbook, obviously Rita's.

Minnie smote a hand to her forehead, as the contents spilled on the carpet. "Damn."

She began to collect the items and stuff them back in the pocketbook, hoping Rita didn't notice the mess. She hesitated when she spotted the last stray item. Curiosity got the better of her, and she examined the photo. Minnie gasped. A young woman with a beaming smile wore cap and gown as she collected her diploma. *It's me.*

The door to the lounge opened. "Hey, Min, I think I left my pocketbook..." Rita stared at her, but more importantly at the object in her hand. "I didn't know you liked to rifle through someone else's personal belongings. You do know it's illegal."

Minnie simply stared at her friend.

"Give it back please. We have that taxi booked for forty-five minutes from now. Believe me, your date will not appreciate your attention to personal detail looking like that."

Minnie turned the photo and read the inscription. I love you, Minnie Barrington. I wish you felt the same, Rita.

"You loved me?" Minnie asked, breathless.

Rita clenched her hands. "Hey, I liked all my students." She shrugged.

"I don't see anyone else's photos here. What about Karen Starling? She was your star at the lectures. Evangeline Rolling, your definition of beautiful. You did a personal mentoring session with her. They adored you. Why my photo? Damn, Rita." Minnie clasped her hands together and dropped her head. "I'm confused. According to what you wrote on this photo, you loved me!" She looked at her friend.

"Minnie, sometimes we do things that make no sense." Rita's cheeks had turned crimson. "It was years ago. You were a young woman on the brink of life. I was ten years older. I doubt, very much, you would have considered going on a date with me at the time. I'd have been an old lady to you."

Those words served up a lot to digest. "I've loved you since the first day you gave a lecture to us," Minnie choked out. "I was captivated, and when we accidentally met when you spilled coffee over me at that absurd conference on trees…. To this day, I still don't understand why you were there. Rita, I love you. For the record, I always have. I figured I didn't have a chance with you on any level."

Rita held herself as stiff as a statue.

God, I've gone too far.

The statue came to life. Rita moved to within inches of her. There were tears in her eyes.

"Are you saying that I've wasted ten years on friendship, when we could have been lovers?"

Minnie touched Rita's soft cheeks and smiled. "And before then."

Pulled hard into Rita's chest, Minnie's lips were captured in a kiss that would be embedded in her mind forever.

"I love you, Min, please don't go on a date with another woman."

Gasping for breath from the kiss that injected her with so many emotions it was impossible to describe them, Minnie cradled Rita's head in her hands. "I'll promise if you do?"

"Oh, that's a given." They kissed again.

"You do know we have to cancel our dates. It's the right thing to do." Their kisses became frenzied.

"Let them sue us. I want you and only you. I've waited a long time for this." Rita captured her lips again.

When they broke apart, Minnie sent up a prayer that Ava and Jackie would understand, eventually. "Take me to bed Rita; we've both waited long enough."

CHAPTER TWENTY-TWO

Forty-five minutes, she'd been sitting at the table Minnie had booked for forty-five minutes. Ava looked at her phone. *Yep, seven forty-five. Should I call? There could be some problem.* She glanced away. *Don't be stupid.* It was way too early to consider this a brush off. She ordered another wine and contemplated being dumped. She was so engrossed in her thoughts, she jumped when a familiar voice spoke her name.

"Jackie, what are you doing here?"

"I'm on a date, but so far she's a no show. Don't tell me you're in the same boat?"

Ava flushed.

"Wow, I'd never have thought Minnie would do that to anyone. She hasn't even called?" Jackie stared at her, and something in her gaze told Ava the woman was secretly laughing—it rankled.

"She hasn't. Maybe she's just late. I guess the same could be said for your date with the lawyer." Her words were sharp. She'd put more emphasis than necessary on lawyer and didn't know why.

Jackie's eyes twinkled. "You could be right, maybe I'm impatient. She is half an hour behind schedule. Do you mind if I sit until she turns up, or Minnie does?" It wasn't really a question; Jackie took the seat opposite her and the waiter appeared with her wine.

"Want a drink?" Ava had never been one to drink alone publicly, privately, that was another ball game.

"Sure, I'll have the same as you." The waiter smiled, saying he'd be right back.

"Do you even like wine? I've seen you only drink beer." Ava sipped the dregs of her first glass, enjoying the lush, juicy apricot and melon flavors wrapped with a warm spicy oak and a touch of nutty creaminess.

"I guess I'll find out in a minute or two. What do you think of the golf club's restaurant?"

Ava shrugged at the table set with pristine white tablecloths and napkins to match. Two lots of wine glasses and the cutlery were set for a five-course meal. The waiter had been very attentive as well, and that was usually a good sign. "I've yet to sample the food, but the presentation and service so far is very good."

Jackie glanced around the half-empty dining room. "In about five minutes this place will be packed, the members are creatures of habit."

"How do you know this?" Ava couldn't see anyone near the entrance, and it was five to eight. "I mean, there isn't a line waiting to get in."

165

Jackie chuckled. "Trust me, they will be jostling to get in at precisely eight, and guess who will be the first one to enter, even if they weren't at the head of the line."

"I have no idea." Ava lifted her hands and waved toward the door of the restaurant.

"The mayor. Wait a couple more minutes, and we will see if I'm right. Want to bet on it?"

Ava shook her head. "Not a chance, you have inside information."

The waiter arrived with the glass of wine for Jackie and placed it down in front of her. "Are you ready to order yet?"

"No, not yet," Ava said. "Please give us another fifteen minutes." He nodded and headed off.

"Are you saying that you'll give your date until eight fifteen and then call it bust?"

"Well, if we both are in the same predicament, then you'll just have to have dinner with me. Neither one of us wants to lose face, right?" Ava rolled her eyes to emphasize her point, then her mouth opened like a guppy and refused to close. She spotted the mayor and his wife, who pushed aside others beginning to form a line. His bombastic entrance seemed typical of what she had heard of him. "You were right."

"About what—" They heard the boom of a voice in disagreement with a softer woman's voice, telling him he had jumped line and he needed to go to the end. "She's got balls."

Ava laughed. "Yeah, I guess. She looks familiar. I'm sure I've met her before."

"Yeah, you're right. She's the woman we saw with her cats before Mrs. Cross, who incidentally will be in that line." Jackie pointed at the ever-increasing queue. Some pushed their faces against the glass entrance door, wondering what was going on.

They both watched, as the mayor finally turned tail. From her body language, it appeared his wife was apologizing to the woman.

"Wow." Jackie took a drink from her glass, and Ava schooled her features not to laugh at the grimace on her face. Several splutters later, Jackie gave her a tight smile. "You really like this?"

"Yes." Ava grinned. "How about we order you a beer?"

Jackie sighed heavily, then winked. "Good call, Doc. She sure does have power over these folks who think they are better than the rest of us."

"Very cynical, Jackie, and not all of them I suspect. Do you remember the woman's name?" Ava pursed her lips in concentration. Names of people she'd only met once didn't register that well with her.

"Not right now. Give me a few minutes, bound to remember."

"Well hello there, I thought it was you two. Are you being well taken care of?" The woman they were talking about appeared out of thin air to stand between the two of them a wide smile on her weathered complexion. "Do you mind if I sit for a minute? I never did get the chance to thank you earlier in the week."

Ava nodded and suspected Jackie did the same, as the woman they couldn't name sat down in a vacant chair and summoned the waiter.

"Sam, take special care of these two ladies this evening. They are my guests." She winked at the young man who nodded vigorously and asked if they needed anything.

"I'd love a beer, please. I guess I'm not cut out to drink wine." Jackie gave a self-conscious shrug.

"Oh, well we have some fine beers from across the globe. My Pete insists on it. Sam, bring this young lady a list." She turned to Jackie. "Sorry can't remember names. It must be part of getting old I guess." She chuckled.

"Jackie." Jackie held out her hand.

Ava smiled indulgently at Jackie's polite gesture. *I guess I should do the same.*

"Well I know you are Doc. Lawrence, the younger," she chuckled and turned her pale-blue gaze toward Ava and back to Jackie. "Hello Jackie," the woman took her hand and shook it.

"We don't know your name. Well actually, I'm sure you said, because I remember the three cats. We must be getting old too, because we can't remember names either." Jackie grinned.

"Speak for yourself." Ava said.

Jackie winked at her and the older woman smiled.

"Evalyn Clancy Derossy."

Ava was about to say her first name to make things less formal, when she saw Jackie's jaw drop. It did, big time. *Wow, she looks like a fish out of water.* All eyes were drawn by Ava's laughter. "I'm Ava."

"Good to meet you Ava and Jackie." Evalyn grinned. "I think Jackie knows the family connections around here, but you obviously don't, Ava. Very refreshing, I'm glad to say." Her gaze traveled to the entrance. "Hmm, got to go. The mayor is acting up again. Anything you two need tonight, go for it. Everything is on the house. See you both soon." She stood and agilely headed to the heated conversation most customers could hear.

"Mayor Blaine isn't happy." Ava remarked, as she rubbed a thumb around her wine glass.

"Ava, do you know who that woman is?"

"Nope. Enlighten me." She took a sip of the wine.

"It's…well if Pam knew who she was, she'd have wet her pants."

"Doesn't make sense, Pam must know. She had to bill her." Ava bit her lip, remembering that she hadn't filled in any paperwork. "Except I think I gave her a free pass."

Jackie stood and reached over the table. She kissed Ava's cheek. "Oh, your uncle is going to be so proud of you." Jackie settled back in her chair.

"I don't understand." Bemused, Ava wanted to touch the skin Jackie had kissed; it felt like it was burning.

Evalyn Clancy is from *The Clancy's*. Oh god, in this state, she'd be equivalent to the Queen of England." Jackie's face was the most animated Ava had ever seen.

"Here you go, the beer menu. Want to take a minute—"

"Oh no." Jackie speed read the menu. Ava was impressed. "Heineken super cold, please."

"Great choice, I'll bring you two. You are a little behind." He winked as he left.

Jackie laughed and turned her attention to the room. They sat quietly, and Ava watched Jackie's countenance change from a smile to consternation as she watched the goings on in the restaurant.

"I guess it's time to order dinner." Ava's words didn't register, her colleague was so enrapt by their surroundings. "I figure it's eight fifteen. Our respective dinner companions are no shows, don't you think?" Still no reply. Ava picked up her drink and wondered why anyone could dislike this wine choice.

CHAPTER TWENTY-THREE

Minnie, sated from love making, gazed at Rita sleeping beside her. Rita had been the love of her life for over a decade, from afar. Unrequited love, she'd always thought. Yet a simple discovery had given her the world.

She gently moved the bangs from Rita's forehead and traced a finger over the faint lines that featured there. "I love you, Rita. God why has it taken so long for this to happen?" Pondering the past, she shied away from the possible future. They had different views on where they wanted to live and lifestyle. *I love my life here, but do I love it more than you? Can I sacrifice everything for you?* She kissed Rita's forehead.

"Hey, god did I fall asleep on you? Shit that is so bad." Rita scrambled up and faced her.

"No, no I guess we exhausted each other." She looked at the clock in her room." It's ten thirty."

"Wow where did the last four hours go?" Rita grinned and pinched a nipple. Minnie squealed.

"That was oh so naughty, but nice. What else do you have in your arsenal?" As she captured Rita's lips and sucked on her tongue.

"Whatever you can offer me, minx." Rita answered breathlessly when they came up for air.

Minnie opened her arms and pulled Rita close, their breasts pressed together. The simplest of touches, yet her body lit up like fireworks. "Just make love to me again and again. I want you so much."

Her body absorbed the vibrations of Rita's groan, pushed back onto the bed. Kisses began at her lips, breasts…and down. Strong hands gently pushed her legs apart. Her clit engulfed by a warm mouth, heaven exploded.

†

Jackie laughed, then stifled the sound by covering her mouth. People either side of their table were staring at her. Ava's explanation of vet college had been amusing, though not overly antic worthy. She hadn't figured on Ava being a rebel. Nope the sober woman didn't strike her as one who would do anything more than achieve her degree, much like eighty percent of people who take up a profession. Yet the conversation had been light and fun, at least to her.

"It's good to laugh, Jackie. In fact, I'm glad you are. Amazed of course." She smiled. "I'll take it I'm not exactly the most boring person in the world, but close." Ava twirled a finger around the stem of her wine glass.

Jackie chuckled. "I didn't want to embarrass you. This is an elite restaurant in these parts."

"You think I care what these strangers think?" Ava shook her head. "Please give me credit for a little common sense. Besides, isn't that the reason why people come out—to entertain themselves? I believe laughing is a compliment to the company you are in."

In that moment, Jackie accepted her instinct of liking this woman, even if others found her stoic. Those words had validated the feeling. "I like the way you think. Tell me why research and not a hands-on practice?"

Ava pursed her lips. "Hmm, I did hands on, as you call it, for my first five years after graduation. Although I've always been drawn to research."

"So, how long have you been a researcher?"

"Almost five years."

"Why the change? Did you just get bored?" Jackie thought she noticed a wince, but Ava shrugged.

"In my first year of practising, there was this particular cat with respiratory problems. The "mom" loved her so much, she would have sold her soul to make her well. The cat was only three. There wasn't a cure. In my spare time, I began that particular quest."

Jackie's brow raised in surprise.

"Stupid right? There are a lot of cats out there."

Propelled from her chair, Jackie managed to deliver a warm hug with a calm that didn't draw attention. "Not stupid at all."

"Anyway, over those five years, I found that this respiratory illness wasn't confined to cats but dogs too. I decided that I needed to try and fix it." Ava smiled. "I don't have a god complex, but I do have a great education."

"Pam might get confused if I called you god, Ava." They both laughed and raised a glass, chinking them together. "Did you succeed?"

"Well, the project was funded." Ava grinned. "My parents were the main contributors to the fund."

"Who cares if it was your parents or others? Did you achieve what you wanted?" Jackie held her breath.

"Research can take years, Jackie. Let's say I'm making progress." Ava took the final sip of her wine.

"You know, I've never considered anything other than hands-on care, but now I have a greater understanding for the people who invent the drugs." Jackie saw Ava pale. "What did I say wrong?"

"No, nothing wrong. My research uses natural herbal treatments."

"Are you kidding me?" Jackie struggled not to spit out the mouthful of beer she had taken.

"No." Ava waved Sam over. He arrived immediately. "We need the bill and a couple of taxis, if you can arrange that please."

"Sorry there is only one taxi in town, he will do two trips."

"Whatever!"

Jackie knew she'd made the biggest faux pas in history, or at least hers. The expression on Ava's face felt so cold. "Doc. I just didn't think you were one of those…"

"One of those what?"

"Well you know, people who think that they can cure stuff from herbs and potions. We all know we need the pharmaceutical drugs to keep us going."

"Well I don't. Nature has her ways too, and my research is based on that. Molly would have had a chance if a natural remedy were available."

"Molly?" Jackie felt like a wonderful evening was turning into a nightmare, and she didn't want that.

"Didn't I mention the name of feline who started me on this mission? Molly. My research program is currently called Mol89."

"That sounds so practical."

"I am practical. The number represents the times I've tried to make the cure and failed. When I go back, it will be Mol90." Ava moved awkwardly. Jackie was sure there were tears in her eyes. *Why...of course. Stupid, stupid, stupid me.*

"Was Molly yours?"

Ava seemed to shrink before her eyes.

"Ava, was Molly your cat?" Jackie kept her voice soft, as she saw tears welling in the electric blue eyes.

"Yes. She appeared a wet kitten on my doorstep one night shortly after I graduated and moved into my apartment. I had the bottom floor. I tried to find her owner, no microchip though. I guess, at the end, I was her owner. She trusted me.... I failed her."

Jackie didn't give a shit if anyone looked or said anything. She moved out of her chair and embraced Ava. "You are one awesome person, Doc. She found the best person to help her."

"But I didn't." Ava whispered.

"You did, Doc, because you tried to help. I bet she had a wonderful time with you right?" Jackie felt tears rolling down her cheeks and didn't give a damn.

"Still have her scratching post and beds in my apartment. I guess I need to get rid of them." Ava sniffled.

Jackie wiped away her own tears. "Not a chance, Doc. One day, we will use them again."

"Thank you, Jackie, you can release me now."

Jackie withdrew. "Sorry." Self-consciously, she retook her seat.

Ava smiled. "No thank you for understanding."

"Always Doc."

The waiter arrived at their table. "Ladies, the taxi is here, but can only do one journey right now. He's busy. He said he'd return for the second passenger eventually. Unless you want to share?"

"Sure, we can share." Ava said. Sam smiled and left.

"I guess this is the end of the evening." Jackie hoped that Ava would want the evening to continue. Maybe she'd ask her to have a nightcap at her place.

"Yeah, to be honest, all I want to do is get out of these clothes."

Jackie laughed. "Maybe you need to say that to someone else."

"There is no one else but you." Ava pursed her lips. "I guess we were both stood up. For the record, Jackie, you were wonderful company, thank you." Ava stood and settled against her walking stick.

Jackie nodded. "Ditto on both," she whispered and followed behind Ava to the entrance.

CHAPTER TWENTY-FOUR

"Danny, I'm sorry you've been brought into this." Judy quietly said, as she placed her head against the broad shoulders of a man she had reacquainted with. Really, her heart had never let him go. *I've been in love with you since the first day we met.*

"Hey, you and I seem to be on the brink of changes in our life. What better way to face them but together?" Danny kissed the top of her head.

"Slightly different circumstances, Danny." She shifted to face him. "I'm homeless without a job, and frankly, probably one of the most hated people in the town. No one's going to give me a job. I'll need to leave town, maybe the state."

"Hey, I'm crashing my career before it even starts. My sister is on the brink of disowning me, because I'm supporting your corner…not your dad's, for the record."

Judy nodded.

"I want to be here with you. We can work out the kinks. Do you feel the same?"

Would it be that simple? Kinks—yeah right. Yet his smile and the genuine look in his eyes made her feel that things could only get better.

"Do you?" Danny's voice was intent.

She cupped his face and gave him a swift kiss. "Yes. First, we have to make amends with Minnie. She's important in lots of ways."

"Yeah? Why does Min appear in my love life suddenly?" Danny grinned.

"Without the Barrington farm, my father is stonewalled."

"What about the Reynolds property?"

Judy took his hand with a compassionate squeeze. "Joyce can't take the pressure. Her assets are mortgaged to the hilt. She had to take out a second mortgage when Ben died. Apparently, he had a few debts in town that took them over the edge." Danny pushed away and stared at her as if she was the second coming.

"Sorry Danny. I know these things; it was my job. As ashamed of him as I am, he's my dad."

"Yeah, but you've encouraged this...no went along with this. You preyed on people who were vulnerable."

Judy stood, her eyes turned heavenward. "Life sometimes isn't that straightforward. decisions we make don't always make sense to everyone."

"Minnie was right about you. You are self-centred. I was such a fool." Danny shook his head as he stood. "Good luck, Judy." He stormed away.

She watched, anger rising as he left. "Fuck you Dad. I've had enough of your actions dictating my life." She reached inside her pocketbook, withdrawing a business card. "Ace in the hole." She called the number and left a message.

†

Ava had reluctantly ended the evening with Jackie. She'd enjoyed the few hours talking about all kinds of things, even those that hurt. The memory of Molly, still raw after five years, brought more tears to her eyes. She wiped them away. Gazing down at her leg, certain it would have ballooned beneath the cast. The ankle hurt like hell. Even the alcohol she had drunk over dinner hadn't dismissed the pain, probably made it worse. She slowly walked into her makeshift room and sat on the edge of the bed. She managed to lever her leg onto the coverlet and lay her head on the pillow. She closed her eyes, and the pain slipped away. *I guess rest is needed. To hell with getting undressed. I'm all in.* As the thought slid into her mind, she began to lose herself to sleep. "Thanks Jackie," she whispered, then knew no more as sleep claimed her.

†

Lizzy watched from her bedroom window, as her parents arrived back from the club. They were early. Usually they didn't get home until one, and it was only eleven. "I wonder why, not that they'd tell me. Isn't that right, Misty?" The cat was lying on her bed cleaning her butt, clearly not interested in the comings and goings of humans in the house. Raised voices entered the home with her parents, another unusual factor for them. Lizzy opened her door a crack to listen.

178

"Robert, you embarrassed me in front of all my friends. How could you?"

"Your friends? Aren't they ours? For the record, they had no right to treat us like that. I've a good mind to resign from the club and see what publicity that will get them."

Lizzy could picture her dad's chubby cheeks turning red from the anger in his reply.

"Well if you resign, I won't be joining you."

"That's ridiculous, Sheena. I'd expect your support in this. I did nothing wrong. We've always been allowed to enter first, regardless of the waiting line. That damn woman was wrong, and she'll know about it when I speak with her husband on Monday."

"Peter Derossy is hardly going to agree with you, Robert."

"I pay my damn fees for that club and they're extortionate. He owes me; I supported his presidency of the club."

Lizzy was getting bored. This was just a stupid spat over something at the club. Before closing her bedroom door, she heard her mother's voice rise over his. Now, that was a first.

"Get over yourself. You have no power over the golf club presidency, I do. It's my money that allows you to railroad people, and I'm getting tired of it. Power has a habit of corrupting people, and frankly Robert, I believe you are. You don't even consider our daughter's feelings in anything, and believe me, that hasn't gone unnoticed."

There was a silence that Lizzy felt sure would never shatter. Time froze...until the thunder clapped.

"It's always been about your money, Sheena. Your parents hated me. Why the hell did you marry me if you don't like me?"

179

"Remember our mistake? I was pregnant and wanted my baby to know her father. The big question is why did you marry me? You hated being a father and barely acknowledged Lizzy as a baby...well at any time in her life, really."

She hadn't been wanted. The revelation came as a heavy blow. Lizzy slid to the floor with a thump and wailed her pain. She was too upset to do more than cradle her arms around her waist and cry. Moments later, a gentle voice at the door drew her attention.

"Hey, Lizzy what's wrong?"

Scrubbing her eyes of the tears, she quietly asked, "Mom, are you all right?" She opened the door slightly to see her mom.

"Yes, Lizzy. Can I come inside?" Lizzy moved away from the door, and her mom walked inside and closed it behind her.

"What's with the tears? Did you hear the conversation downstairs?"

"I was a mistake. I always felt like a third wheel, but I didn't know you regretted..." Her mom pulled her close and kissed the top of her head.

"You were never a mistake...well maybe a little for all of ten seconds. I was only eighteen." Her mom lifted her chin, and they stared into each other's eyes. "Never a regret for having you or loving you. I have regrets on other fronts. That's my problem, not yours. I love you. You are cherished, and when I saw the first scan, oh so wanted. You have been the highlight of my life, and all I want is for you to be happy, healthy, and safe."

Lizzy wanted to cry again. This time, because she knew the words her mom spoke were genuine. "Dad doesn't feel the same way, does he?"

Her mother inhaled a fierce breath, hands clenched together. "As I said, I've made a few bad decisions. Truth be told, my darling, I don't know what's in your dad's heart about you...actually me too. He's never been the most demonstrative man."

"Why spend over thirty years with him?"

Her mother shrugged. "I was in love back then and so happy he chose me as his girlfriend. He was handsome, and believe me, he had a sports bod that his friends envied. He was twenty and on a sports scholarship." Lizzy saw the faraway look on her mom's face. "Back then, I do think we were in love."

Lizzy felt better, at least knowing that her mom loved her. She couldn't see her dad as a sports jock. He was plump, and the most exercise he did was two rounds of golf a week. *Wow I need to see those old photos, for sure.*

"Mom, I'm in love and you probably...you won't approve of him, I'm pretty sure. I'm scared that I'll lose you and Dad, but mainly you." Lizzy anxiously held her breath.

"The Reynolds boy, Jerry, right?"

"Yes, how did you know?" Lizzy's eyes widened and she breathed again.

"I'm your mother; I know everything." Her mom chuckled and pulled her close. "Frankly, he's...well what makes you happy is the most important factor of all."

"You have reservations, I know. It's in the tone of your voice."

"I'd be a bad mother if I didn't have reservations, except he does tick all the boxes." Lizzy became bugged eyed at the statement.

"How?"

"He has a decent job, doesn't pay much, but enough for a small family. He'll never cheat on you. He comes from a good family. Most important, he loves you. I call that a win-win relationship."

The words floated in Lizzy's mind, and all she could do was smile.

"I guess that's the answer you wanted."

"Oh yes, Mom, oh yes. Can I bring him over for Sunday brunch?" Lizzy enthusiastically took up the opportunity.

"Yes, does eleven sound good?"

"What about Dad? We usually have brunch at ten."

"Your father doesn't make the decisions in this house, I do. If he doesn't like it, he can go to the golf club for brunch." They both laughed. Lizzy hugged her mom hard.

"I love you, Mom. Thank you for bringing me into the world."

"I love you too, Lizzy. I'm blessed I did bring you into the world. You are an awesome person. Right, I'd better go and see what your dad is doing, probably hitting the whiskey bottle."

"Why didn't you divorce him?"

"Darn that would be so simple." Her mom gave a sigh. "I love your idiot dad. I'm just hoping that one day he'll admit it was the money that tempted him, and the rest was all me. A girl can live in hope. Now, off to bed for you, because I know you get up early for those secret assignations with Jerry." Her mom wriggled her eyebrows

"Mom, we walk Sinbad, his dog!"

They laughed again. "Good night, my love, and sweet dreams."

Lizzy shut her door and closed her windows. If her mom had issues with her dad, then it was their personal problem. An eavesdropper, even one that loved them both, wouldn't help.

"Wow, I hope Jerry will accept the invitation to brunch and not be intimidated." She walked over to her bed. "Misty, how will you like a brother for companionship? He's called Sinbad, and I think he'll protect you, big time." Misty didn't move from her sleeping position. Lizzy drew back the covers and settled into bed. Misty shifted to snuggle up next to her, a gentle purr accompanying the movement.

"You know, Misty, I think I finally know what's important for me." Misty licked her hand, as Lizzy gently stroked her. "Love you too." Sleep wasn't far behind her words.

CHAPTER TWENTY-FIVE

Minnie woke at her normal 5:00 AM. It was tough leaving Rita, who was spooned into her side. The animals weren't going to be pleased if they weren't given breakfast. An hour later, she entered the house and saw Danny's sneakers neatly standing to attention underneath the coat hooks. *Oh, so he is home. I feel guilty at treating him the way I did yesterday. He didn't know the background, and I shouldn't have been so negative. Seymour is the problem, not his daughter.* She saw a notification on her phone, as she waited for the coffee to percolate. "Oh crap, Ava." Minnie read the text message asking if there was a problem. "Damn we both forgot to cancel our dates." A part of her fretted over her total lack of concern that she'd stood up a date. The other part recalled the lovemaking with Rita. There was no contest. "Better late than never."

Sorry, Ava, I won't lie to you. An old friend turned my night inside out. I apologize profusely for not contacting you and leaving you in the lurch. I'll pay for your dinner and taxi, whatever you decided to do. I'm so sorry for wasting your time, I hope you can forgive me.

After sending the text she sat and wondered what would happen next. *Rita hates animals and the country. Am I prepared to live in the city full-time?* The idea depressed her.

Time to set things up for breakfast. Her stomach fluttered at the thought of sharing her first breakfast with Rita after their lovemaking. *I hope Danny stays in bed.*

†

Jackie woke refreshed for the first time in months. She might have been stood up, but her evening had been great...no, better than great, just at this moment, she wasn't sure of the word. Climbing out of bed, she had the absurd idea to call Ava. She twisted her mouth over the thought. It wasn't a date. They were both stood up and had a mutual, save-face kind of evening. Yet, if it had been a date, she'd definitely want to see Ava again. She scratched her right eyebrow in consternation. "I cannot fall for Ava. It would be emotional suicide. She's obviously not interested in me on the romantic level. I might have been having those flutters in the stomach, but she appeared as impassive as ever...until she mentioned Molly. I wasn't expecting that." She headed for the bathroom. All that beer was now bursting her bladder.

Fifteen minutes later, she sat on a stool against the kitchen counter, waiting for the coffee that would replace the beer. She picked up the local paper that arrived every Wednesday, without fail. She never read it until the weekend. Normally, she'd read the contents inside out within ten minutes. She was having difficulty getting past the second page. The new owners of the golf club, Peter and Evalyn Derossy, were smiling beside a golf cart. Judging from that photo, he was at least ten years younger than her, maybe more. *I wonder if he married her for the social status and money.* Jackie cringed at the uncharitable thoughts.

She slipped off the stool, padding over in stocking feet to draw a cup of coffee. The phone rang before she took the first sip. She debated leaving it to voicemail but swiped to answer on speaker. She nearly choked on the hot coffee when she heard the caller's voice.

"Are you all right?"

"Yes, yes I'm sorry. The coffee was too hot. How are you this morning, Doc?" Jackie figured her grin would give the Joker a run for his money.

"Good. Is this too early?" There was a pause. "Hmm it's only eight, but I wonder if you're a morning person like me." Ava seemed to be asking herself as well as Jackie, who closed her eyes. *For you, Doc. I'll be a morning person.*

"Yeah, mostly. I'm up and having coffee, so it can't be too early right?" She could almost see that trademark twitch of Ava's left eyebrow, as she decided if it was true or not.

"Yes, I guess."

"So, how can I help?" Jackie hoped it was simply that she wanted to chat about their evening. The next words deflated that thought, and her smile disappeared.

"I had a text from Minnie, albeit around seven this morning. She gave an apology."

"Really, what was her excuse?" Irritation began to rise at the topic.

"An old friend turned up, and she couldn't make it, apparently."

"Are you good with that?" Jackie wondered who the old friend was, then it dawned on her. The only person it could be was Rita, her errant date. It made sense, since they had both been stood up.

"I guess. She offered to pay for the meal and the taxi. We know there isn't a meal to pay for. I had a good time last night. I'm certainly not going to let her pay for our taxi." Those words soothed every negative thought that had formed through this conversation. Jackie's smile returned. She cleared her throat, then took another sip of her coffee.

"Are you still there?" Ava asked.

"Yeah, sorry. I think that was very generous of you, in the circumstances."

"What circumstances? It was a first date. Frankly, I wasn't that interested. It was a gesture after she took care of me when I had the injury to my leg."

"Yeah, but it was on her land. She was probably hoping you wouldn't sue." Jackie enjoyed their shared laughter. "I know Minnie might have slipped up on your date, but I don't know another person who is more caring in this area. It's not like her."

"I'd better let you get on with your Sunday. I'm sure you will want a rest from people involved in your day-to-day work routine. Mrs. Dank is due to arrive in an hour and ensure I have an adequate breakfast and have managed to make myself presentable should anyone arrive when she's not here." The words were matter of fact, but there was an intonation that made Jackie imagine Ava was giving that small, indulgent smile she rarely used, unless it was something she genuinely liked. *I guess Mrs. Dank comes under that umbrella.*

"Yeah well, I wouldn't exactly want to spend my private time with Pam, but any of the others, not a problem. I'll try to get by sometime next week to see you Doc. Take care of—"

"As you are now alone, why don't you come over and have breakfast with me? Mrs. Dank makes a Sunday breakfast that would put a Michelin star restaurant to shame." The alone part stung, not as much as it had in the past. As ever, Ava was direct.

"I can be there in forty minutes. I need to shower." Jackie accepted so quickly it sounded to her like she was desperate.

"Great and thank you. See you in forty minutes then." The phone call ended.

"Darn, I wish she didn't just end things so suddenly." Jackie tossed that comment away. She didn't care. This was what she wanted after their dinner, another chance to...to do what? Make an impression? "Stupid, she's lonely. That's the only reason you're invited." *I'll take it.* She headed for a shower.

†

"You were right, Min, she played me." Danny said quietly, as he slumped in the seat opposite her. The heavy wooden table had been at the farmhouse for at least three generations that she knew of.

"Judy?"

"Yes, of course. Who else? You told me, and I didn't believe you. I'm sorry." The words spent forcibly, at the same time, the sadness in her brother's eyes told another story.

"You liked her a lot, right?"

He nodded.

"Nothing is what it seems. I've found that out recently...very recently. What makes you think she played you?" Minnie gazed at the clock on the wall; it was almost eight thirty and no sign of Rita yet.

"Well, I think she wants me to put pressure on you to sell. Apparently, you are the problem, not the Reynolds."

"Oh, but Joyce won't sell either. How does that work?" Minnie was fascinated and not surprised at Judy's possible tactics. She'd certainly used worse with others in town, from what Minnie heard on the grapevine.

"Judy said Joyce is mortgaged to the hilt. She doesn't have the funds to follow through for the long term." Danny dropped his head in his hands. "You know, I think I might have been falling for her. I always liked her at school, but she was always with the wealthier kids."

Minnie felt for her brother. She'd felt that way about Rita, look at them now. At least.... The door opened and her tousled-hair lover entered, sans her tortoise-shell glasses, which were quite the Rita trademark. She looked endearingly lovely. Minnie stood.

"Hey, sorry. You weren't in bed, and I came to see if you were going to come back or not." The words seemed louder to Minnie than they were. Danny gave her an undisguised smirk.

"Well..."

"Rita, good morning. I'd forgotten you were staying the night. Had a good night I see, so the date was successful?" He smiled at Rita, who blinked rapidly. She opened her mouth, then shut it.

"Yes, for the record, we had a great night and Rita didn't go on a date. She and I, well, we talked and..."

Danny held up his hand. "Say no more, Sis, I do not need details." He stood and headed for the door with a wink at Rita. "Incidentally, it's about time. I thought you two would never figure it out." He laughed and shut the door behind him.

Minnie didn't move. She gave Rita a weak smile. "I'm sure he didn't mean that."

"He's right, isn't he? We have waited a long time." Rita enclosed her in a warm hug. "Now you know what I look like first thing in the morning, not a pretty sight." Rita's gentle finger against her lips hushed Minnie's reply. She kissed it. "If you think that you can put up with this the rest of your life, then I think we could have a future together." Rita grinned.

Minnie didn't answer. She simply kissed the lips that had given her heart the world.

†

Jackie arrived at the Lawrence homestead in thirty-seven minutes and hoped Ava wouldn't notice she was three minutes early. Sounded absurd, but the woman had a habit of noting timings, especially with her appointments. That look Ava had through her reading specs was a chill, and not in a good way, especially if someone was late by more than five minutes. Less than that, and she'd raise an eyebrow. Worked for being early too. *I guess, working in research would make attention to such detail paramount.* She parked her car next to a silver Buick LaCrosse. *Nice.* Her fifteen-year-old Honda Civic was the poor pony on the drive. Nonetheless, it had served her well and was the one thing she had refused to change. Sue-Ann had always nagged about getting a sports car.

She walked up the five steps onto the front porch, then looked behind her before knocking on the door. Rolling hills and beautiful pastures exploded into her vision. She saw the donkeys in the closest field, Doc Lawrence's passion since his wife died. Probably before, she figured. She rapped on the door and waited.

The door was swung open by Mrs. Dank, who gave her a once over and smiled. "Good, you aren't late. When Miss Lawrence said you were attending breakfast, she was adamant you'd be here in forty minutes. You are early by a couple of minutes."

"Damn, I was hoping I'd wasted a few looking at the view before I knocked." Jackie chuckled, and the older woman did the same.

"Yes, she's a timekeeper, that's for sure. Not a bad thing. Come along inside, Jackie. I'm glad you came by. I worry about her being here alone for most of the day, especially now she's not able to do as much as she could." Jackie knew by gossip about Mrs. Dank being overprotective, but meeting her and having a conversation, it was obvious she was an empathetic woman.

"Thank you. I guess I'd better be prepared for a raised eyebrow for being early." Jackie grinned at the belly laugh from Mrs. Dank.

"Miss Lawrence is on the back patio. Coffee or orange?" Mrs. Dank pointed to a door at the end of the corridor.

"Coffee thanks." Jackie walked across a polished oak floor; it was the real thing, no imitation vinyl. Taking a deep breath, she opened the sliding door and walked onto the patio. Ava was sitting with her leg resting on a makeshift bench, oblivious it seemed, to her entrance. She took a moment to watch the view Ava was enrapt in, more rolling hills, a paddock that was closer to the house, corralling more donkeys.

"Hey, how are you doing?"

Ava shifted around and simply stared at her. The expression was disconcerting and caused a knot in Jackie's stomach. "I see you are a few minutes earlier than you said."

"Sorry, am I forgiven?" Jackie wanted to smile at the arched eyebrow but refrained, unsure what to expect.

"Nothing to forgive. I'm a bit sensitive about timings, I guess. Take a seat. Do you mind if we eat outside?"

"Absolutely, no problem. How could you not with this view?" Jackie tentatively took a seat next to Ava, holding her breath under the weight of Ava's full gaze.

"I like it too—wasn't sure at first. I'm a city girl, born and bred. There's a donkey out there who likes me."

"Cool, does the donkey have a name?" Her heart was beating so wildly, she wondered how the hell Ava couldn't hear it.

"Theo. He's quite old and loves apples. Until I did this"—she pointed to the raised leg— "I used to feed him one every day. He whines, because the only time he gets one now is if I persuade Mrs. Dank to take him one. She isn't keen." Ava sighed. "Have you heard from your errant date?"

"Nope, and don't expect to. You do know that my date and yours are old friends, and she was staying at Minnie's last night?" Ava's eyebrows knitted together. Without her glasses the expression didn't look as harsh.

"I didn't. At least if she said, I took no notice. You suspect that they went out to dinner together and left us both high and dry?"

"Yes." Jackie decided an explanation that going out to dinner probably wasn't on their menu would be lost on Ava.

"I hope they enjoyed it."

"I know I enjoyed my dinner." Jackie examined the intricacies of the wicker chair and its pale green seat cushion rather than Ava's expression

"Hmm, drinks rather than dinner, though we had a good time, didn't we? We must do it again, including eating before I leave. My uncle has sequestered me for another session. Would you believe he's getting married again? My parents are going to be horrified he hasn't invited them to the wedding." Ava softly chuckled.

"You're joking right?"

Ava shook her head.

"Wow, he's coming back right?"

"I assume so, he loves this place. If he sold, who would take on the donkeys?" Ava shook her head.

"You maybe?" A risky question. Jackie hoped her smile hid the fact she was holding her breath again.

Ava laughed. "Even if I wanted too, I couldn't afford a place like this. Way above my pay grade."

The door to the patio opened, Mrs. Dank arrived with a tray.

"Here you go my dears, croissants and orange juice. The butter is on the table, and I'll bring your coffee in a moment, Jackie." After serving, she retreated to the house.

"God, they smell divine." Jackie's fingers were itching to take up the baked treat.

"Don't overindulge, Jackie, this is just the beginning. Trust me, I learnt that after the first Sunday breakfast she brought me."

"I'm in heaven. I love croissants, all that butter and deliciousness. Sorry, I can't resist." Jackie tore one apart and began spreading butter over her snatched goody.

Ava laughed and Jackie looked up. "What?"

"You are like a kid in a candy store. I like them, but they don't give me the buzz they obviously give you. Go for it."

"Are you indulging me?" Jackie stuffed part of the croissant in her mouth. Ava gave her a shrug and smiled.

"Sure, I like indulging you."

CHAPTER TWENTY-SIX

"You need to front up, Rita, you haven't even apologized for missing the date with Jackie."

"That was a month ago. Why bother to bring it up? I'm sure she's over it." Rita scrolled through her notifications.

Minnie slapped away the phone. "Because it's the right thing to do. If you intend to have any interaction in this community, you need to think beyond the city mentality."

"City mentality, what do you mean?" Rita frowned.

"In a country community, we need our neighbors. Friends are so much better than enemies. Are you going to switch that damn phone off and come with me or...?"

"Oh, that important, really. She's a vet nurse, Minnie. I'm sure she doesn't care." Rita sighed and tucked her phone in her pocket. "I'll come with you."

"Good. I need special kibble for Ginger. She's almost run out." Minnie climbed out of the truck, parked outside the Vet office. Rita slowly followed.

As they entered the reception area, Minnie was surprised at how many animals were waiting with their humans. She walked over to the shelves, surprised that they weren't full. Fortunately, Ginger's kibble was available. Another surprise as a bubbly young woman greeted her.

"Hi, I see you knew what you needed, thankfully." The freckle-faced girl grinned. "I'd have taken a few minutes. I only started last week, and I'm still finding my way around the merchandise. Do you need anything else?"

Minnie turned to Rita and raised her eyebrows.

"What?" Rita hissed.

"Oh, forget it." Minnie shook her head and turned back to the receptionist. "Thanks this is all I need. Is Pam on vacation?" Passing the time of day was preferable to looking at Rita, who was aggravating her right. She wasn't sure if her jaw dropped at the next words, it certainly seemed that way.

"Oh Mrs. Dawber, she's on extended leave." The girl pointed to the register. "Cash or credit?"

"Cash." Minnie laid the bills on the counter. "Is she ill?"

"Not sure. Oh, here's Jackie, she'll know." The young woman waved to Jackie, who nodded, smiling as she headed over. Her smile disappeared when she saw Rita.

"Hi Jane, is there a problem? Hi Minnie, hopefully not Gertie or Ginger?" Jackie pointedly stared directly at Minnie, ignoring Rita.

"No, thanks for asking, Jackie. Look, I know this is awkward. Any chance we can have a few minutes alone, right Rita?" Minnie tugged on Rita's sleeve to concentrate her attention.

"Right, please, or my life isn't worth an iota." Rita muttered.

Jackie shook her head. "We're busy right now, as you can see. We're heaving at the seams. Can it wait?"

"Sure." Rita answered.

Minnie snorted. "What about when you leave? We could meet you for a drink or have dinner?" At Jackie's raised eyebrow she scratched the back of her left ear. "Sorry. Please, just tell us a time and place, and we'll be there. Won't we, Rita?"

"Yes. I'm sorry Jackie about…well you know." There was silence for a few seconds, and Jackie chuckled.

"Forget it. You did me a favor. I'll meet you over at Ray's around six. I'll need to bring Ava. I'm her go-to-girl for getting her home after four."

"Sorry, Jackie, Mrs. Parson's appointment is due, and Doctor Lawrence doesn't like things late." Jane interrupted them.

"So very true." Jackie smiled.

"We will meet you at six. Thank you, Jackie." Jackie nodded, walking away to the next patient.

As they headed toward the car, Minnie glanced at Rita who kept touching her jacket pocket. "Answer it for goodness sake, Rita." She pressed the open button on her key fob, then climbed into the truck. At that moment, she didn't care if Rita didn't come home with her. How could she have such an uncaring attitude toward Jackie, especially after her recent breakup? Rita appeared oblivious to someone else's emotions. What if they argued? Was this an indication of what might happen? *God I hope not.*

The passenger door opened, and Rita climbed in.

"Min, I need to see a client. Can you drop me off at the farm and I'll take my car?"

"It's four. We are meeting Jackie and Ava at six. Will you make that?" Minnie scowled.

"Not sure. I'll try."

The roaring revving engine mirrored Minnie's frustrations. "Great, so I'm having drinks with the person you are apologizing to. Rita. This isn't right."

Rita grinned and pulled her forward into a passionate kiss. "It will be, trust me."

Minnie had no antidote to Rita's kisses. *I hope so.*

†

Ava's raised eyebrow didn't deter Jackie, as she ushered Mrs. Parsons into the surgery with a dog called Shamus. Only an owner could love Shamus. Equal parts pit bull, Alsatian, and Heinz 57, he had the goofiest ears she'd ever encountered in her time as a vet nurse. The eyebrow remained raised.

"Sorry Doc, Minnie Barrington and her friend blindsided me." Jackie deposited the dog on the examination table as gracefully as she could. Ava struggled to stand for too long and crouching down was even harder for her.

"I like Minnie, known her since she was a whipper snapper. Not sure about her friend, seems cold, doesn't smile much." Mrs Parsons received a sloppy face washing from Shamus.

"What seems to be the problem with Shamus?"

"He is struggling to breathe most nights but settles during the day. He sounds worse than I do with my asthma."

Ava smiled. "Can't have that, can we Mrs Parsons." Jackie watched deft hands examine Shamus. As always, Ava kept her expression noncommittal.

"Do you need me, Doc.? Jane is struggling with the increase in business, and I want to make sure that your time scale isn't interrupted too much more." Jackie smiled. Ava gave a short nod, her eyes narrowed. *Hmm I guess she's going to have words with me later about something.* "Want me to send Jerry to help?"

"Yes." The curt reply said it all; she was upset about something. "See you later, Mrs Parsons." Jackie left the exam room and looked over the crowded reception area. Who would have thought Evalyn Derossy's influence would draw people who normally used facilities miles away? Didn't matter, it kept her in a job. With a bright smile, she headed to the frazzled looking Jane.

"What's the problem, Jane?"

"Oh Jackie, you are sent from heaven. I'm afraid the computer is waiting for me to do something, and I sure can't remember what."

Jackie chuckled. "Let's see, shall we?"

†

Judy Seymour drew a deep breath in the kitchen of the house she rented in Fieldstown, twenty miles from Sterling. The papers laid out on the wooden top of the kitchen counter nearly vibrated with intensity. Once she signed this document, her father was finished as a businessman in Sterling.

"Is there something that you want changing, Judy?"

Judy shook her head, contemplating the words in front of her.

I, Judy Seymour, revoke Sean Seymour as a controlling trustee of the trust fund established by Claire Allen Seymour to benefit their children.

The declaration came along with lots of other jargon. For her, this was the important part. Did her dad think she was foolish enough to not know she had this right once she reached twenty-five?

"Look, you came to me, Judy. If it isn't what you want to do?"

"I do, it's just hard." Judy gave a tear-filled glance at the lawyer. "This will destroy him." She gave a sob. A gentle hand settled on her shoulder.

"Sometimes, it's just the right time. If he loves you, he will understand."

"What if he doesn't?"

"Love you?"

"Yes…I guess, since the accident he only loves Blue, his Dalmatian, and maybe Delsey, his second wife. She will be in for a shock when this happens." Judy hated the sick feeling gripping the pit of her stomach.

"They will understand eventually. If they don't, you hold all the financial cards. Trust me, he won't want to piss you off. I'm sorry, Judy, I made a promise to be somewhere else at six. I don't want to rush you. Take more time to rethink this, and we can…"

Judy picked up the pen from the wooden surface and found the signature page. Seconds later, she signed the document and pushed it towards the lawyer. "It's done."

†

Jackie looked over the reception area, finally empty at six fifteen. The last patient was taken in for a consult five minutes ago. She sighed. Jane looked shattered.

"Hey are you okay? I'd invite you for a drink after time but…"

Jane chuckled. "Too young. Mom will have dinner waiting, and Dad will not have his usual two beers until I'm home. He doesn't drink and drive."

"Cool parents. When you are twenty-one, the first drink's on me. You've been great. It was the most hectic ever in my experience and I've worked here since …a long time." Jackie laughed.

"I couldn't have gone through the day without you, Jackie. I'm sorry things became mixed up with the last three patients. Do you think the vet will be mad?"

"Don't worry, I'll smooth it over. Besides, you are going to be a great receptionist. You know all the computer jargon, and if you don't, you take it in quicker than I ever would."

"I couldn't today."

Jackie grinned and placed a hand on her shoulder. "Bet you remember now, don't you?"

"Sure." Jane smiled.

"Took me weeks to remember." They both laughed. The door to the exam room opened and Mr. York trotted his Scottie toward them. "I'll leave them to you, Jane. Then please go home to dinner, can't have your dad waiting for his beer." Jackie winked and headed where Mr. York came from. The room was empty—unexpected. She opened the door to the hospital wing.

"Hi Jackie, phew busy today." Jerry grinned as he pulled on his overcoat.

"Sure was, Jerry. Are you heading home?" Jackie was only half listening, looking around for Ava. The words penetrated her brain and she stared at him. "What did you say Jerry?"

"I'm having dinner with Lizzy and her mom. We are going to the golf club. I've never been there before. Do you think I'm presentable?" He opened his coat.

Jackie looked at the dark blue jersey with many tiny dogs as the pattern. His trousers were black. She could almost see her face in his highly polished shoes. "Perfect Jerry. Have a great time. I'll want to know, tomorrow, all about your exploits."

He blushed and laughed. "Sure, but it will be Monday. We have Sundays off remember?"

Jackie grinned and smacked a hand to her forehead. "I must be overworked. Off you go, Jerry, and have a wonderful time." She watched him leave with a huge grin on his face.

"So, are you going to tell me?"

Jackie didn't turn to the owner of the voice for a few seconds. She took a deep breath first, then spun on her heel and almost cannoned into Ava, who was less than a foot from her. "Tell you what?" *Here we go. Elevated eyebrow time.*

"What did Minnie Barrington want with you?" Ava crossed her arms, her expression stern.

"Oh." Deflated at the question, Jackie bit the lower part of her inner lip.

"And?"

"Not really your business is it?" Jackie turned away. A light touch on her shoulder called her back. "Yes?"

"When it affects my work routine, it does. What did she want?" Ava gazed into her eyes, and Jackie tried hard to be mad. It never happened. This woman disarmed her just by a touch or soft word, the more time they shared together.

"To meet and let her friend Rita apologize. Although I'm sure it's Minnie's idea. I said I'd meet them at Ray's for a drink at six." Glancing at her watch. "Twenty after, maybe she'll think I've stood them up as they did us."

Ava dropped her hand. "Do you need me to take a taxi home?" The quietly spoken words indicated that Ava was apologetic, not that she really ever said. Jackie had figured out Ava's way in the months they'd known each other.

"Actually, I was hoping I could still be your taxi and you'd have a drink with me and them. I will have the perfect excuse to leave early. What do you say?" Jackie wasn't confident Ava would agree.

"Good idea. I'll get my things."

Blown away, Jackie rapidly replied, "I'll need ten minutes to check on the hospital wing."

Ava gave her a smile. "Efficient as ever." Jackie's stomach did a somersault, as she watched the vet hobble through the door marked private.

Jackie thrust open the door to the hospital wing. "Hey Francine, how are we doing?" Jackie addressed the vet nurse in charge of the hospital cases.

"Pretty good, but we need more space. I hate to say this, but she needs a home or go to the local cat shelter." She pointed to the cage that held an errant kitten.

"Give me twenty-four hours, and I'll work something out." Jackie walked over to the kitten, who purred when lifted from her cage. "You are one cute kitty. About time you had a loving home." She kissed the top of the kitten's head and placed her back in the cage. "I'll be back, sweetheart, promise."

"See you tomorrow, Francine."

"No rest for the wicked, hey Jackie? I hope Dr. Lawrence gives you overtime."

Jackie smiled and left the room.

CHAPTER TWENTY-SEVEN

Minnie sat in a corner of Ray's bar, alone, a club soda warming as she nursed the glass. Several people had been staring at her in speculation. Some she knew, others were strangers. One guy, who appeared to have had too much to drink, slurred an invitation to join him. She smiled but shook her head. Memorabilia from sixties movie icons surrounded the clock on the wall. Six thirty. There was shift in the air, and a seat was pulled up next to her.

"Why are you in a bar alone, Sis?" Danny placed his beer on the table and straddled a chair.

"It wasn't my intention to be alone. Rita was supposed to be here, and I'd arranged to meet Jackie Cochran for a drink at six. She hasn't turned up either." Minnie sighed.

Danny nodded. "Jackie probably doesn't leave on time." He flashed a smile. "How are things with you and Rita?

When I came home last night it seemed tense." He held up a hand when Minnie glared at him. "Minnie, I'm your bro. I love you and want to see you happy. That's why I ask."

"I know you do, Danny, I'm sorry I sound grumpy. Rita and I had a difference of opinion about putting right something that happened last month. I guess she really only gave me lip service." Minnie sipped the warm soda and grimaced.

"Why don't I get you a refill, or something more alcoholic?" Danny stood, pointing at the drink she held.

"Oh, I think I'll call this a bust and go home. I'm beginning to think that the only place I'm comfortable is on the farm with the animals." She stood, and Danny pulled her into a hug.

"Love you, Sis. It will all work out as it should. A sage person once told me that, and I believe her." Danny released her. She looked at him and saw their mom's eyes, and she felt the safety net go around as family enclosed her.

"How did the exams go? I haven't seen you long enough to have a conversation." Minnie touched his tousled, sandy hair.

"Good. I've had lengthy discussions with lecturers about what's best for me to do. I'm going to arrange a meeting with Doc Lawrence and hope he might offer me a junior post." Danny grinned.

"Danny, he isn't due home for at least another eight weeks. Ava is running the show, as far as I know, or as best she can with her own disability. Have you thought of asking her? At least she could give you the contact details for Doc Lawrence, wherever he is in the world." The crestfallen expression on her brother's face hit her hard. The door to the bar opened, and Jackie Cochran entered with Ava Lawrence.

"You might have a golden opportunity." She whispered, as Jackie saw her wave.

Danny turned. "Wow, talk of the devil."

Ava slowly made her way to them, as Jackie peeled away toward the bar.

"Sorry, we're late. The surgery was hectic today. Jackie needed to double check on the hospital wing. She's very efficient." Ava softly remarked. "Hi Danny, Jackie didn't say you'd be here. How are things?" Ava smiled, balancing on her stick.

"Great to see you, Ava." Danny grinned. "Please take this seat." He pulled out the seat he had originally taken. "Good. Now all I need is a job."

"Thanks, I'm dead on my feet. Don't tell Jackie; she's very protective. Good luck with the job. I'm sure you'll find a place easily." Ava sat, and Minnie noticed she closed her eyes for a few seconds. Obviously, Ava was ready to relax and not have any more drama for the day. *Damn, and I've brought them here under false pretences. Rita isn't here to apologize to Jackie.*

"Look, if it's a bad time we can…" Minnie said.

"Jackie deserves an apology. I received one, and she hasn't. I find that…. Well, you don't want to know what I think. Where is Rita?" Ava gave her a glacial look.

Minnie had no words. *What can I say, my lover has bailed?* Jackie appeared with drinks and plonked down next to Ava. The woman's infectious smile was never far away.

"Here you go Doc. The best wine they have here. Not sure it meets the golf club standard or even yours, but you need it. We've had a helluva day." Jackie placed the glass next to Ava.

Sniffing the wine before taking a sip and gave then Jackie a small smile.

"I know I brought you here Jackie, but it appears that…"

"God damn, Judy." Danny interrupted her. They all turned to the entrance.

"Rita?" Minnie whispered.

†

Rita had loads of experience of being cold to people's emotions. She had to. Getting excited and losing the threads of a case because of emotion wasn't going to work in her profession. At the same time, in the last four weeks, she'd achieved her ultimate personal goal. Someone she loved reciprocated, and Rita didn't want to avoid that emotion. She'd pushed the envelope in this situation and was grateful her lover had been understanding. The big question was for how long? Minnie was intelligent, empathic, and certainly not stupid. *Damn I love her so much. Please understand.*

"You came?" Minnie's said.

"I'm sorry I'm late. I did say…"

"Yes, you did!"

Rita recoiled from the harsh tone.

She turned to the others around the table. "Sorry, I'm late. Can I buy anyone a drink?" The negative shake of heads around the table made her feel worse. "I'll get Judy and I a drink." She inclined her head toward Judy. "What's your poison?" A phrase she'd used for years, whenever she was on the hunt for prospective bed partners. As the words rolled from her lips, Rita hated every single one of them.

"I'll have bourbon and soda, thanks."

"Great, are you sure anyone else doesn't need a drink?" She didn't make eye contact with Minnie.

"Actually, Rita, I've changed my mind, and so has everyone else." Rita saw the surprise in the others gazes as they looked at Minnie. "In fact, this evening is on you." Rita had never experienced the wrath of Minnie Barrington before. Her lover was on a roll.

"Sure, it isn't a problem. How about I open up a tab at the bar and we go from there?" Rita walked away slowly, hoping that Minnie might follow and give her that charming smile that melted her heart—no such luck. As she approached the bar, part of her wanted to simply walk out the door and say to hell with it. The best part of her though recalled the lovemaking with Minnie and how her life had changed for the better since they had become a couple. Each day was worth getting up for, and it hadn't been like that in a very long time. It was time she realized that the couple part became more than that…marriage. As a divorce lawyer, she'd seen so many train wrecks. Maybe that was why she'd been reluctant to make the final commitment to anyone. *God, why am I doing this to myself?*

"Yep, what can I get you?" The barman polished a glass with a towel.

"Right, yes. A bourbon and soda. Can I see your wine list?" The bartender shot her a glance and pointed to the bottles behind him.

"That's the choices. Red or white?"

"Do you have a merlot?" Rita tried to make out the names and types, but she'd left her specs in the car. *Damn vanity!*

"Lady, I wouldn't have a clue. Red or white?" He reached over and collected a couple of bottles. I'll be right back. I have another customer." He left the bottles in front of her and walked to the other end of the bar.

Rita sighed. *This is not my day.* She peered at the labels. Things were looking up. *Markham Vineyards Merlot – Napa Valley, not bad.* The other was a chardonnay from First Press Winery. "Have you decided?"

"Yes, I'll take both."

"Oh." He reached for glasses.

"Nope I want the bottles. Do you have more?" Rita figured a place like this wouldn't, then was surprised again.

"Yeah, Ray has a few bottles in the cellar. I figured they would just collect dust…seems I'm wrong. Anything else?"

"Yes, I need an open tab for the table over there." Rita waved to the table.

"Ah the Barrington's, sure. You do know Danny boy doesn't drink wine, right?"

"Nope, I didn't. I do now. Anything they want, drink, food, whatever, I have the bill?" Rita began to take out her credit card.

"Not necessary. If you are friends with the Barrington's and Jackie, we trust you. I'll bring the bottles over with glasses." He gave her the bourbon and soda.

"Thanks." She made her way over to the table, where the talking stopped as soon as she came into listening zone. "Here you go, Judy." She placed the drink next to her client. She then took a seat next to Ava Lawrence, who barely acknowledged her.

"Aren't you drinking, Rita?" Danny asked with a smile.

Thank god not everyone around the table hates me. "It's on the way."

†

Sheena Blaine had never thought she'd be entertaining her daughter's boyfriend without her husband, unless he was dead—he wasn't. Jerry Reynolds wasn't what they expected for their only child, that was true. He was from a less wealthy family. Most were, except the Seymour's, and that old family money came from Carol. Jerry was also intellectually disabled, compared to many. Except he had a rare rapport with animals, and that had to count, big time. How could that equate to him not being good enough for their daughter? Lizzy loved him. Sheena saw the yearning in her daughter's expression whenever she talked of Jerry. Lizzy was an innocent as far as Sheena knew, and Jerry probably more so. Did it matter? No! They were happy.

"So, are we ready to eat? Have you both looked at the menu?" She knew the menu by heart; it hadn't changed in ten years. Evalyn Derossy had indicated change was coming soon. That didn't sit well with Ben; he hated change.

"Mom, are we having starters?"

"You two have what you want. I'm having garlic bread." She saw Jerry's eyebrows move to a heavy frown, then Lizzy took his hand and he smiled. *Wow, I'd fall for that.*

"Jerry, do you want to share garlic bread? I know for sure Lizzy loves it." Jerry grinned and nodded.

"Anything you want to know regarding the dishes on this menu? I know them all." She winked at Jerry and her heart missed a beat at his smile. *Darn I wish I was thirty years younger. He's perfect for my daughter.*

†

"I'm sorry, Jackie, I was callous not to call and explain. I don't expect you to forgive me, but for what it's worth, I have never behaved so badly regarding a missed date."

Jackie had been surprised when Rita followed her to the bathroom. Now she knew why; they were alone.

"Hey, it wasn't a big deal. In the end, you did me a favor." Jackie opened the first stall.

"I did, how?"

Jackie looked at the lawyer, her face was taut. It was obvious she was having a tough time with Minnie ignoring her. The lines etched on her perfectly made-up face were testament to that.

"Yes, I got to know my boss, Ava, better. We're friends now, as well as working colleagues." Jackie entered the stall and shut the door.

"Right, I'm glad it wasn't a waste of your time. Want me to get you a refill? You've barely drunk anything."

"Nope, I'm the designated driver. Thanks anyway." Jackie sat on the stool hoping the woman would just leave.

"Oh, of course. See you at the table." Jackie held her breath until she heard the door close. A thought niggled away as she peed. *Are Ava and I friends, or am I kidding myself?*

A few minutes later, she returned to the table and sat next to Ava, who gave her a brief smile. "Are you doing ok or do you want to go home?" Jackie quietly asked.

"I'm good thank you. What about you? It's Saturday evening, and you have to chauffer me about. Want me to go home in a taxi so you can join the party?" Ava whispered, as she discreetly gestured around the table.

Jackie considered the option. It had been a hectic week.

"You aren't going, are you?" Minnie's words sounded sharp; unlike the woman she knew. Minnie was not her usual self. *I guess the honeymoon period is over.*

212

"Well, it's transport for Ava..."

"Forget that. Ava, are you up to having dinner here with the rest of us?" Minnie directed her question to Ava.

"I guess, although Mrs Dank will have..."

"Great. I'll organize a lift for you. Don't worry. Let's get the party started. Shall we girls?" Minnie left, presumably to organize something.

Jackie frowned, and that changed to surprise when Ava touched her forehead with a tapered finger. "You'll get lines. If you want to go, we can. Has she apologized?" Ava turned her gaze to Rita, who had her back turned. She was looking at Minnie, standing at the bar.

"Yes."

"Good."

Jackie wasn't sure what to do or say. "I'll be right back. If we are staying, I need something more fortified than ginger beer." This was going to be an interesting evening, for sure.

†

Ava shook her head. At least that damned lawyer had finally apologized. *What does Minnie see in her?* Her gaze traveled to Rita, and she saw the taut expression. *Worry, big time.* She'd seen similar expressions on the parents of her patients. The empathy gene hadn't skipped her entirely. To do her job, she needed to be impassionate. Molly had changed that for a while, then reinforced it big time when she died.

Danny Barrington looked solemn as he cradled his beer, his eyes fleetingly gracing Judy Seymour, who looked equally as serious. *I think going home might have been a better choice.* Jackie could have joined her for dinner. Mrs. Dank always made enough for a tribe.

She looked back to the bar and saw Jackie making her way toward the table, a laden tray in hands. Jackie saw her and gave a smile. Ava smiled back.

†

They'd made it through the evening. Glancing at the time, Jackie chuckled. "Hey, guys I'm at work tomorrow. I do not need another shot. What the hell was it called again— a fireball? —fierce."

"It's Sunday, we're closed." Ava blinked rapidly. Jackie saw that her eyes were dilated. *Way too many wines and not much food.* Ava sipped from her glass and dribbled some of the liquid down her chin. *Cute.*

"For some, yes. Except I always check on the hospital Sunday morning, first thing and late afternoon." Jackie shrugged at Ava's astonished expression.

"I'm so glad, Jackie. I often wondered what happened when it was the weekend and a pet was in the hospital. Thankfully they have you. That's why I love Doc Lawrence's practice. He might not be Dr. Doolittle, but he sure has some of the magic." Minnie's face was red, and her eyes were most definitely not focusing properly. All those Moscow Mules, Jackie figured.

Danny laughed out loud. "Sis, you've had too much. Why don't we go home?"

Jackie wasn't sure who was more surprised at Minnie's next words, the rest of them or Danny.

"I love my farm." Minnie glared at Judy. "Your company isn't taking it. Joyce, her boys, and me will stand firm. Who wants another drink?" Minnie's slurred words matched her movements, as she stood, or rather swayed. Rita rose and placed a hand on Minnie's arm to steady her.

"We know you do, Min. Sometimes, it isn't that simple." Rita quietly said.

"I know you hate the country. Why don't you go back to the city and do what you always do?"

"What's that?" Rita's words a whisper.

"Don't give a damn about anyone." The explosive words reverberated around the table.

Silence ensued.

"I think I'm the bad seed here." Judy Seymour whispered, as she stood.

"No!" Danny shouted. The rest of the bar looked around for a few seconds, then went back to their own business.

"We've all had a few to drink, and sometimes things get out of proportion. Before anything is said that can't be taken back, let's just take a moment and ...reflect." Ava sagely retorted.

Jackie decided in that moment, she was in love, truly in love. It didn't matter if the feeling wasn't reciprocated. A part of her had known for a while that Ava was becoming more and more important in her life. At that moment, she would have loved to pull the vet into her arms and kiss her. *My dear vet.* The words floated in her mind.

"What the hell does that mean, reflect?" Minnie demanded, glaring glassy eyed at Ava.

"Your farm is safe, Minnie. So is the Reynolds property." Everyone was surprised when Judy spoke up. "Rita and I have been ironing out the details. She was under strict instructions not to tell anyone." Judy turned to Minnie.

"Especially you, Minnie. Rita was reluctant to take the case because of that." Judy's eyes moved to Danny. "This may sound stupid, but I love you, Danny Barrington, have since I was seven years old. Will you forgive me enough to at least be my friend?"

Jackie had tears in her eyes. They all waited, some with open mouths, for a response to the confession. Danny stood, shook his head, and left the bar.

Another silent moment.

"Why didn't you tell me?" Minnie whispered, as she grasped Rita's arm.

"Hey, I think I did, except you weren't listening." Rita gave Minnie a smile. "Why don't we go home, and I'll tell you everything." Rita half carried Minnie away from the table. "Sorry guys. I will pay the bar tab on the way out."

"No problem, Rita, take care." Jackie wasn't sure what was happening. Everyone was disappearing, and that left her, Judy, and Ava.

Ava slid next to Jackie. Under normal circumstances, she would have been turned on. Ava snuggled into her shoulder. Seconds later, she fell asleep.

"I guess it's just you and me. What a night." Jackie smiled down at the snoring woman nestled to her shoulder. "Pretty crappy for you though, hey Judy?"

Judy picked up her drink and downed the remains. "Yes. I'd better go."

"You were very brave tonight."

"What do you mean?" Judy frowned.

"You actually fronted up, knowing that it might cost you the one person you love."

Judy dropped her head and didn't answer.

"I know it's hard to make a decision that releases you from the norm. I did it myself and a part of me will always miss the woman I used to know when I first fell in love with her. I also know that there comes a time when you need to move on for your own sanity. Time for you to do that, Judy. Either try to make it work with Danny or accept this is it." Ava nestled in closer, and Jackie was certain her body recognized Ava in a profound way. It just felt…normal.

"She obviously feels safe with you." Judy shrugged.

"More likely she's had too much to drink." Jackie smiled. "Ava was tired out before we came here. Several wines with only a snack to eat wasn't going to cut it." Jackie caressed the top of the blonde head. "You think you are the odd one out, take lessons from this one." Smiling, Jackie looked down at Ava. "She doesn't have the best bedside manner with her patients' owners, and yet the practice is thriving. What Ava lacks on the personal front, she more than makes up for with her skills as a vet. Please don't ever let her know I said that; she already has a big ego." They both chuckled. Ava moaned and moved even closer to Jackie. "I'd better get her home."

"Thank you, Jackie. I'm sorry you lost the love of your life."

"Oh, I don't know about that. She was my first love. You never forget that, but I'm hoping there is someone out there who loves me as much as I love them, and I'll get my happy ever after." Jackie chuckled. "Darn, I'm getting all cheesy."

Judy stood. "Do you think Kevin will take me to Fieldstown. Rita gave me a ride here."

"That's twenty miles away. He will have a fit, you know Kevin only likes the local taxi runs. Why don't you take my spare room for the night? Before you say anything, it is no trouble."

"Thank you, Jackie, I really appreciate that. I'll go order the taxi." She left, and Jackie looked down at Ava.

"Well my dear vet, I think you might have to take my room, because I'm damned if I'm going to leave you on your own in that rambling house in your condition." She whispered.

Five minutes later, Judy arrived back at the table with a couple of drinks. "It's going to be half an hour at least. Hope this was okay. I know you said that you're at work tomorrow."

Jackie laughed. "I've decided Ava can stay at the house too. So sure, another drink for the road. Cheers Judy." They chinked glasses.

CHAPTER TWENTY-EIGHT

Ava peered at the unopened letter Mrs. Dank had placed near her breakfast plate before rushing away. Normally, the woman was gregarious to say the least. The plate consisting of two bacon rashers, with mushrooms and two hash browns and a poached egg had to be consumed quickly, unless you enjoyed cold food. Yet the housekeeper's obvious desire to vacate the vicinity while the letter was read fascinated Ava.

She began to consume the food and her stomach relished every single morsel. Freshly squeezed orange juice was a staple for her breakfast. Taking a sip, her thoughts traveled to the Sunday morning, a month ago, when she woke up in Jackie's bed and wondered what the hell had happened. Thankfully, nothing other than embarrassment on her part that she'd fallen asleep. Jackie's idea of orange juice for breakfast was some weak supermarket brand that gagged in Ava's throat. She'd drunk it anyway.

"Miss Ava, have you finished?" Ava was surprised; normally Mrs. Dank left her to read the newspaper before that question was asked.

"Well, yes thank you, Mrs. Dank. Delicious as always." Her hand went to the envelope. "I guess I'd better read this." Ava could have sworn that the woman paled.

"I'll be right back." Mrs. Dank scurried out of the dining room.

"What the hell?" Ava smiled, ripping open the envelope. She unfolded the single sheet of white paper and read the contents and sighed.

†

Jackie grumbled, as a rough tongue licked her cheek. *I know I'm awake, but she doesn't. Maybe if I play dead...* Then came the demon nudge of the nose and a pathetic whimper, and she was lost.

"Monster kitty, we've had this discussion. Sundays I can sleep in." Jackie tickled the ears, and Monster purred in delight. "I'll get up and give you breakfast." She trudged to the kitchen. Monster followed, almost steering her to the room. "I know where it is, you little minx."

Five minutes later, Jackie watched the cat tuck into her wet food. She strolled over to the coffee machine and set it in motion then looked at the time. Almost seven. She'd binge-watched the first five episodes of Star Trek Discovery the night before. Sue-Ann had hated anything space related; except under the odd drug she took. *Nope bad, that was bad, I did not think that.* Jackie grinned, as Monster curled around her legs. "Had enough, hey? I bet you want out now, right?" She smiled at the marmalade cat, who gazed up at her with an innocent look. Jackie walked over to the sliding door and let Monster out into the garden. Not big in the grand scheme of things, but Monster seemed happy and never strayed. Jackie looked at the sky. "I think it's going to be a beautiful day, Monster. This afternoon, you and I will chill in the sun. How does that sound?" Monster had gone, at least as far as the garden shed. The kitten was fascinated with a small hole that went underneath the structure, a mouse hole or maybe not.

Jackie headed back indoors as the coffee percolator gurgled for attention.

†

Ava stared at the letter in her hand and frowned, then placed the paper on the table. On cue, Mrs Dank appeared out of nowhere. From the side door to the kitchen.

"Are you sure?" Ava asked the housekeeper.

"I'm sorry, Miss Ava, but yes. My son wants me to go back home with him and spend time with the family. I miss seeing the grandkids grow up." Mrs. Dank collected the unused items from the table.

"My uncle will be upset. Do you think this might be short term or…"?

"Not sure. At least six months, my son said. I think he wants me to settle there and be close. His wife, Shania, was buzzing when I talked about coming to stay. She's a nice girl, a bit like me. City life isn't her normal."

221

Ava digested this information. "Uncle Gerald is due to call me shortly. I'll let him know." Her phone rang and she looked at the ID. "On time, as always."

"Thank you, Miss Ava." Mrs. Dank whispered, scuttling away.

"Hey, how are things my darling Ava?" Ava smiled at the upbeat sound of his voice.

"Good. I'm more interested in your news though, now that you've been a newly married man for the last two weeks."

"Wonderful. This is sudden, I know, but I'm arranging to sell up."

Ava sucked in a breath. The news was totally unexpected, but she composed herself. "The practice, the homestead, or both?"

There were a few moments of static.

"Both."

"Why?"

"I've spent forty years in Sterling. it's time for a change of direction for the last years of my life." The solemn last words hit Ava hard.

"You do know that you'll outlive us all, Uncle," She chuckled. "The new wife didn't have anything to do with this decision by any chance?"

"Gail isn't really keen on spending her life in a rural town. She had a full-on career in nursing, until she retired six months ago. She wants to spread her wings, and I want that for her. I'm sorry, Ava, if you think I've duped you these past months. I can honestly say I only decided to take this path recently. If you want to leave and go back home, that will be understandable."

"What about the practice, the staff, and your clients?" Ava rarely allowed her voice to rise in irritation. Years of schooling herself to be nice to someone whose failure to learn basic care had resulted in cruelty to an animal was a benefit at the moment.

"I'm sure whoever takes on the practice will keep them on. I have a good team." Ava raised her eyebrow at that statement.

"Then there's Mrs. Dank, although she's also decided that living here isn't for her either. She gave her notice today, effective next weekend."

"Finally! Her son has persuaded her. I'm glad. She deserves a new life." There was a low chuckle at the end of the line.

"Apparently. Look, when are you making arrangements to sell, and what about your donkeys?"

"I'm going to miss them, for sure. I'll try to make the house a package deal. I saw a lawyer yesterday. He will make all the arrangements. I said you would be the first point of contact unless you want me to ask your dad?"

"No, no. Who is this lawyer?"

"I'll email you the details. He was going to be in touch about the staff...." The line went dead. Ava cradled the phone to her ear. *Old man smitten syndrome, it had to be. He was right. Maybe it was their time to see the world while they could. Who the heck knew what was around the corner? The bigger question she wrestled with was what did he mean about the staff?*

CHAPTER TWENTY-NINE

"What the fuck?" Jackie's reaction was understandable.

"He's selling up, the business and the homestead. Personally, I think he's crazy. It's a very lucrative business, and the house is grand. It's his decision, not ours." Ava replied, surprised by the tug at the edges of her white coat.

"You've worked your butt off to grow this business, and he's taking advantage." Jackie snorted, then released her and walked to the door of the office.

"Jackie, I thought you loved my uncle?"

"I love…fuck." Jackie wiped a hand across her face, opened the door, and left the room.

Ava felt the velocity of the simple statement from across the room. Moments later, there was a knock and the door opened. Jerry tentatively entered, then stepped back holding the door handle.

"Yes?"

"Sorry, Doc Lawrence, we have an emergency. Blue, Mr Seymour's Dalmatian, is in real bad shape."

Ava didn't hesitate, she picked up her cane and headed for the door. "What's the problem Jerry, do you know?"

"Convulsions and he coughed up blood on the floor when he came in." Jerry's expression tearful. "I'll clean it up, Doc Lawrence, I promise. I know you don't like mess."

"Jerry, let's see to Blue, shall we? We can think about the mess later." She touched his shoulder.

"He's real sick. He might die." Solemnly, Jerry kept his head down as they entered the reception area.

"Not on my watch." Ava whispered. They made their way to the reception counter, where Mr. Seymour was making a scene. She looked down at the prone animal by his side. "Take Blue to the exam room, Jerry. I'll be right there."

"You can't do that. I demand to see Doc Lawrence, not some floozy." That was a description Ava never had or would associate with herself.

"I am Doc Lawrence. If you want to take your dog elsewhere, by all means do so. Jerry." Jerry turned to her, his arms enfolding the large dog. "Mr. Seymour isn't happy with me treating Blue. Return him to his owner. You'd better get him help soon. He isn't doing so well."

"I know that! Why do you think I'm here?" Mr. Seymour ran a finger along the collar of his red shirt.

Ava looked the man over. He wasn't what she'd expected. How the hell had he held an iron grip on this town for so long. Judy had derailed his plans and intimidation. Now, he looked like anyone else who wanted to save their pet, desperate.

"Doc Lawrence, Blue isn't so good." Jerry said. The dog vomited blood over his arm.

"Take him to the surgery, Jerry. We'll fix this."

"Promise?" Ava half expected the words to be from the owner, but they were from Jerry. "Promise, not on my watch, Jerry, remember."

Jerry grinned and pushed open the door to the surgery.

"Mr. Seymour, I'm going to do my darndest to save Blue. Answer me these questions. Has anything happened that is different to his normal routine? When did you notice his condition?"

†

Jackie watched as Ava moved away from her patient after doing a stomach wash. Her attention to detail and the questions she'd posed Blue's owner had saved him. He was ready to be moved to his recovery cage.

"He'll need to be watched during the night. Not sure we got to him in time. The rest is up to Blue and a little help." Ava turned to Jerry and winked.

Jackie was astonished. When had Ava ever winked? Jerry's huge grin made her smile, and a happy bubble soared inside.

"I'll stay and watch over him Doc Lawrence." Jerry pulled a chair close to the cage.

"Thank you, Jerry." Ava slowly made her way over to the door into the reception area. As she did, she glanced at the empty cage where the kitten had been.

"Ava?"

"Yes?"

"I'll do the night shift on Blue."

"It isn't necessary, Jackie. I've got that covered." Ava left the room.

Jackie had been duly told. Did that mean Ava was taking point or she'd asked someone else? Francine might, of course, though this was her evening off. There wasn't anyone really qualified except for her after that.

"Hey, Jerry. It was a good call you made going direct to the doc. Not frightened of her now are you?" Jackie smiled and he grinned back.

"Nope, not now. Lizzy said she was nice, and I wasn't to be afraid. I thought and thought about that." He went silent, his eyes squarely on the sleeping Blue.

"And?" Jackie prompted.

He gave her a long stare. "How can anyone be bad when they heal animals? Blue was real sick, and Mr. Seymour was getting upset at reception. He was loud. I figured Doc Lawrence would know what to do." He went back to his vigilance over Blue.

"You were right. The doc was the right choice. Let me know if you need anything before, I leave."

"I will Jackie, you are ace like Doc Lawrence. We make a great team, don't we?" Jackie nodded. "Yeah we do." She walked away as the internal phone rang and she answered it.

✝

Ava allowed her eyes to wander over the three clients waiting, excluding the one she was about to talk to. Making her way over to an area partitioned by a wall from the main area, to see one of the most hated men in the town, possibly the area. She stood beside him and he stared at her his eyes red rimmed.

227

"Have I lost him?" The bleak words were a surprise considering what she did know of the man, people called him heartless.

"No." Ava sat down next to him. "If my diagnosis of him consuming a pesticide is correct then we might have treated him in time. He's had a stomach wash and we've sedated him so he can sleep. We will know for certain if he will recover in the next couple of days. He will be tired and weak, expect that."

"Can I see him?" Tears welled in his brown gaze.

"Yes, but only for a few minutes. Jerry has volunteered to keep a close eye on Blue until his shift ends this evening."

"What happens then?" When Ava frowned at his tone, he softened. "I'm sorry. He's my boy and I'm worried."

"We have the facilities to take care of patients overnight. I'll arrange for someone to take you to see Blue. Please wait here." Ava began to hobble away.

"Thank you."

Ava turned and nodded. "Perhaps you need to reflect on this situation and think about what losing someone or even *something* important means to people. I'll be in touch." She turned back and made her way to her office. Opening the door, she looked around as the door closed. Sure, it was still mainly her uncle's stuff. Though her personality was prominent in some things and the more she looked, the more realized she had been taking over his personal space in the five months she'd been here. *Do I want to leave? Is it the practice or someone who is keeping me here?* Taking a seat at the desk, she picked up the phone to let Mrs. Dank know she'd be staying in town to care for a patient.

†

Ava settled in the hospital recovery room. She flipped open her laptop and downloaded her email, particularly the one her uncle had sent earlier that day.

My Dear Ava,

I know you are disappointed in me. I heard your disapproval on the curtailed call. I promise that the donkeys will not suffer. I love them dearly. You must know that. I wish you were more interested in practice work than research. I'd happily discuss a deal that would work for both of us, for you to buy me out. I doubt you'd want the burden of the homestead. I'm promising you the animals will all be well looked after.

My lawyer is Ferdinand Cross. He's from Chicago. He's a good man, Ava. I've told him that you will make all the final decisions. I trust you. I'll call you at our usual time and day.

Love you and thank you, Ava.
Uncle Gerry

Closing her eyes, Ava didn't know what to think—worse, what to do. A first for her since high school. "Do I want this?" The words were barely out of her lips when there was a response.

"Want what?"

Ava struggled not to drop the laptop on the floor. "What are you doing here?"

"Nice welcome. For the record, I always check on the night staff if we have a critical patient. First time I've ever seen the resident vet doing the night shift."

"Jackie, don't you have a life?" Ava felt her heartbeat faster at the presence of her senior vet nurse.

"I try. Somehow this place calls my name. Call me dedicated." Jackie dragged a dolly chair over and sat next to Ava.

"You don't think I can do this, do you?" Ava closed the lid of her laptop and placed it on the table next to them.

"Wholeheartedly I do. Though I figure a friendly face might help for a few hours. Gives you at least one pee break." Jackie winked.

Ava laughed.

"I'm sorry about earlier when I.... Well I wasn't expecting your uncle to bail on us." Jackie's solemn apology resonated with Ava.

"Truth be told, I was as shocked as you. I'll miss that damned donkey." They both smiled.

"I guess you'll be leaving sooner than planned. Getting back to your research projects." Jackie stood and walked over to Blue's cage.

"My uncle expects that. Probably everyone does." Ava shrugged.

"I don't. Regardless of the cold research type you originally portrayed, you love saving animals on the front line. I think you are doing a disservice to yourself not being a full-on treatment vet." Jackie headed for the door. "Want a coffee?" Ava nodded.

"Have you considered that you only see a shell, Jackie, not the real person? I'm helping family. It doesn't mean I want to spend the rest of my life doing this." The distraught look she received had her heart in pain.

"I guess I was wrong. Hey, a habit for me, seeing something in a person that doesn't exist. I'll get that coffee." Jackie left the room.

Ava had the distinct feeling she'd made a critical mistake with her words.

Blue moved and opened his eyes.

"Hey guy, how are you feeling? I'm no Dr. Doolittle. Give me a clue." He wagged his tail, "Good enough." She opened the cage and checked his temperature. He was still groggy from the sedatives but seemed to be coming around ok. "Blue, be less inquisitive and avoid the pesticides." His blue eyes stared trustingly at her. "I guess that's how you were named Blue." Ava smiled.

"He likes you." Once more, Jackie had caught her off guard.

"I wouldn't go so far as to say that." She closed the cage and took the drink Jackie offered. "Thanks."

Jackie retook the seat next to Ava. "Welcome."

They sat silently for a while.

"Jackie, you aren't wrong about people in general. I'm just not sure I live up to your idea of me. I came to help family, and I'll always do the best I can in my professional capacity. Is this what I want to do for the next thirty years? Frankly that decision scares the hell out of me. I applaud people who commit a lifetime to one thing and don't turn a hair. Can I do that? I don't know." Ava sipped her drink and contemplated the plain green mug in her hand.

Jackie shifted on the chair and faced her. "I remember a special person telling me the only answer to any question is, does it make you happy?"

The words echoed softly around the room.

"At this moment, yes, it does. I can't remember a time when I've been happier. How can you know that it will last through?" Ava sighed

Jackie smiled. "You can't. It's a leap of faith. Will returning to the city and your research job make you happy? If the answer is yes, then you've made your choice. I don't

231

know what other factors come into a decision that huge, and it is huge, Ava." Jackie looked over at Blue.

"Do you think you made the right decision, with hindsight? I don't want to open old wounds. Your relationship died here. She wanted the city life, from what I've gathered. You don't talk much about your ex-partner."

"Unequivocally yes. Sue-Ann wasn't my motivator for the choices I made, Ava. I love working with animals. Since I was a kid, I used to tell my foster mom I was going to mend all the broken animals."

"I didn't know you were in foster care."

"Why would you? We haven't exactly been tell-all friends, have we? Anyway, my foster mom, Marie, encouraged me to learn. I managed to attain a scholarship, and the rest is history." Jackie took a deep drink from her mug, then placed it on the table. "I guess I'd better leave you to your vigil."

"Don't go." Ava swallowed hard. This woman was important in her life. It had taken her a long time to work it out, but the thought of letting Jackie slip away and never seeing her again was unthinkable.

"Why?" Jackie stood in front of her, and Ava's heart somersaulted. *God what is happening to me?*

"I'd like to know more about Marie. She seems a really good person." Ava defensively replied.

"Nope, you got that wrong. She was fricking awesome. You will be leaving soon, Ava, and the chances of us ever seeing each other will be remote. We both know when the practice goes on sale it will be snapped up. You've made sure of that with the increased clientele. What would be the point of making Marie casual conversation? That's something I'm not inclined to do." Jackie shook her head. "I'll see you tomorrow, Ava. I arranged for Francine to relieve you around two. It will give you time for a few hours' sleep on the couch in Doc Lawrence's office, before the day shift starts. Good night, Ava." Jackie simply left.

Ava looked at the closed door, then at Blue, then back at the door. She hoped that it would open, and Jackie would be back with that gorgeous smile that scintillated every cell in her being.

"I know, finally, where my happiness is." Ava whispered and reached for her laptop.

CHAPTER THIRTY

"She's not here?"

"Nope, and we have clients booked." Jackie watched, as Jane waved at the four people in the waiting area.

"Did you check the office?" Jackie pointed to Doc Lawrence's office.

"First thing I had Jerry do. He's upset by the way. Can't quite understand why. Can you find out? You're good with him."

The door to the practice opened, and Mrs. Ross arrived with her Pomeranian. She always had a huge smile and it was no different today, as she headed for the counter.

"Oh god, what do I say?"

Jackie raked her hands through her hair. Damn. *Has she just left us in the lurch? Crappy!*

The door opened once more. A tall man entered and walked over to the reception counter. Jackie stared at him and knew who he was before he spoke. "Hi, I'm James Lawrence. Doctor Gerald Lawrence is my brother, and my daughter asked me to help out. She's had to deal with a personal situation. Show me where to change, and I'll get right to it."

Jackie was as stunned as Jane.

"Mr. Lawrence, this way. I'll show you to the office and get you kitted out for appraisals." Electric blue eyes, the exact match to Ava's, stared at her. She bit down on her lip. *Ava didn't leave us in the lurch. She sent reinforcements.*

"Are you Jackie?"

"Yes."

He smiled. "I know I'm in good hands. My daughter thinks highly of you."

Jackie opened her mouth. Words became a whirlwind of spit in her mouth and she spluttered. Embarrassed, she just smiled. "This way."

†

Minnie watched Rita feed the chickens. Rita had insisted that accepting the daily routine would help their relationship. Her city-slicker lover tried to avoid every piece of chicken crap. A feat worth a trophy. *I love you, Rita Temple, now more than ever.*

She turned back to the kitchen and saw Danny. He'd passed his finals and was looking for a position. She'd kinda hoped it would be here with Doc Lawrence. He'd been tight lipped about staying in town.

"Hey, any luck on finding a position?" She went to the percolator and poured two coffees.

"I'm working on it."

"Danny, I love you. That will never change." She placed one of the mugs beside him. "You need to make big decisions for your future and anyone else who joins your journey in life. I waited a long time, too long maybe, lots of wasted time."

"Min, when did you ever not think things through and do the right thing? It can't have been the right time, until now." He picked up the coffee cup. "Thanks."

"Welcome. I'm not perfect, Danny! Look at me; I gave up a potential career in law for the family farm." She raised her hand. "I love it. It's perfect for me. I'd never do anything else or regret that choice." Minnie smiled. "If you take a look out the window, you will see that people sometimes accept a need for change."

Danny moved to look over her shoulder. "Wow, I hope Rita bought some serviceable footwear, other than her usual trendy heels." He laughed. "She really must love you to do this."

"I know she does. She's trying to fit in here, though is that fair of me? Rita loves the city and her work there. I think I'm prepared to let her go where her heart is. I'm sure we can compromise and still have a relationship, just not the ideal of waking up together every morning." Minnie's heart sank. She'd been thinking about it a lot but had never actually said the words out loud.

"Min, I'm twenty-seven. It's hard to make those kinds of choices. I've spent most of my adult life in educational institutions. I feel like I'm a weakling. Judy is so strong in comparison. Look what she did." Danny threaded his hand through his hair.

"A very brave woman and worth maybe sticking around for, I'd say. She owns the family home. Her dad can hardly keep her from living there. Rita said he's penniless without her benevolence."

Danny lifted his head. "I didn't know that."

"Oh yes. Judy Seymour is quite the heiress, on a par with Lizzy Blaine I figure. Danny, do the right thing for you. If fate is kind, everything else you want will fall into place. Besides, if you do want to court Judy, you will most definitely need a job." Minnie chuckled. "Right, I need to save Rita from the ornery ducks, who hate new people feeding them."

Danny stood at the same time and wrapped his arms around her. "I love you, Min, thank you."

"I love you too, Danny. It will work out how it's supposed too. Go find that job."

"I think Rita will stay." He grinned and left the room.

Minnie took in a huge breath, as she looked out the window. Lady, the duck's matriarch, would chase Rita if she didn't approve of her feeding the flock.

†

"Well, I have to say, this practice is very busy. My brother must have been run off his feet. I can see why he needed a vacation, big time." James Lawrence threw off the white coat onto the chair nearest him. "A good set up too. That young man is a wizard. I would love to have him in one of my practices." He walked over to the chair Jackie now thought of as Ava's. The scene niggled even though it was Ava's dad.

"Ava has a lot to do with the increase in volume of clients. I think we've grown in the last five months by at least 25%, but then I'm not the accountant." Jackie shrugged, watching Ava's dad wander to the window. He could see a view of the yard, where the hospitalized animals could exercise.

"Do you think Jerry"—James Lawrence turned back to her—"that's his name right?"

"Yes." Jackie frowned. Where was this conversation going?

"Do you think Jerry might consider a move to the city? I'd definitely make it worth his while, money wise." He turned back to the yard. "He is excellent with animals. A gift I call it—only seen it once before in the raw. Most of us just like animals and want to help. Then there are the rare ones who are almost in tune with the animals." He sighed. "Better check my phone. Ava said she was going to be back this evening."

Jackie released a deep sigh of relief. She's coming back, thank you, thank you, anyone who is listening.

"Ah, a delay. Sorry you've got me for at least another day."

"Nothing to be sorry for. You were great. Mrs. Ross was smitten and will probably ask for you next time." There was a low chuckle, and Jackie's heart somersaulted, it was so like Ava's.

"The Pomeranian, right?"

"Got it in one, Dr. Lawrence. Ava has that instant recall too. It's impressive." Jackie was surprised at the intent gaze she received.

"Call me James. Do you recommend a place to eat? I told the housekeeper to go home, and I'd take care of things."

Jackie was reluctant to say there were only a couple of places open. The town of Sterling wasn't exactly renowned for eating out early in the week.

"Not much, right?" James Lawrence smiled, and Jackie felt her heart skip. *Damn, Ava's smile is so like her dad's. I wonder what mannerisms, if any, she has from her mom.*

"I don't want to be too familiar. I have a pot roast with potatoes in the slow cooker—only need to microwave the veggies. If you want to join me?" Jackie held her breath.

"I can't take advantage of you, Jackie. Thank you, I'll find something in the fridge at the homestead."

"It isn't an imposition, unless you don't like beef pot roast." There was that smile again, and her heart throbbed, if only it was his daughter.

"Ok, sounds good to me. Do you mind if I ask you a few questions about the area over dinner?"

"Nope, I've lived here all my life."

"Let's go then. To be honest, I'm starving." They both laughed.

"I'll see you out front in ten minutes."

†

Rita knew something was on Minnie's mind. She'd avoided conversation all day, found tasks to do that avoided contact. Maybe it was that time of the month. *God knows I'm like a bitch.* At lunch, they'd sat so far apart she almost needed to shout to be heard. She watched Minnie fill a bowl with piping hot spaghetti and bring it to the table.

"Help yourself." Minnie sat opposite Rita, then began to ladle spaghetti into her bowl. "You can have as much as you want. Danny went to look for work in Smithtown. He'll be back in the morning." Minnie began to spoon sauce over her pasta.

"That's like a hundred miles away. Surely there must be something closer. I bet the Lawrence vet practice could do with the help. It seems to me that it's a one-man band. Ava had to work when she was injured, hardly practical." Rita took a small portion, twisted the pasta around her fork, and took a mouthful. "Wow, this is great." For the first time that day, Minnie smiled.

"My mom's recipe, not sure if it's a family tradition or just something she threw together. Danny and I always loved it." Minnie looked as if she was recalling a memory. "Spaghetti night usually accompanied a trip to the movies and chips after. Treat night we used to call it."

The smile lingering on Minnie's face made Rita's heart lurch. "Treat night huh? And this happened how often?"

"Until we inherited the farm. When mom received her tips, must have been twice a year."

Rita wanted to throw caution to the wind, wrap Minnie in her arms, and say she could have spaghetti every damn night of the week, with a movie and chips, if it made her happy.

"My folks gave me TV dinners every night except Sunday. They were both busy with careers. I was one of those latchkey kids. I don't think they ever watched a movie with me in my life. Might watch movies now, I wouldn't know."

Minnie frowned. "Even now? When did you last see your parents, Rita?"

Why did I say that? "Two Christmases ago, I was ordered to attend a family get together." Rita replied nonchalantly.

"I thought you were an only child?"

"Yes I am. My family has a legacy of longevity. I have three uncles and two aunts alive, and ten male cousins, all of them bachelors." Rita placed food in her mouth and let the burst of flavor cleanse the ashen taste she'd had at this turn in conversation.

"That's good, right?" Minnie shrugged. "I mean the longevity part. All bachelors. Wow, that means the family line is going to die out, right?"

"Maybe. On the longevity part, I hope so. Anyway, they were the same studious parents I'd always known." Rita sat back in her chair. "Minnie, are we good?"

Minnie's eyes flared. "What do you mean?"

"You've kind of been distant today, after you saved me from that duck from hell. If I didn't say already, thank you." Rita sighed. Minnie put down her utensils and shrugged.

"I need to tell you something, and I hope you'll understand."

Rita's heart plummeted to the wooden floor at her feet. *I can deal with this, I can.* "Go for it, I'm a big girl." *How crap is that!*

"I really don't want to upset you." Minnie dropped her gaze and ran her fork through the spaghetti. "I think you need to go home and do what makes you happy. I'm being selfish asking you to give up everything to join me here. We can see each other when I visit the city, or you can come over and visit."

Rita had thought she felt hollow echoes in the farmhouse before, but this time it was real. Her throat constricted.

"Rita, I love you, but I'm not going to let you sacrifice all the things you love to accommodate my lifestyle." Minnie dropped her fork and stared at her.

Rita stood and faced the cupboards. With her hands on the counter, she counted to ten. When she turned back, she saw the devastated expression staring at her. "Do you really mean it when you say you love me?"

"Yes, I've loved you since almost the first time I met you. You are the reason I never let anyone else into my life. A sad sack, right?" There were tears in Minnie's eyes.

"Minnie, in my lifetime, I've been with a lot of women. The only one who holds my heart is you. As time moved on, I figured we were never meant to be. A friend made me realize that if you love someone beyond yourself, it's worth everything, and I mean everything. You are the reason for my life, Minnie Barrington, please don't let me go." Rita clasped her hands together.

Minnie was crying. She seemed unsteady as she stood. "I can't offer you much beyond farm life. Look at how it turned out today—you were almost pecked to death."

Rita laughed.

"I come from good stock, my love. All that matters to me is,will you please love me back and keep me in your bed?"

Minnie rushed toward her. Being shoved against the counter hurt like hell, but the kisses she received healed any injury. When they disengaged from the kisses, Rita held Minnie close. "I take that as a yes. Is it too early to take you to bed?

"God, no."

†

Jackie smiled, as James Lawrence sat back, patting his stomach after eating his second helping of pot roast.

"Haven't eaten this good since…oh when I was a boy. Reminds me of my mom and her home-cooked meals." He smiled, "Thank you, Jackie."

"You're welcome. You can definitely come again with praise like that."

"I might take you up on it. My mom was a farmer's daughter and knew how to feed her children. Trust me, my dad was an overweight and very happy man. You must have learnt from your mom." James took a sip of the dark beer Jackie had found at the back of the fridge, a memento from the last party held at the house.

"My foster mom would be laughing like a train at that comment. She couldn't cook worth any beans. I figured that if I wanted something edible to eat once I was old enough, it was worth giving it a try. I like cooking, but simple meals are mainly my forte." Jackie shrugged and removed the plates from the table.

"I'll help with the washing up. In fact, if you point me in the right direction, I'll wash and dry." James stood.

Jackie chuckled and pointed at the appliance tucked under the counter. "My trusty dishwasher will do all the hard work. Thank you, James, it was a kind thought."

"Next time then." James gazed at her intently. It was disconcerting.

"You wanted to know something about the town. Anything in particular?" Jackie retook her seat at the table and James followed.

"Yes, Ava tells me that my brother is selling up and taking some "me" time. I totally applaud that. He's been mourning Megan long enough and working himself to the bone." He took a sip of his beer.

"You do know he's married again?" Jackie bit her lip, maybe it was a secret. A loud chuckle followed, and she relaxed.

"Yes. I'm glad he's found someone to share his life with again, though not happy we didn't get a chance to be at the wedding and meet the woman." He pursed his lips. "Ava tells me you are upset that he's selling." Jackie partially closed her eyes.

"It was a shock. I have to admit. I love working for Doc Lawrence." *I love working for Doc Ava more.*

"Tell me, how many people actually live in Sterling, and who are the big players as far as influence?" Jackie was surprised at the questions.

"There have been a few changes of late...."

†

James looked at Jackie and smiled. "Thank you for a wonderful evening and the added bonus of taking me home."

"You're welcome. Mrs. Dank obviously had the foresight to put on the lights for you. I'll see you in the morning, sleep well." Jackie smiled. He gently squeezed her shoulder and climbed out of the Honda.

"Goodnight Jackie." He watched, as she reversed and drove away. With a nod to himself, he took the steps to the porch. The door opened before he reached for the knob. "Hey, you said it might be tomorrow before you came back or I'd have been earlier. Or maybe not." Engulfed in a hug, he chuckled.

"How was your country field day?"

"As always, to the point."

"Would you have it any other way?"

James crushed his daughter closer. "Never. You take after your mom, and we both know how much I love her."

Ava grinned at his remark. "Jackie brought you home, it's later than any surgery hours."

"Oh, a touch of jealousy." He winked

"No!"

James laughed. "Oh my dear, you protest too much. Don't let me regale you again with how me and your mom got together."

"Can you and Mom help?"

He watched as Ava sank into one of the porch chairs. It was a lovely, clear evening, a bit cold. His jacket worked but was too warm. He perched on the arm of the seat next to Ava.

"Yes."

"Great—"

His raised hand cut her off. "There are conditions." Ava pierced him with that radar-direct gaze that scared the living daylights out of most people who didn't know her well.

"What?"

"Simple. Make it a family concern." Ava dragged her hands threw her hair and looked puzzled. "When I mean family, I mean family."

"It will be family. Uncle Gerry owns it now. You and Mom are helping me keep it in the family."

James shook his head. "Your family, Ava. If it's what you want to do for the foreseeable future." He stood.

"Dad, we've been through this. I'm hardly likely to give you grandchildren, no matter how much you and Mom want it to happen." Ava sighed.

"Let me get a sweater and explain to you that family isn't just about having children, though that would be good." He kissed the top of her head. "It's someone to share your life with." He headed inside. *I hope Gerry still has a decent Highland Scotch hidden away somewhere.*

CHAPTER THIRTY-ONE

Ava strolled along the path she'd gone that fateful day when she'd injured her ankle and wryly smiled as she reached the now-decimated hedge. She stopped and simply gazed at the field beyond and the Barrington farm in the distance. Her life had changed dramatically that evening. Lost in thought, she didn't at first hear the voice that called her name. When she did, she grinned. Danny Barrington, her saviour of that event.

"Hey Danny, I haven't seen you for a while." Ava walked closer to the hedge to face him.

"I've been looking for a job." He shrugged.

"Any luck? It isn't always easy. Not sure I'd have got a job initially, if it hadn't been for my folks."

"Really?" his eyes widened.

"Yes. I bet you are being romanced by a few practices to join them."

Danny shook his head. "I wish. I was in Smithtown looking for opportunities. No real openings. I'll need to look further afield."

Ava scratched the top of her left eyebrow. "You don't want to work in Sterling?"

"There's only Doc Lawrence's, and on the grapevine, he's selling up. Sorry, I know he's your uncle."

"Don't be. It was a surprise for me too." Ava frowned. "Want to have a trial? I'd need you to start tomorrow. If things work out, you might end up permanent. If you find something better before that time, it's all good." Ava watched him drop his head, then quickly lift it, his smile beaming.

"You have a deal…boss." He reached over and took her in a bear hug.

"Great, means my dad can go home. He hates being away without my mom. I'll see you bright and early tomorrow, Danny." She disengaged from his arms.

He nodded his head, the huge smile undiminished. "I'll be there and thank you." He turned and ran over the field toward the farm.

Ava laughed softly. "Now to convince others onto my side." Ava turned at the sound of an engine revving up behind her. She couldn't see what type of vehicle through the mask of trees. Shrugging she set off back to the homestead. *That darn donkey will want his treat for the evening.*

†

Jackie was not sure what to expect as she donned her blue uniform. Ava's dad was nice, at least he had been to her, but she wanted desperately to see Ava. The door opened and Danny Barrington entered.

"Hey Jackie, I was told by Jane to come here for a fit out."

"It's seven thirty, Danny. What fit out?"

"I'm the new vet, at least a temporary one." He frowned. "Did she change her mind?"

"Ava?"

"Yeah, talked to her last night over that darned hedge of all places. I guess she didn't have time to update you." Danny stood arms folded. "Said I couldn't be late. Adamant about that."

Jackie laughed. *Damn the woman was so predictable.* "Welcome Danny." She pulled him into a hug. "I'll get you some gear."

"Thanks. I'm excited. You know it's been a dream of mine to work here."

"Yeah, mine too. Working here is a dream." There was a discreet cough behind her.

"Good to hear." Ava gave her a nod, and Jackie's heart missed a beat. "You took me at my word, Danny, excellent."

"Sure, did boss." Danny grinned, as Jackie handed him a white coverall.

"Great, why not familiarise yourself with the rest of the practice before we open our door in half an hour." Danny nodded and left the room.

Jackie sucked in a deep breath. Her heart was beating fast, and she knew why. Could she get over Ava leaving as easily as she had released Sue-Ann from her life?

"I'm sorry I didn't have time to tell you that my father was going to stand in yesterday. He's going to be here again today for a short time."

Jackie shrugged. "You don't owe me an explanation. I'm just an employee, remember?"

The expression on Ava's face was puzzling; she looked upset. "I understand. Well, I need to speak with my dad. I'll see you out there." Ava nodded and left the room.

Did I miss something?

The door opened again, and Jerry popped his head around the door. "Jackie, it was great." He grinned and left. As the door slid shut, Jackie wondered if there might be one day when she could cut a break and be that happy. She looked at her name tag for inspiration. "Just another day at the office."

†

Ava scratched the top of her head, looking at the figures on the pages in front of her. She closed her eyes and sucked in a calming breath.

"Darling, it isn't that difficult. I've explained this to you several times in the last hour." James Lawrence hovered over the desk where the papers were strewn.

"I'm a vet Dad, not an accountant."

"You are going to have to be both if you want this to work."

"I thought you said family was enough." Ava grimaced.

Her dad laughed and wrapped a comforting arm around her shoulders. "Just like your mom, no head for figures. Give us that grandchild, and I'll do all the numbers for the rest of my life."

Ava groaned. "That's not fair Dad, and you know it."

"Sure I do" he winked. "What is it that puzzles you the most?"

"How can I do both? My savings, with the sale of my apartment, will cover three-quarters of the lawyer's asking price for both. It's the salary. How can I cover the mortgage repayments?" Ava dropped her head into her hands.

There was a knock on the door, and Ava automatically said, "Enter." Jackie walked inside.

"Sorry to interrupt. Mr. Seymour is here. He insists he needs to speak with the vet."

James moved toward the door.

"Sorry James, he means Ava." Jackie looked at her and gave that heart-beating smile.

"Dad, scribble down a few options. I'll be back soon."
"Ava stood. "Want to have lunch before you leave?"

"Yes. Can I invite someone else?"

Ava frowned, preoccupied, as she collected her stick and walked toward the door. "Sure, I'll be back." She left the room and followed Jackie to the reception area. Her senior vet nurse's ass had her clenching her fingers and wanting to touch—sexy.

†

"I think she will make the right decisions."

"You always do, my love. I agree, because she's our daughter and has never done anything that we aren't proud of. Maybe, if we hadn't been so engrossed in taking care of other animals, we should have let her have a pet growing up." James frowned. Had they been focused on making services available to others and not their own child? Something to ponder.

"God James, you have a memory like a sieve. We tried several animals, and she was allergic. We never tried a cat because we were both allergic. For whatever reason, our baby has an affinity to cats and isn't allergic. We didn't think that far."

"No, we didn't. I'll be home by seven."

"Want take out or go out?"

"I want to take my wife out. I love you. Choose where you want to eat."

"There's something you are not saying."

"Yes." James chuckled. "I'll tell you over dinner. I love you. Now I need to have lunch with our daughter."

"Give her my love."

"I will, bye."

†

Jackie watched, fascinated by the tenderness between Ava and her dad. There was a lot of love there. A part of her wondered about her own father.

"I'm sorry, Jackie, are we boring you? I had to tell Ava about her mom's apple pie episode." James grinned.

There was nothing to forgive, and if there had been, that smile would have won her over.

"My mom is not the best cook in the world, and baking"—Ava shook her finger—"Burnt offerings, right Dad?" Ava's eyes held Jackie's as she smiled.

"Yes. Jackie, my daughter here takes after her mom in this area. Please don't accept anything she's baked or even cooked."

"Now, that's unfair." Ava chuckled. "It's true, Jackie. I was so grateful for Mrs. Dank."

"Oh, she has a fine reputation around these parts for her skills with meals and looking after folks." Jackie smiled.

"I agree. Jackie here is rather good too, Ava. If you're lucky, she might invite you for dinner one evening. I can vouch for the excellence."

Jackie flushed. "Well it was only pot roast, nothing special."

"Maybe, if you invite me, I can be the judge." Ava caught her gaze again, and they stared at each other. Jackie's breath caught in the back of her throat. She could hardly breathe.

"Well, I'm sorry to have to rush off, but I promised to be home by seven. If I go now, I can catch the train in Fieldstown and be on time." He stood and Ava stood and hugged goodbye.

"Safe journey, Dad, and thank you for your help."

"Anytime, my love." He released her.

Jackie stood and held out a hand. He accepted, then pulled her into a hug. "Thank you, Jackie, for taking care of me and my very stubborn daughter. She has found a fine friend in you. One day, perhaps, you'll head our way. You can meet, Eva, my wife. Perhaps give her a tip or two on how to bake an apple pie." He winked, and with a wave, headed out of the café.

They were silent for a few minutes.

"I like your dad. He's kind of different to what I expected."

Ava looked at her and took a sip of her water. "What did you expect?" Her eyes became hooded.

"Oh, a more mature you, I guess, with your funny ways. He's more like your uncle, but sophisticated looking." Jackie shrugged.

"Funny ways?" Ava's top lip curled.

"Hey, I was waiting for the arch of the eye and that totally absorbed look you get when you concentrate. The usual mannerisms I've become used to." Jackie grinned.

Ava shook her head and laughed. "I get those from my mom. She's very intense. I think that's why she can't cook worth a damn. Mom and I never cared about making meals. Takeouts were good. Dad can make a mean breakfast and a wonderful Thanksgiving turkey dinner."

Jackie crossed her fingers under the table. "I'll miss you. I did miss you, and you'd only been gone a day. Any news on when the sale will be announced?" *There I've said it.* She wasn't sure she felt any better over saying the words.

"Thank you, Jackie, I'll miss you too. My dad is right; you have been a good friend." Ava glanced at her wristwatch. "We need to get back, or Jane will be worried."

"Sure, I'll get the bill." Jackie moved, about to head to the cashier. She was disappointed Ava didn't catch the clue she was interested in her.

"Taken care of, my dad's treat." Ava stood and reached for her stick. "Can't wait for five days' time when I can finally walk without this darned thing." She pointed to the stick.

Jackie laughed. "If you didn't have it, I'd have to hold your hand. How would that look?" She was unprepared for the speculative look in Ava's eyes.

"Wouldn't be the first time, right?" They both laughed.

CHAPTER THIRTY-TWO

Ava stood at the bottom of the stairs leading to the vet practice, briefly recalling the early days when her attitude was so very different. *I now own all of this.* With a smile, she climbed the few stairs and entered to a delightful banter of voices. She heard the odd bark from a canine unhappy at being restricted. A definite baby cry announced a disgruntled cat Ava guessed had been there before. Someone was prodding and poking the poor thing. A smiling Jane was explaining that the vet was busy but there would be an opening in an hour. The young woman had her back turned to Ava, but the Dalmatian was familiar—Blue Seymour.

"Sorry I'm late, Jane. Theo was cantankerous this morning." Ava walked up to the counter. "Hi Judy." Ava stroked Blue's head, and his stub tail wagged vigorously.

"Hi Ava. You've transformed the place in the few weeks you closed for renovations."

Ava looked around at the modern practice, but not too much to scare the local farmers away. They liked the traditional look, until free barista-style coffee was on offer. Suddenly they didn't mind changes at all.

"Thanks. Reception needed updating, but the major work was the extra two exam rooms and better facilities in the hospital wing." Ava was proud of the changes she'd made. The staff were impressed too, at least they hadn't been vocally against the changes.

"Want me to see Blue, or..." She winked at Judy, who blushed. "Jane, Judy will wait to see Doc Barrington." Jane wrinkled her brow at their laughter. "Judy is Danny's girlfriend, Jane."

The young woman's eyes bulged. "Oh I'm so sorry. I didn't know." Jane looked mortified.

"It's new. We haven't been stepping out for long." Blue growled at the miniature Jack Russell terrier taking shelter under the taller dog's belly.

"Oh god, I'm so sorry. Malcom behave." The owner dragged the errant dog away.

"I'll take a seat. Good to see you, Ava." Judy walked away.

Ava nodded and headed toward her office, then decided to check on the surgery area. Everything from trollies to instruments gleamed, as the sun shone through the window into the freshly painted room.

"Hi, Doc Lawrence. Is there anything I can help you with?" Francine was covering the day shift for a change.

"Just checking on things."

"You sound just like Jackie." Francine laughed. "When is she back?"

Ava contemplated the question.

"Tomorrow. She said not to get too comfortable working the day shift." They both chuckled.

"That's typical Jackie; she loves working here. I remember your uncle taking her on full-time, fresh out of college, even before the results of the exams. She'd worked here for years during school holidays. "

"I didn't know that."

"Well, why would you?" Francine smiled. "I don't know anyone more dedicated to animals than she is, maybe Jerry." They smiled. "He, by the way, is fretting over why she didn't turn up for work at the beginning of the week like the rest of us."

"Ah, I guess I'd better do my diplomatic bit. Jackie usually solves these things for me."

"Well, if you say so. I think it's in her blood. She hates to see people and animals in pain."

"Yes, an admirable trait. Thank you, Francine, for your help and support." Ava walked over to the door that led to the outside exercise area. She spied Jerry talking to a feline patient, in a room with a view, as Jackie called it. *Jackie!*

"Doc Lawrence, do you need me?" Jerry stood straight up to attention.

Ava wanted to laugh but knew that would be a no-no with this sensitive man. "Good morning, Jerry. How are things?"

"Good." He turned to the cage she had watched him talking too earlier. "Misty is doing well. Doc Danny made her well again. Lizzy is happy."

Ava nodded and pursed her lips. "Yes, he did. Jackie will be back tomorrow." Not subtle but it didn't matter. Jerry's features stretched to the ends of the earth as he smiled.

"I miss Jackie. She's my friend." Jerry nodded. "We share secrets."

She's my friend, and I miss her too, more than I thought I ever would miss anyone, other than my mom and dad. We don't share secrets though.

Her phone began to ring. Retrieving it from her pocket, she saw Jackie's ID. "I need to take this Jerry, good work." She pressed *accept* as she walked away. "Hi, how are you doing?"

"Relaxed, pampered, and ready to come home."

"Hope that includes work?" Ava's her heart swelled.

"Absolutely."

"Good to hear. Francine is ready to give up the day job." Jackie chuckled, and Ava's eyes welled up with tears. "A little bird told me you've made big changes."

"Not big!" Ava shook her head when Jackie sniggered. "Better. I've had no complaints from the staff or the clients."

"That's because I'm not there. You need my approval, right?"

"Did anyone tell you that you are rather sassy?"

"Yes."

Ava shook her head again. "For the record, I did ask you about a certain aspect of the renovations."

"Oh yeah, you were permanently on the fence about the damned color scheme. For an intelligent woman, Doc, you can be indecisive."

"Whatever." Ava sniffed.

"You hate it when you can't make a decision." Jackie chuckled.

"Come home, and I'll make decisions." Ava sucked in a breath. "I miss you, Jackie Cochran. See you tomorrow." She ended the call. The phone rang again. Expecting Jackie, her smile faded when she saw the number of her lawyer. "Lawrence."

†

Jackie sucked in the fresh air of Sterling. No matter where in the world you call home, you'll recognize a distinctive smell that washes over you and says life's OKAY. Even if it isn't, you have the chance to make it great.

"Jackie, wonderful to see you. I heard on the grapevine you were on vacation."

"Hi Mrs. Derossy, good to see you too. How's business?"

"Great. Your boss is one of our best customers. I figure she can't cook." Evalyn Derossy winked. "She orders simple food, like her lunch sandwich. I'd never complain, of course. I'm wondering if she's one of those people who gives back. She was grateful for the clients we sent her way. I would have done it regardless. She is the best vet I've ever been to."

Jackie smiled. A bubble of pride puffed up inside. *Stupid, it happened anyway.* "Maybe she's too busy since buying out her uncle and taking on the renovations."

"What are you really saying, Jackie?"

"She can't cook." They both laughed.

"Well, you're home now. I guess I'd better downgrade our budget projections." At the pip of a horn, Evalyn grinned. "Got to go, see you soon."

How does my being home lower the club's budget projections? I guess I could invite Ava over for a pot roast. Jackie's heart warmed at the idea, as she headed home.

†

"Theo, this is your last treat, and behave tomorrow. I don't want to be late again." The donkey's brown eyes gazed at her. "I will not be taken in by doe-eyed looks." He greedily took the last half of the apple, the munching far louder than the fireflies in the air. Ava surveyed the house paddock and the one beyond, where five other donkeys grazed. She turned to the homestead, a humongous place for one person and lonely. Her apartment in the city had never felt that way. Although, living in a box was quite a different proposition. She pulled the ringing phone out of her jacket and smiled.

"Hi, are you telling me you're home or delayed again?" There was a delicious chuckle at the other end of the line.

"I'm home, and you'd know that if you were."

Ava frowned. "I am home."

"Ah, talking to Theo, right?"

"Yes."

"That explains it."

"Are you at the front door?" Ava began to walk slowly back to the house. She wanted to run, but the doctor advised she take it easy on the ankle for another month.

"Yes, I brought dinner."

Ava speeded up. "Give me a few minutes." Finally arriving, she thrust open the front door and gestured for Jackie to enter. "Hi, good to see you." Her heart raced at the sight of Jackie. She had missed her so much. The divine smell on the porch had Ava drooling.

"Same here. Just chili and rice. I prepared it this afternoon and decided you might be too busy to make anything yourself." Jackie wiped a hand across her mouth, but not before Ava saw the smirk.

"Evalyn Derossy told you I've been there a few times, right? Damn, you can't do anything in this town without someone commenting." Ava scrunched her nose and followed Jackie inside.

"Small towns, rural ones, have a habit of being informative, even if you didn't want to know. I bet Evalyn knows the exact brand of toilet roll Sheriff Beaker uses."

"Gross, why would anyone want to know that?" They made their way to the kitchen.

"I can. See, other than the odd drink, you don't use the facilities much."

"You know I can't cook." Ava poked Jackie and moved over to one of the cupboards. "I can find the plates and utensils, and I know how the dishwasher works."

"I'll need to warm this up for a few minutes. A pan would be good." Jackie lifted the aluminium foil from the two dishes she took out of a carry bag, then re-covered them. "Changed my mind. Let's just put them in the oven for a few minutes. They're still pretty warm."

"I'll deal with it." Jackie laughed at Ava's frown.

"How was your vacation?" Ava watched, as Jackie checked out the oven and placed the items inside.

"Ten minutes, tops, should be sufficient." Jackie turned back from the oven and smiled. "Great. Marie has never been to Florida, never left the state. I'm glad you suggested I take a vacation and mentioned my foster mom. She loved Disneyland." Jackie laughed. "You do know I bought something for everyone at work, even you."

Ava smiled. "Wouldn't be you, Jackie, if you didn't. Will I regret what souvenir you decided to buy me?"

Jackie laughed. "All depends."

"On what?" Ava tapped her fingers on the kitchen countertop.

"Why don't we change the subject? You'll find out tomorrow. How did the renovations go?"

"The building firm Mr. Seymour recommended was efficient and in budget."

"I don't care about the builders, Ava. What did our staff think?"

Our staff. Ava held on to those two words. "Our staff approve. At least, they haven't said anything different."

"Well they wouldn't to you, not directly that is." Jackie's words were chosen for levity. Still, they hurt. Ava still hadn't garnered the people skills. It hadn't mattered in her research work. She felt like an explosive device waiting to trigger. "Tell me more of your vacation. I've never been to Florida." All she wanted was to talk to Jackie and be near her, a voice inside her head said. *Tell her you love her.*

†

James Lawrence finished a call with his brother and turned to his wife.

"Was it all good?" she asked. "I'm looking forward to meeting Gail. The chats we've had over video media have been entertaining."

"Yes."

"What's wrong?" Eva put an arm around him.

"Why would you think anything was wrong?" He gave a tight smile.

"I've known you for forty years, James Avenger Lawrence. Eventually, focused people like me can join the dots."

"Gerry has cancer. Terminal, in fact. He's decided to go to Luxembourg." A warm embrace did not mitigate the tragic news but made him feel better. "I think he knew when he went on his journeys."

"What about Gail, and why Luxembourg of all places?"

James bit his lip. "She's in the same position. I think they tried to do everything they could until the illness prevented them." The hug became tighter.

"Do you want to travel to Luxembourg and spend some time with them?"

James nodded, tears in his eyes.

"Make the arrangements."

"That's the reason I love you the most. You just know what I want."

"I love you; it's a done deal. Time to book those tickets. I need to make plans for our vacation with the staff."

"Shall I tell Ava?"

"No."

"Why?"

"Because she's on the brink of making her forever life. This might derail her for a long time."

"Forever life?"

Eva grinned at him. "You are my forever life. From what you told me, Ava is on the brink of hers."

James smiled. "You really are quite the romantic, my darling Eva."

"I'm no such thing. Now get on with it." She winked and gave him a kiss.

"Oh yes you are." He whispered as she left the room. The tears ran free. He hadn't told her that Gerry and Gail had a mutual pact for going down the path of assisted death in Luxembourg. That would come later. Knowing Eva, she'd probably guessed.

CHAPTER THIRTY-THREE

"What's up?" Jackie perched on the side of Ava's desk. She looked upset.

"The usual paperwork. It gives me a headache." Ava's voice was quiet. Her eyes never left the papers on her desk.

Jackie gave Ava's downturned head a serious look and moved to stand next to the woman. "You look upset. Can I help?" She received a sharp glance, then nothing. Ava picked up a pen and began to draw on the envelope in front of her.

"Great stick man. I hope that isn't a representation of me." Jackie saw a definite lift of Ava's lips.

"Hardly, you are far from a stick person." The words were merely factual. Jackie knew they weren't meant to hurt.

"True, although I did lose a few pounds for Florida."

"I noticed. You look good." The compliment was so unexpected, Jackie almost keeled over in shock.

"Why thank you. Tell me, please. I'm your friend, and I don't like to think you're upset." Jackie pierced her with a gaze, and Ava's eyes locked with hers.

"My parents called me a few minutes ago. They're traveling to Luxembourg to meet up with Uncle Gerry and his wife. "

"What's wrong with that?"

"Dad never mentioned it when he was here, and a trip like that requires planning. They would have said when I called home last week. They're on a flight out this afternoon." Ava sounded perplexed.

"Sometimes spontaneous is a good thing." Jackie said.

Ava shook her head. "My mom is not a spontaneous person, trust me."

"People change, or circumstances force them to change. It doesn't necessarily mean that there's a problem." Jackie walked away from the desk. "Look, we finish in an hour. Want to come for a drink at the bar?"

"I'm not that good company at the moment, sorry Jackie."

"Never be sorry to me, I understand. I do have an alternative suggestion." Jackie crossed her fingers.

"That is?"

"Join me at the pub for a drink, and we can have dinner there. I'm hungry but can't be bothered to cook. We both know you …well, will end up at the golf club for dinner or have nothing at all."

Ava frowned. "I can make a sandwich."

"Well, I heard on the grapevine you used the club for making sandwiches too. Tell me I'm wrong." Jackie grinned, and this time Ava reciprocated.

"Got me there. Don't expect any in-depth conversation; I need to think."

"How about idle chatter, will that work?" Jackie wriggled her eyebrows, and Ava burst out laughing.

"Jackie Cochran, you are something else. Thank you, I'll happily take you up on your offer of dinner."

Jackie opened the door, about to leave. "I never mentioned actually paying for dinner." Ava threw a paperclip at her, as she left the room chuckling.

†

Two people were seated at the bar, and about four tables had patrons, one with children. Ava thought they all looked happy.

"Here we go, a wine for you and a beer for me." Jackie took the seat opposite her and looked around. "Quiet, just as I like it on a Wednesday evening."

"Oh, you come here on a Wednesday often?" Ava looked puzzled.

"Hey, I just like being in company once a week and have a drink before going home. If there is one thing I miss about not having Sue-Ann around, I guess I get lonely." Jackie sipped her beer.

"How strange. I was thinking the same thing myself, the evening you arrived at the homestead after your vacation." Ava picked up her wine glass and took a sip. They lapsed into silence, until a familiar voice called hello.

"Hey Danny." Jackie waved at him.

Ava gave him a nod and one to Judy, who was holding his hand. As they neared the table, she indicated they take up the vacant seats. Judy sat, and Danny disappeared to the bar to order drinks.

"It's official then?" Jackie grinned at Judy.

Judy laughed. "That he's finally accepted that he can date me. Yeah, I think so. Thank you, Ava, for believing in him and giving him his first post. He loves working with you all."

"You can't tell." Jackie chuckled. "He's such a grouch in the morning." Judy laughed, but Ava wrinkled her face.

"He is?"

Jackie placed a hand on Ava's. The heat it generated had Ava's pulse vibrating. "Well yes, but you, my friend, can be even worse. Especially if Theo is playing up." They looked at each other and Ava nodded.

"Yes, Theo can be a problem and makes me late. I hate being late."

"Don't we know it." Danny took his seat next to Judy.

"Am I that bad?" Ava pursed her lips, then her hand was squeezed. She hadn't realized Jackie hadn't let go.

"Not always Doc. Right Danny?" Jackie winked at the man.

"I love working with you, Ava. I think it will take me a lifetime to be as good as you. That's my dream."

The words were impractical. "If you work hard for the next ten years, I'm sure you will know what I know now."

"My dear vet, you really don't understand, do you?" Jackie whispered into her ear. "He has a crush."

"I'm a lesbian!" Ava announced. All eyes turned to her, including those from the two tables closest to them. She picked up her drink and drank more in one gulp than she should.

"Are you having dinner, or eating at home?" Jackie asked the couple.

"My dad is still in the family home until the end of the month. Danny is with Minnie and Rita at the farm. This is the only place we can have alone time." Judy's eyes darted to Ava, and she whispered. "Is she okay?"

266

"Yeah, busy day." Disengaging her hand from Ava's, Jackie took her beer. "We were going to have dinner as well. Don't feel pressured to sit here. Have a nice dinner together at another table."

"Are you trying to get rid of us, Jackie?" Danny said.

"Nope."

"I'm sorry for my outburst. How about we have dinner together on me? Did you say a burger and fries Jackie?" Jackie nodded. "I can work with that. Are you going to join us?" Ava looked at the couple.

"Sure, if that's okay with you, Judy?" Danny said.

"Great." Judy gave a tight smile.

"Good." Ava closed her eyes for a few seconds. *I'm definitely not good at this. Why the hell am I here?* Her eyes tracked to Jackie, who was nursing her beer and appeared disappointed. *I'm such a lousy friend.*

Two hours later, Ava faced Jackie in the parking lot. "Out with it."

"What?"

"You look like a sour lemon. I understand that you could be with my poor contribution this evening. Danny and Judy were nothing but nice and polite."

Jackie stared at her. For one of the few times in her life, Ava felt that she was on the back foot.

"Yes, they were."

"What is the problem, other than I'm my usual self?"

"Ava, you will never say this, and perhaps I shouldn't, except I need to do this. I love you, Ava Lawrence, with every fibre of my being. God, I miss you so much when you aren't around. I've never felt as connected or in tune with someone as I am with you. I know it's a long shot that you might love me too." Jackie shook her head. "I thought I could take the crumbs of your affection, but it isn't enough. If you don't love me, I will have to leave town."

Ava stood unmoving, as Jackie walked away. She didn't know what to do. Jackie was already so far away.

"You can't leave!"

Jackie turned and looked at Ava across the parking lot. "Why not?" She held her breath.

"Because." Ava seemed smaller somehow, or less confident.

"Because? Because what?" Jackie didn't close the gap between them. She'd done her part. Now it was up to Ava.

"I miss you too when you aren't here. I said as much when you came back." Ava looked distressed.

"Do you love me?" Jackie's heart palpated so much she thought she might have a seizure while waiting for the answer.

Ava scraped her booted foot in the gravel. "Yes."

Jackie had a feeling of floating on air and expecting someone to pop that bubble, sending her descending to the ground in pieces.

"You do?" She figured the words were a whisper but maybe not.

"Yes. I just didn't know how to tell you." Ava moved forward slowly, and eventually they were only inches apart. "Jackie, please don't leave me."

Jackie reached out and touched the frown above Ava's eyebrows. "I'll never leave you. I love you." She pulled Ava into her arms, and the sweet kiss they shared erased all her doubts.

CHAPTER THIRTY-FOUR

Ava nervously looked around her practice. The fact that it was hers should have settled her nerves. She'd arrived early—big time. The minute hand clicked to the nine on the clock above the reception counter. A quarter before seven. She made her way to her office and quickly shut the door behind her, her moves akin to a mystery movie and she the villain.

Walking across to her desk, she sank down in the chair and sighed. They didn't have any hospital patients, ensuring that no one was in the building.

"What the hell am I doing?" She smote a hand to her forehead and shook her head. "Jackie loves me, I love her, and I'm nervous about meeting her today. God, I feel like a teenager. I'm thirty-five not seventeen." Her thoughts traveled to the previous night.

As they came up for air, Ava smiled and caressed Jackie's bemused smile. "You really want to go the long haul with me?" A question she'd never expected to ask in her lifetime.

"Absolutely, my…dear…vet." Jackie kissed her at each word and disbelief evaporated.

Enclosed in Jackie's arms, Ava sighed softly. "I'm not sure what to do, right now. It isn't as if I've never asked a woman to my bed." Jackie placed a finger over her lips.

"I don't want to be any woman you take to your bed. Ava, I want to be the only one from now on." They kissed again. Her body thrummed with an over-excited desire to have sex in the parking lot. "We'll work it out tomorrow, Ava." Jackie moved away. "I love you, my dear vet, sleep well." Ava watched Jackie walk away.

Tomorrow was today, and she simply didn't know what to expect. She left her office and went to the staff area. She missed the usual aroma of coffee brewing, and she really needed a caffeine fix. How hard could it be to set the machine up? There was one at the homestead. After fiddling for five minutes, she gave up. The phone rang, and the answering machine kicked in. It was still only seven.

"Hi, it's Minnie…Minnie Barrington. Can someone come as soon as possible please? I have an emergency."

The phone went dead. Minnie sounded desperate. Ava went back to her office and picked up her bag. She left a message for Jane.

†

Jackie practically bounced into the staff room at seven thirty. She opened her locker and placed several items inside.

She went to check on the recovery area, forgetting that they didn't have any cases under observation. It was quiet, and she basked in that silence.

"Hi Jackie."

She turned at the interruption, half hoping it was Ava and knowing it wasn't. Jerry's voice was definitely male.

"Hi Jerry."

"Morning, Jackie. It's quiet."

"Sure is, but not for long. I noticed there were at least three messages on the answering machine when I came in. Gonna be busy as always." Jerry chuckled.

"Doc Ava is really good, isn't she? I loved Doc Lawrence, but she's something else." He grinned. Jackie swore she saw adulation shining from his brown eyes. Ava would be happy. Jackie's belly fluttered.

Damn I love that woman. Why didn't I take her to bed last night? We could have made love all night? "Yes, Jerry she is." The door to the staff room opened, and Jane entered.

"Hi guys. Ava is on a case."

"On a case, what do you mean?" Jackie asked.

"She left me a note. Said she'd gone to attend Minnie Barrington's emergency. She must have arrived early." Jane removed her coat and hung it in her locker. "Kind of odd she was early. Normally, she's just on time, or dare I say, even late occasionally." Jerry laughed and disappeared into the yard.

"Must have." Jackie wondered why Ava had arrived in the building so early.

"I'll call Minnie and see how things are going," Jane said.

"Why don't I do that? You can deal with the other emergencies."

Jane laughed. "Yeah, Mrs Grey and her Pomeranian with a nervous complaint, and I bet you Mrs. Ralph and her goldfish." Jackie chuckled. *Yep Mrs. Ralph and her goldfish was a certainty, if the son hadn't been around in a couple of weeks to clean out the tank.*

"Jane, you have a great memory. Mrs. Ralph's son has a shift change every month, and he misses the usual time to call on her. Do you know what emergency Ava has gone to the Barrington farm for?"

"Not yet, it's just a note on my desk. Right, better get out there. We are ready for business in fifteen minutes." Jane left.

Jackie ground her teeth. "Why were you here so early, my dear vet?" She whispered and went to find a phone. The call went to voicemail.

"Hi Minnie, it's Jackie does the vet need any backup? If she does gives us a call." Jackie hoped someone might pick up. They didn't. All she wanted to do was rush over to the Barrington farm and help. She wondered why Danny was late. Jackie headed for the reception area for an appraisal of how busy they were going to be. As she entered reception, Danny turned up.

"Morning Danny, Ava is at your sister's farm. There was an emergency." She spoke quietly, so no one else could hear. His flushed face told its own story. *Damn why was I so noble? That could have been my expression this morning.*

"What's wrong?"

"We don't know. Ava was here early and caught the message. I tried calling but no answer." Danny frowned and she felt for him.

"Damn," He stroked the fine stubble on his chin. "Will you let me know if you get news?"

"Sure." Jackie touched his shoulder and smiled.

Danny gave a brief smile and headed to the staff room to change.

"Jane, what kind of day are we going to have today, do you think?"

"Busy." Jane laughed.

Jackie grinned and looked over the schedule.

†

"My girls are tough old birds." Minnie said, as she walked Ava over to the barn housing the chickens.

"Hmm, don't let anyone outside this conversation hear you say that. They might take umbridge." Ava sighed.

"Don't be silly, it's a term of affection." At Ava's raised eyebrow, Minnie relented. "Ok, maybe not to everyone."

"I hope you say more flattering things to Rita, because I'm sure she wouldn't like to share the sentiment with chickens."

Minnie saw a smile lift the thin line of Ava's lips.

"Are you going to tell me exactly what the emergency is other than a problem chicken."

"It's Mr. Pip." Minnie said.

"Mr. Pip? I hope it doesn't have anything to do with Miss Havisham. As a kid, I was frightened of her."

Minnie laughed. "Ah a reader of the classics. I have to admit, I did name him after the character in *Great Expectations*." Ava shrugged. "I figured Miss Havisham was hard done by, don't you? All in the name of love."

"Hmm maybe. This Mr. Pip, where is he exactly?" Ava looked around the barn they entered. Straw and dust drifted in the air, as several chickens still in the barn gave strangled cries and flew outside.

Minnie slowly made her way to a small bird that was lying on its side. "This is Mr. Pip. He's the oldest rooster I have, by a long way. I know it's stupid to keep old birds around, but I'm not going to cull him unless he's suffering."

"You made an emergency call for this?" Ava pointed to the colorful rooster.

"It's Gertie's husband. She might go off and die somewhere if he dies. Look, she's trying to coax him to get up." Minnie knew the more she said the more ridiculous she sounded. *Not ridiculous to me.*

Ava looked at the rooster, its mate, then back at Minnie. "Well, we can't have that can we? Love is a powerful thing." Ava knelt near the bird, and Gertie squawked. "I'm here to help, Gertie. I'll do the best I can to have him back to you." Gertie didn't move too far away, as Ava picked up the listless bird.

Fifteen minutes later, Minnie handed Ava a cup of coffee. "I can't thank you enough for being so good with Mr. Pip."

"Thanks." Ava drank some of the hot beverage. "He's getting old, Minnie, and that younger rooster is picking on him. I've tended to the cuts, but I can't do anything about his mood. If he's decided it's time to call it quits, who are we to stop that?"

Minnie sucked back a sob. The hall door opened, and Rita entered the kitchen.

"Morning." Minnie stifled another sob.

"Is there a problem?" Rita frowned.

"Mr. Pip, he might be dying." Minnie said. Rita rushed over and enclosed her in a hug.

"Darling, I'm so sorry. You love that old rooster. He might not die, right Ava?"

Ava shrugged.

"Yeah, I do." Minnie sniffled. "But if it's his time…"

"I have a suggestion." Ava stood and gulped down more coffee.

"What? I'll do anything."

"Why not have a small compound for Mr. Pip and Gertie to see out their retirement together, without interference from the macho usurpers." Ava picked up her bag.

Minnie gaped at the vet, then rushed the few feet between them and dragged her into a hug. "Thank you, thank you for understanding. I now know why everyone in the area is talking about how wonderful you are. However, I already knew that."

"Hey, keep up the good vibes. I have a mortgage to pay." Ava chuckled and headed for the door.

"Thank you, Ava. This means a lot to Minnie, both of us," Rita said, as she placed an arm around Minnie's shoulders.

"You do know there might be a hefty bill? It is out of hours." Ava smiled and shook her head. "Call this a freebie marketing exercise." Ava went out the front door and headed for her car. Minnie watched her leave the property, knowing why Danny said he'd found his perfect job.

"She's not going to bill us?" Rita looked surprised.

"Nope." Minnie grinned, as they shut the door and went back to the kitchen to have breakfast.

†

Jackie tapped her fingers on her lunchbox. Ava had been back for hours. Somehow or other, they hadn't been in the same place together. Jane had been right, almost. The day was manic. Tom Rush brought in Rock, who had somehow manged to eat his way thought layers of plastic and wasn't feeling that good. Danny had taken on the bull mastiff. After a stomach pump, his diagnosis was the dog would recover.

She heard the door to the staff room open but kept gazing at her unopened lunch.

"Not like you to leave your lunch." Soft words smothered her with a soothing balm.

"I haven't. Kept hoping a certain special someone might turn up and share it with me." Jackie replied, then held her breath.

"Thank goodness. What's for lunch today?" Ava dropped down on the seat next to her. Next to, not opposite. *Yes, yes, yes.* Jackie's heart soared.

"Are you special?" She looked at Ava, and her heart tripled its rhythm.

"Well, all depends on personal preferences. If you want me to do tricks, might be difficult, I leave that to our patients." Ava grinned. "There is a simple test."

"There is?"

Ava moved closer and kissed her. "May I share your lunch?"

Jackie's heart was racing so fast, she wasn't sure she could answer, then burst out. "I love you."

"Good to know. I love you too. What's for lunch?" Ava prodded the packages.

"Tuna and mayo." Jackie removed the wrap and offered a sandwich to Ava, who bit ravenously into the soft bread. "Didn't you have breakfast?"

"Kind of missed that. This is tasty."

"You were early at work this morning; couldn't you sleep?" Jackie probed gently, as she watched Ava demolish the sandwich in record time.

"I was nervous." Ava bluntly replied and took another sandwich.

"You and nervous don't compute." Jackie tipped her head in disbelief.

"You said you wanted to get it right. So do I. I have never had more than dates, sometimes accompanied by sex. You lived with someone for years and knew she was right...at that time."

Jackie paused. Ava was right to be nervous. I didn't even think that my relationship with Sue-Ann might be a problem.

The door opened and Danny walked in. He removed a small package from the fridge and sat down near them.

"Wow, that was a tough morning. I heard from my sis you are one awesome vet. I knew that, of course. Thank you, Ava. If I'd been there..." He dropped his gaze to the cellophane-wrapped object in front of him.

"You would have done exactly what I did. Jane tells me we are fully booked this afternoon." Danny groaned good naturedly. "You need to find something more substantial for lunch, Danny." Ava stood. "See you on the battlefield." She snagged another sandwich half, winked at Jackie, and left the room.

Danny turned to Jackie. "I love that woman." He grimaced at his lunch. "I think I'll take something out of the snack machine. See you later, Jackie."

"Well that was unexpected, and I love that woman too." Jackie glanced down at the single half sandwich, picked it up, and ate. "

CHAPTER THIRTY-FIVE

Ava sank down in her chair and let out a deep sigh. It was seven on Friday evening, and she was exhausted. The hectic workload was exactly what she needed to pay the bills, giving her little time to do anything else other than take advantage of Jackie's generosity on the meal front. For the last three weeks, Jackie had brought her lunch every day and also a meal for her to take home, when she did finally leave. "What the hell was I thinking? How can I have a romantic relationship with Jackie? I'm either too tired or working." She shook her head and groaned at the pile of papers on her desk. At least she had the weekend free if you could call it that. She needed to go over the bank payment schedule and review the essential supply orders for the practice to run smoothly. Dropping her head, she ran her hands through the sides of her hair, unaware that someone had entered the office.

"Hey, you look even more whacked than I am." Jackie smiled and walked toward her. Ava grinned, the stuff on her desk forgotten, as she gazed at the woman she loved.

"Why, thank you."

"A pleasure, my dear vet." Jackie walked around the desk and lifted Ava's chin, then gave a soft kiss on her lips. "Whatcha doing?" Jackie perched on the side of the desk.

Ava shrugged and glanced at the papers. "Trying to decide if I need a truck to take this lot home with me."

"I thought you had the weekend off. Danny said he'd cover the Saturday shift, didn't he?"

"Yes. I own the place, remember? The work doesn't stop when the day ends." Ava pushed several papers in her briefcase. "What are you doing tonight?" All Ava wanted to do was say to hell with the paperwork and ask Jackie to dinner. It would be so easy to play hooky.

She saw Jackie hesitate before answering, then with a small smile she replied. "I figure my girlfriend needs help. If it's good with her, I'll follow her home and we can work on stuff together. I'll cook dinner, what do you think?"

Ava wanted to agree. They hadn't even been on a proper date, just the two of them, somewhere romantic, since confessing their love for each other. "Jackie, I'd be taking advantage of you."

"And that's a problem how?" Jackie frowned.

"We haven't even been on a proper date yet."

"Am I going too fast?" Jackie moved to the other side of the desk.

Ava stood and pulled Jackie close, spotting tears in her eyes before kissing pliant lips. As they broke apart, she shook her head. "I don't want you to think I'm using you.

Right now, that's what it feels like to me. I don't even have the time to say hi to Theo."

Jackie smiled "Are you comparing me to Theo?"

"No, I didn't mean it like that!" Ava sighed. Her pulse raced, as Jackie placed a finger to her lips.

"I'm luckier than Theo. I get to spend my working day with you. We have lunch together when we can. I'm happy to ensure you eat something when you get home in the evening. Every moment I have with you, Ava, is a date for me. I can't explain it any better than that."

There was no better explanation, as Ava pulled her close and they lost themselves in kisses. She knew, for her, these were a first. Her body simply vibrated on a different level when she had Jackie in her arms.

Eventually, they pulled apart both breathing heavily. "I guess, you'd better stay over, this work could take all night."

Jackie's face flushed. "Sure unexpected, but I love it. I just need to make some arrangements for Monster."

Ava laughed. "Monster? You called our cat Monster…why?"

"I didn't even know you knew I'd taken her home. She was supposed to be for you." Jackie raised her eyebrows.

"Well, in that case, you'd better bring her too. She's family." Jackie kissed her so passionately, Ava didn't know if she'd survive—she did.

"I love you, my dear vet, so very much. You continue to amaze me."

"I love you too, and believe me, it's reciprocal on the amazing part." Ava threw more papers in her briefcase. "The sooner we go, the sooner we might have some free time together."

"I'll be quick." Jackie blew her a kiss and headed out the door.

"How the hell did I get so lucky?" Ava smiled, picked up her personal stuff and her briefcase, then headed home.

†

"Wow, I can't believe that's happening." Jackie blew out a breath, as she put together the Spanish omelettes she'd made and placed the two plates on the kitchen table.

"According to this invitation, it is, and I can bring a significant other." Ava grinned and waved the embossed wedding invitation in the air.

"A bit soon, don't you think? It's not as if they have to consider a nine-month problem. Though Minnie has waited a long time for Rita to settle down, I guess."

"Nope, not the baby problem." Ava chuckled. "Although they could be considering adoption. Neither one of them is getting any younger."

"Ohh, to the point as always, my dear vet. If I thought about adopting or having kids, do you think I'm getting a bit old?" Jackie sat opposite Ava at the table. "Enjoy." She pointed at the food.

Ava picked up her fork and began to eat, then suddenly stopped and laid her fork on the plate. She stared at Jackie. "Do you want children?"

"To be honest, I've never thought about it, at least not with Sue-Ann—would have cramped her party style. Do you?"

Ava picked up the fork again and began to play with the food on her plate. She gave Jackie a concentrated look. "Never thought it would be a part of my lifestyle." She took another forkful of the omelette. "This is good, wonderful actually."

"Would you want a child of your own, if you thought it would work out?" Jackie continued eating her meal.

"With the right person, I'd be open to the situation." Ava quietly answered.

Jackie laughed. "You liar, you don't want kids, do you?"

"My parents do." Ava scrunched up her nose and rolled her eyes. "Please, is it the only thing in life that we are supposed to offer our parents for their gratification in old age."

Jackie almost choked on the food in her mouth, laughing. "I'm sure there is more to your parents than that."

Ava shrugged, then grinned. "I love them, and to be honest—like I said—if it was the right person, then yes, I'd be there with bells on. Does that answer your question?"

Jackie dropped her utensils and stood. She walked over to Ava and placed a kiss on her surprised lips. "Yes." Ava's arms wrapped around her, and they nestled together for a few minutes.

"Our food will be cold." Jackie pointed to the plates on the table.

"I know. Sometimes there is something a little more substantial to the heart than food."

"Yeah, what?"

"Having the woman, you love in your arms and knowing that it's almost perfect."

"Almost?" Jackie stared at Ava, lost when they locked gazes. "How much more work do you need to do before we can call it a day?"

Ava frowned. "I could be up until after midnight."

Jackie nodded.

"Give me an hour after dinner, then I need to see to Theo and…"

"Stop Ava."

Ava looked like she was in the middle of the road with an oncoming car approaching.

"We will do all these things together, and remember we have Monster. Trust me, by nine she will want all your attention and to sleep on the bed."

"Sleep on the bed?" Ava's looked aghast.

Jackie chuckled and kissed her. "We will work things out, trust me."

"Can we finish our meal? I'm starving, and it's becoming cold and less appetizing."

Jackie laughed and moved away. "Do you like fast food?"

"Do we have fast food in Sterling?" Ava frowned.

"Oh yeah, will you trust me?"

"That's a given."

Jackie grinned and pulled out her phone from her trouser pocket.

"Hi Steve. It's Jackie Cochran, I have an order. Will you deliver to Doc Lawrence's?" Jackie laughed. "Great, my usual times two. Hey, don't be smart. Thanks Steve, two hours is just fine." She placed her phone on the table. "Right, my dear vet, what's first, the paperwork or Theo?"

"Theo." Ava grinned and they both headed outside.

†

Replete from the huge amount of food that had been delivered, Ava shook her head. "That was the best Kung Po chicken I've ever had in my life. Do you really order this much food for yourself?"

"Well, this was a double order, but yes. I've the perfect excuse; I cook for myself all week. On a Saturday, I indulge my fast food fetish." Jackie winked and settled her hands over her belly. "I'll be putting those pounds back on sooner rather than later, I'm sure."

Ava smiled and walked around the kitchen table and touched Jackie's shoulder. "Want to snuggle up on the couch and chat? I can provide the beverages."

Jackie stood and pulled Ava into her arms. "Sounds great to me. I'll pass on the drink. Right now, I'm full to the gunnels." She kissed Ava's lips, tasting the spicy sauce from the dish she'd consumed. It wasn't unpleasant. Their mouths opened and tongues entwined. The kiss lasted for a long time, and hands moved over clothing, desperately.

"We could take this to bed, what do you say?" Ava gasped, as they stopped to take breath.

"Are you sure?" Jackie looked into the glazed eyes of the woman she loved.

"Oh yes, very sure." Ava grasped her hand and virtually dragged Jackie to her room. Clothing seemed to have a mind of its own, as pieces dropped away. Jackie gently pulled Ava onto the bed and lay on top of her, their breasts touching.

"Positive, no backing down now?" Jackie looked at the pale skin of Ava's heaving breasts.

"You talk too much, Jackie Cochran. Let's make love." Ava pulled down Jackie's head, and they lost themselves in each other.

†

Ava awoke to a faint scratching sound at the door. Puzzled, she listened intently. Her eyes softened at the feel of the naked woman spooned next to her. There it was again, then a faint meow. *Ah Monster*. Reluctantly extracting herself, Ava went to the door. Sure enough, Monster was sitting outside the door as if she didn't have a care in the world. With a flick of her white tail, she walked inside the room and sniffed around, then leapt onto the bed. She settled next to Jackie on the side of the bed where Ava had been.

"Hey Monster, don't steal all the bed." The words were seemed sensible, though Ava was sure Jackie was still sleeping and it was an automatic response. She smiled, located her dressing gown, and quietly closed the door behind her.

Don't' want to disturb my lover. Hmm, lover sounded good. Smiling, she entered the kitchen and headed for the faucet. She drew a glass of water, looking out the window onto the dimly lit porch and the yard. Theo would still be happily asleep with his pals. She glanced at the clock on the wall, a quarter after three. She headed to her study and saw the piles of paper she and Jackie had been working on. She had to admit, Jackie was full of surprises and had the majority of orders worked out for suppliers before Ava had even worked out the bank payment schedule. They made a great team. Her belly fluttered, as she recalled their lovemaking, exciting, tender, sensual.

Picking up her phone she called a familiar number. Not really expecting an answer she was delighted when her dad answered.

"Hey there darling, it's early for you. Is there a problem?"

The sound of her dad's voice grounded her, not that she needed it. "Hey Dad. I couldn't sleep. Thought I'd check in and see how you all are enjoying your vacation."

"Nice country. We've pretty much gone from one area to another at lightning speed. Your mom is chatting up a local barman for information on our next stop."

"Uncle Gerry usually does that kind of stuff. Are you and him drinking them dry?" Ava laughed.

"Gerry and Gail retire early. Just me and your mom. How are things going at your end?" Ava heard a sadness in her dad's voice she hadn't heard since her grandmother died ten years ago.

"Good, I'm worked off my feet. I could use you to work out the bank—"

"Hey, I was lonely. Can't you sleep? Was it anything to do with Monster?" Jackie walked up and wrapped her arms around Ava and kissed her neck.

"I'm on the phone." Ava heard a deep chuckle down the line.

Jackie moved away. "Sorry." She walked toward the door.

"No. Dad I'll catch up with you tomorrow? Text me a time."

"I bet this is family business, right?" Ava shook her head at her dad's intuition.

"Yes, family business. Love you Dad, give Mom and Uncle Gerry a kiss for me." Ava ended the call and looked for Jackie, she was gone.

Damn.

She looked in her bedroom and Monster was snoring in the middle of the bed, no Jackie.

Damn.

The kitchen was the next port of call. Nothing.

Damn.

She saw a movement on the porch and could vaguely see Jackie sitting on one of the chairs, simply staring into the darkness. A few minutes later, Ava opened the door to the porch and walked toward her lover. She sat down next to her, placing a wine cooler and two glasses on the table in front of them.

"Hi."

"Hi." Jackie quietly responded.

"I think I offered you beverages earlier. I brought wine, my favorite, is that ok?" Ava's stomach rolled waiting for the answer.

"Sure."

"I was talking to my dad. The times are hard to correlate to have a decent conversation with my parents. I'm usually working, or they're asleep."

Jackie frowned.

"Monster woke me, she took over my side of the bed." Ava didn't know what else to say; it was the truth.

"Are you going to pour us a drink?" Jackie took her hand and gently squeezed.

"Yes. Am I forgiven?" Ava poured the drinks and at once took a sip from her glass.

A slow smile graced Jackie's lip. "Hey, that's why I call her Monster." She picked up her glass and took a drink." How is your family?"

"Not sure, really. Anyway, I'm going to set up a video chat, then I'll know for sure."

"Good wine." Jackie sipped from her glass and screwed up her face.

Ava laughed. "You hate it. Jackie, I love you." She fumbled her glass and didn't care it turned over and spilt everywhere. She knelt before Jackie. "I know this is sudden but…"

"Don't." Jackie placed a finger on her lips. "Let's go back to bed."

"I like your thinking." She stood and held out her hand, Jackie took it and kissed her lips.

CHAPTER THIRTY-SIX

Music softly played, as the tables in the room were moved around to make a decent-sized dance floor. People busied themselves with getting drinks or simply talking to friends and family. The stars of the show were laughing with three older people, possibly parents. Certainly, one of the women looked like Minnie.

"Hey, are you daydreaming?" Jackie took the seat next to Ava, grinning as she set their drinks on the table. Ten minutes ago, it had seated four other people, none of whom she had met before. As it turned out, they were colleagues of Rita's when she lived in the city. They had all left to chat to people they obviously knew.

"Nope. Observing. Thanks for the drink."

"Don't thank me. It's all free. Besides, a club soda would hardly break the bank." She took a sip of her beer. "It was a nice wedding, don't you think?"

"Yes it was. The celebrant did a great job. I think the golf club was a great choice too. The Derossys certainly know how to put on a wedding feast." Ava watched several others heading their way. "I think we're going to have company we actually know."

"Thank god," Jackie said. "Those lawyer types can be so…intense."

Ava chuckled. "Hi Danny, Judy, Lizzy," She looked behind Lizzy and smiled. "Jerry, does this give you ideas?" The shy man gave her an anxious look and blushed.

"Well, I never thought Minnie would ever get hitched, especially to Rita. They are good for each other," Danny said, as he sat down opposite them. Judy took the seat next to him.

"Here Jerry, sit next to me." Jackie smiled at the big man, and he sat, with Lizzy taking the seat opposite him.

"It's a good turnout. I have to admit I was a bit surprised. We aren't exactly known for being that liberal around here." Danny smiled.

"Hey, we've changed a lot since you left for college, I'll have you know." Judy gently punched him in the side. He feigned a hurt expression, then took her hand and began to absently swivel the diamond ring around her finger.

"Your turn next then guys?" Jackie asked, looking at the cluster of diamonds.

Judy shook her head and chuckled. "We've decided to take it slowly. Danny needs to get a year or two under his belt working. I've inherited several headaches, business wise, from my father. Rita, bless her, has been a godsend helping me navigate the mess."

"Hmm" Ava nodded. "The last four months have been an eye-opener for me too, especially after my uncle and his wife passed." The table went quiet. A hand took hers under the table. Jackie had probably cried more tears than she had when her parents had told her the truth on why they were in Europe.

"Yeah, Doc Lawrence was a lovely, gentle man. What will happen to the donkeys?" Lizzy quietly asked.

Ava saw Jackie roll her eyes. She knew what was coming next.

"Ava loves those critters more than anything, and old Theo is her favorite. She inherited the house on the one condition, she keep the donkeys until they die of natural causes."

"How long do donkeys live?" Lizzy asked.

"If they are taken care of, a good twenty-five to thirty years." All eyes turned to Jerry. "It's the truth. Doc Lawrence Sr. told me."

"Oh Jerry, I didn't know you knew so much. One of the reasons I love you—you amaze me." Lizzy gushed, then blushed as the eyes all turned to her.

"He knows a great deal, Lizzy. I'm grateful he decided not to take my dad's offer of work in the city," Ava said. "So, what's the new gossip in town? We haven't had the time to do anything but work and sort out the property."

Danny dropped his gaze. Judy did the same. Ava looked at Lizzy, who turned away. Turning to Jackie, she saw an equally perplexed expression.

"Ok guys, what are we missing?" Jackie asked.

The answer came from an unexpected quarter. "You and Doc Ava," Jerry said.

Ava looked at Jackie. "We're the gossip around town, why?"

"Yeah why?" Jackie frowned. "What have we done to warrant the gossip mongers?"

"It's all good, Jackie," Lizzy timidly replied.

"Good or bad, what is it?" Jackie shook her head and took a big drink from her glass.

"Ok, there's a sweepstake that was started at work. It might have gotten a bit out of control." Danny shrugged. "The rest of the town seem to be involved somehow, and I do not have a clue how that happened."

"Oh you liar. Sure you do, Danny. He was drunk one night, about a month ago, and told everyone at the bar. Do I need to say more?" Judy rolled her eyes. "He didn't do it maliciously; he loves you both."

Ava had never heard such a ridiculous thing in her life. Jackie started to laugh, and Ava's forehead grew deep creases. People talking about them and a sweepstake, what the hell was that about? "I don't understand."

Jackie turned to her and smiled. She squeezed Ava's hand she still held under the table. "You wouldn't, that's why I love you...why we all do."

"Exactly." Judy announced.

Ava didn't have the chance to say more, as the happy couple appeared and stood at the head of the table.

"Are you all good? Did you have a nice meal?" Minnie asked, her hand held by Rita.

"Great celebration, Min, and the meal was awesome." Danny stood and hugged his sister.

"You would say that. You're my brother."

Ava stood and nodded and affirmative. "I think he said it all. Now, please don't tell me you've decided on country dancing and we have to find boots." Minnie hugged her hard then released her.

"Not likely." Rita said. "We do want to thank you all for coming though, it means a lot to us. Thank you, Ava, for closing the practice so everyone could attend and celebrate."

"Happy to do it. I'm on call until six, then I can indulge in the good stuff, if there's any left of course." Ava shrugged.

"Doesn't matter if they have run out. I can go home and get your favorite," Jackie interceded.

Everyone laughed, but Ava disapproved with a shake of her head. "You can't go home from a great party. Don't be silly, Jackie. You never said the music?"

Minnie chuckled, as she snuggled close to Rita. "Would you believe my...wife"—Minnie stopped and kissed Rita—"She loves Judy Garland. In fact, it was one of her songs playing at a college party the day we met. Outside of teaching hours, of course. That was the day I fell in love."

"Minnie, Rita, your aunts want to say goodbye." A gangly guy with a wispy beard stood at Rita's shoulder.

"Sorry guys, see you all later." They drifted toward the aging women.

"Over the Rainbow?" Judy asked. "Is that the song they feel in love to? Dah, Danny she's your sister. Where's the insider info?"

Danny raised his hands. "No idea. My sister and I do not trade romantic entanglement secrets."

"Take my bet?" Judy asked.

"My dad likes the old performers. He has some Judy Garland. I think it's *Get Happy*." Lizzy grinned. "I like it too."

Ava shook her head. "I don't know any of Judy Garland's songs."

"Who is Judy Garland?" Jerry said.

"Jerry, you and I are on the same team. Please is it almost six, so I can be like the rest of you."

"I'm the same as you Doc Ava?" Ava a saw his puzzled expression.

"Jerry you most certainly are. Maybe we should stick together."

Ava was stunned at the man's reaction to her comment. "Sorry, I love my Lizzy. She's my soulmate." Jerry smiled and took Lizzy's hand from across the table.

Ava was careful not to laugh, because she was sure Jerry would take it the wrong way. For a moment the table guests were lost for words.

"Jerry, Ava meant you and she are not the best for a music quiz." Jackie said.

Jerry nodded digesting the words. "Got it. I do like music, Jackie. Lizzy and I watch that show on a Saturday, don't we Lizzy." He beamed at his love.

"*America's Got Talent*," Lizzy explained with a smile. "Not sure we like Simon Cowell though, he's pretty harsh."

"Oh, did you see that episode where he was so critical—"

"Everyone, our newly married couple is going to get the dancing started with a medley of songs from a favorite singer of theirs. You are welcome to join them," the DJ barked into her mic, while standing at a small table surrounded by equipment. The intro carried a distinctive Big Band sound and led into the happy tones of a woman's voice. Jackie whispered in Ava's ear, "That's Judy Garland."

Ava listened, as she watched the happy couple dancing close together and singing the lyrics to each other. Jackie was talking to Lizzy and Jerry. Danny and Judy excused themselves to dance. Ava was enjoying watching several couples on the dance floor, then she felt a vibration from her phone. She pulled it from her trouser pocket and looked at the screen. She stood and gently tapped Jackie on the shoulder. "I have an emergency. Remember, save me some of that wine."

"Damn, it's a quarter to six. I'll keep the seat warm." Jackie smiled and gently squeezed her hand.

"I'll be back as soon as I can." Ava reluctantly walked away.

†

By eight, there was still no sign of Ava. The room was thinning out of the older crowd. Minnie and Rita were still around. They'd said they were leaving for a honeymoon on Sunday afternoon, a three-week cruise around the Caribbean Islands.

"Jackie, what did you think of today?" Evalyn Derossy plonked down next to her. The woman looked exhausted but always had a ready smile.

"Wonderful." Jackie grinned; thankful someone was sitting at the table with her. Lizzy and Jerry had left an hour earlier to see his mom, who had the flu. Danny and Judy had simply disappeared once they went on the dance floor.

"You aren't just saying that are you?" Evalyn asked, as her eyes scanned the room.

"No, not at all. If I ever get married, I know this is the place I'll book for my reception, and that isn't bullshit." Jackie shrugged and looked at her watch.

"Need to be somewhere?"

"Nope, hoping a certain someone will be back to have at least one dance with me before it finishes."

"Ava?"

"Yeah Ava." Jackie nodded. "She's on an emergency call. If I know Ava, she will probably go home once she's finished, thinking it's too late to come back." She looked at the time again. "Maybe I will too. Nothing worse than sitting alone at a wedding event."

Evalyn gave her a concentrated look. "Keep the faith, Jackie, I think she'll be back, unless she can't." There was the distinctive sound of a bell ringing. "Oops, got to go. Time to bring out the evening snacks. Got to say, there's more food for snacks than there was for the main meal. All that fancy stuff for the wedding feast, would have made me hungry. Keep smiling, Jackie, Ava will be back."

A slow ballad by Adele began to play. Many wandered away, but Judy half dragged an unimpressed Danny to the dance floor. Jackie listened to the music and wished Ava were there. More and more, Ava filled her mind. She had no doubts about the love she felt for Ava. It was both a joy and a curse. They spent so many hours together, professionally, it was a pleasure to go to work each day. The time they did spend together on a personal level was intense and satisfying. Yet the simple fact was that the personal times were restricted, making Jackie want to scream. As the song came to an end, she peered at the empty glass in front of her. Time to go home.

"Hello," Jackie's heart tried to escape her chest at hearing the sexy voice that haunted her waking and sleeping moments. Two drinks were placed on the table and the chair legs of the seat next to her scraped the floor, as Ava took a seat. "Sorry it took so long. Bob Moore's award-winning bull decided to get his horns stuck in the field gate. Apparently, he wanted to go with Maisy, his newest 'wife', Bob's words, to the calving arena. Anyway, long story short, it took longer than expected to extricate him. I think I gave him enough drugs to put an elephant to sleep." Ava took a sip of her wine and smiled, her eyes drifting around the room. "Did you miss me?"

Jackie wanted to get up and leave. It was an irrational reaction, she knew, because there was no way she was going to do that. Ava was loving in private, but in public, sometimes it was a bit hard to call. "Of course, I did. I thought you might have gone home."

Ava caught Jackie's gaze. "Why would I do that? You were waiting for me."

Was it that simple?

The announcement that the evening food was ready for consumption brought a huge smile to Ava's face.

"Oh great, I'm starving. The food was wonderful at the reception. I don't know about you, but it wasn't that substantial. I've become used to a lot more food on my plate these days." Ava took another drink and winked at her. The reference to larger portions was not lost on Jackie, after all she was the perpetrator.

Yes, it was that simple.

"Got to keep my girl happy. Let's go." Jackie stood and held out a hand to Ava, who took it.

CHAPTER THIRTY-SEVEN

Ava traced a gentle finger over the curve of Jackie's naked breast. She slept close enough they were almost joined. Monster had woken her, wanting to go out. She dutifully responded to the command. Dawn was about to break, and Monster would venture only as far Theo's field. She'd sit on the fence post and watch the day begin, as was her habit on the homestead. Ava slipped back into bed, waiting for her hands to warm before she touched her lover. Jackie was, as usual, comatose through Monster's routine. By six, she'd be awake and ready for the day. Ava grinned. That meant one thing. On Sundays, they'd spend the next two hours making love, before sharing a leisurely breakfast. They'd make love some more, until the donkeys had to be fed. She loved spending her time off with Jackie, no matter if they were embroiled in looking over work papers or simply enjoying each other's company. Her finger touched the dark nipple she wanted to slowly suck into her mouth and bring her lover to arousal. Jackie deserved this time to sleep. Satisfying her own needs would be selfish.

"Are you going to kiss me or just watch? I know what I'd prefer." Jackie's sleep-filled voice made Ava smile.

"Faker, I thought you were asleep." She snuggled closer and took the left nipple in her mouth, hearing Jackie's heart pick up a beat. Ava groaned, and they made love.

Later, Ava cradled Jackie close to her chest. "Are you happy?"

"Happy, asks the woman who just made me scream so much the roof rattled. Yes." Jackie moved so that she was eye to eye with Ava.

"I want you to be happy always; am I being silly?"

Jackie reached up and pulled her face close, tenderly kissing her. "If I had my way you could be silly all the time, with thoughts like that." Jackie sighed.

"I meant it last night." Ava wrapped her arms around Jackie's belly, then moved her left hand lower to trace the hair at the apex of her legs.

"I know you did." Jackie's hand touched hers and pulled it further down.

"You never gave me a definitive answer." Ava placed a kiss on Jackie's neck.

"You talk too much, my dear vet." Jackie pressed Ava's fingers to her clit. "I love you."

Ava took the hint, and they made love again. When Jackie fell back to sleep, Ava cradled her lover close and thought about the end to the previous evening.

"Perfect song for us." One of the brides' classic songs began to play. It was the third to last song, according to the DJ.

"What do you mean?" Jackie asked, as Ava's arms drew her closer.

"Zing went my heart strings, when you entered my life, Jackie Cochran." She pulled Jackie even closer as they danced. "I love you."

"I love you too." Jackie smiled at her.

"We are in perfect harmony"

"Yes, I hope so." Jackie frowned. Ava touched the worry lines.

"I love you. I still recall the thrill when we met." Jackie gave her a perplexed look. "God Jackie, I thought I was the dense one. I said this song was ours."

Jackie pulled her close and sang into her ear. "Dear vet, when you smiled at me, zing went the strings of my heart."

Ava's heart zinged; she was sure of it. "I think zing will be forever pulling at my heart strings when I'm with you."

"Then we'd better make sure that happens." Jackie whispered and snuggled into her shoulder.

"I thought that too, marry me."

Jackie pulled away and simply stared at her. "Bad timing at a wedding."

Ava never got the chance to ask what she meant. Jackie crushed her close, with a passionate kiss on her lips.

Ava, extricated herself from Jackie and collected casual clothes before leaving the room. Five minutes later, she was outside and looking at the clearing skies. It was going to be a nice day. Lo and behold, Monster was sitting where she expected. Theo was munching grass ten yards away. It appeared the cat and the donkey had an affinity, which was good, at least Ava hoped so. Monster saw her walking over and delicately pranced toward her. She rubbed against Ava, purring incessantly. "Morning girl, we really should find another name for you." She stroked the feline. Theo lifted his head and began to make his way toward them. "Hey, our friend is on his way. Did you know he's not even an old man, just middle-aged." Ava chuckled and leant her elbows on the wooden fence.

Theo arrived and nuzzled her arm. "Good morning, Theo." The donkey neighed, and she pulled out an apple core. Monster jumped on her shoulder, butt in her face. "Monster." She fished in her pocket and found three treats to place on the fence. Monster deserted her. "It's Sunday guys, a day off, at least for me. Jackie will be up soon. We love Jackie, and we want her to stay." Ava sighed. "Even if she doesn't want to marry me."

"Yes, I do."

The hair on Ava's neck stood on end. Her throat constricted, and she had no words. She simply turned, smiling.

Jackie moved forward with a few more treats for Monster and a full apple for Theo. "I'm taking your best friend away for a while, guys."

"Where?" Ava wrinkled her forehead.

"We need to check out rings, if you're marrying me." Jackie grinned and held out her arms. Ava entered them, relaxing immediately. This woman was simply the right fit for her.

Ava looked up at Jackie and smiled. "I have a ring, but you might not want it."

Jackie's eyebrows crossed. "Why not?"

"My uncle left me his estate. That included his rings from his first marriage. Not compulsory, in the short time…"

"Ava. I loved them both. I'd be honoured to wear the engagement ring. We still need to find a ring for you."

"You are the best thing for me. A ring is just the icing on the cake."

"I love you."

"Let's leave our family." She nodded to Monster and Theo. "I think it's time you made me yours, now that we are newly engaged."

Jackie chucked. "God, you are so focused. I love it and you."

Hand in hand, they walked toward the house and their new future.

ABOUT JM DRAGON

_____

JM Dragon is a New Zealand citizen, living in the beautiful Canterbury countryside. She loves to garden, travel, write, take care of her animals and family, and pursue her business interests—Affinity eBook Pressny.

She is a keen reader of sci-fi, crime/mystery, classics, and romance, which help to feed her imagination for her own stories.

Currently published by Affinity eBook Press NZ LTD.

You can contact JM by email at:
jm1dragon@yahoo.com
or
on Facebook at:
http://www.facebook.com/julie.dragon

OTHER AFFINITY BOOKS

Always in My Heart by Samantha Hicks
What do you do when you are in love with your best friend's wife? Haze Evens is pleased Gabby Turner has everything she wants, expecting her first child, and happy in her marriage. Even though it breaks her heart she has it with someone else, her best friend Nicole. Everything changes when Gabby turns up one night needing a place to stay. As they spend time together, their mutual attraction blossoms, but neither are willing to cross that line. Tension between Gabby and her wife increase when the baby arrives, leaving Gabby with a traumatic choice, her child or Haze. Not willing to give up either, she decides to fight Nicole in any way she can.This is a story about unrequited love, betrayal, and finding your soul mate. Can the heart really have it all?

One Shot at Love by Annette Mori

Blair returns to her hometown after the death of her sister. Always an activist she vows to use her voice to advocate for better gun control. She meets Maribel, an irresistible, sexy woman who proves to be an enigma to Blair. Maribel can't help approaching the weeping woman and learning the origin of Blair's grief, Maribel thinks she is the last person who should form a friendship with Blair. Ultimately, the allure is too much for Maribel, but how long can she keep her secret and continue to nurture their burgeoning feelings for one another. A committed left-wing social activist could never fall for the poster child of the NRA. Unless taking that one shot at love matters more than anything else.

The Mountain Whispers by Ali Spooner

Arriving home and discovering the betrayal by her best friend and lover, Eli Fortner leaves to run off her anger and hurt. A chance stop at a convenience store and the purchase of lottery tickets sends Eli's life into a whirlwind of change. Able to now pursue her dreams, Eli heads off to see what else fate has in store for her.

Whit Brewer, Eli's neighbor, is everything Eli never knew she needed and wanted. But can she let go of the betrayal long enough to let Whit in? Thirteen black cats, a baby goat, and Cruz, her furry best friend, join Eli on her adventure, new life, and the possibility of real love.

Charlie by Erin O'Reilly

At fourteen, Hannah Garvin met 'the one,' Charlene Gaines, and her life was never the same. They were inseparable and spent every moment they could together. One day, Charlie left without a word and again, Hannah's life took a dramatic change. Hannah vowed to never fall in love again. When she meets Mick, a new arrival to the small Texas panhandle town near her family's farm, her heart remembers what being in love was like, and yearns for more. Will Hannah let the memory of Charlie go so she can start a new life with Mick? Or will her heart betray her and hold on to her love for Charlie?

Misha's Promise by Renee MacKenzie
Misha Wyatt has settled into a peaceful existence as a healer in Karst, New America. When an airplane crashes in the meadow outside of Karst, Misha hurries to help the pilot. Misha is not expecting the pilot to be alive...or so beautiful. Will her uncontrollable desire to keep the pilot safe be her downfall? Can *they* survive their journey? The last book in the Karst series brings our characters to their physical and emotional limits. Don't miss the culmination of this exciting series!

Heart Strings Attached by Ali Spooner & Annette Mori
Socialite Remy has her world shaken. Bartender Chancy has her orderly life turned around. A mutually beneficial business agreement between Remy and Chancy turns into undeniable attraction. Will the two ignore culture norms to explore their intense desire for each other?

The Panty Thief by Annette Mori
Someone is stealing panties, but who? And why? Joey Hartford is a fourth-year medical student who insists she

doesn't have time for a relationship. A new tenant in her apartment building is proving too tempting to ignore. Sabrina is in her final year of her doctoral program focused on completing her dissertation. Meeting Joey is dangerous for so many reasons. Add a suicidal ex-girlfriend who suddenly reappears in Sabrina's life and Joey's jealous friend-with-benefits, and things get complicated quickly.

Country Living by Jen Silver
Peri Sanderson achieves her dream of moving from London to a cottage in the English countryside with her wife, Karla. Peri sees their future as pastoral while chatting with the locals in a quaint village pub. Sexy urbanite, Karla, has other ideas. Secrets are everywhere. Peri quickly senses something not quite right among her rural neighbors and also with Karla. Temptation, betrayal, and intrigue combine to change the lives of both women beyond anything they could have imagined.

Before the Light by Samantha Hicks
One year after her long-time partner Meredith's abduction, and their subsequent break-up, Kathleen Bowden-Scott's life is spiralling out of control. She meets Bethany Jones and despite an instant attraction Kathleen shies away. In this fast-paced, romantic suspense, lies are exposed and hearts unite as Kathleen and Beth fight for their future.

Wanted for Christmas by JM Dragon

Belle Farrow knew what she wanted for Christmas–work. She had little to offer but a minor degree in cookery and household management. Certainly not enough for a decent chef or housekeeper position. Then she saw an advert in the local newspaper. Wanted: Housekeeper/cook/nanny for the period of Christmas until the New Year. This is Christmas. Perhaps Santa reads the ad column too and pushes a little spirit of the season to that request.

Dreams in a Jar by JM Dragon
When you believe your life is a never-ending spiral of despair and the only personal joy you have is inside of a novel, would you grab a chance to hide away in the local bookstore and dream of adventures? Thea's life is about to embark on a journey she never envisioned when local bookstore owner, Marion, is taken ill. Her niece, Sheryl Appleby, takes over the reins and her presence provides Thea the courage to take a leap of faith. Can she embrace the butterfly effect, or are Thea's dreams bottled in a jar forever?

Pleasure Workers by Annette Mori
Alex Cortez is accomplished at two things, fixing broken equipment and pleasuring women. She is happily doing both at the Ranch in Nevada. Danna Nichols, newly widowed, feels lost and alone. When her good friend Lindy invites her to check out the newly established Trophy Wives Club, it awakens dormant feelings and desires. An instant attraction happens and the two form a bond under unlikely circumstances. Will the challenges of their social status tear

them apart before they can enjoy the pleasures of their new love?

The Trophy Wives Club by Ali Spooner
What happens when under-appreciated professional women are offered their dream jobs? When one of Atlanta's elite businesswomen and wife of a prominent judge sets her sights on a goal, life begins to change for these women. Friendships and romance bloom in a unique fitness club on the outskirts of Atlanta, where more than a workout is offered.

Affinity
Rainbow Publications

eBooks, Print, Free eBooks

Visit our website for more publications available online.

www.affinityrainbowpublications.com

Published by Affinity Rainbow Publications
A Division of Affinity eBook Press NZ LTD
Canterbury, New Zealand

Registered Company 2517228